INTO THE FIRE

Morgan Mason swung his axe in a wide arc and knocked away a burning chair as he plunged into the inferno. Squinting, coughing, he advanced one step at a time in the face of intense heat. Never in his life had he reacted without thinking, but another man's life depended on what he did now.

"Can you get out? Come towa_____ He waited to see if the miner responde_____ swung back and forth to hack a ___

He quickly saw wh_____swer. The miner lay stre_____the filing cabinet. A falli_____ him on the top of the hea_____ay forward and reached the man_____im with the butt of the axe handle.

He then reached ___ ___ put his hand on the other man's shoulder. The smoke billowing about obscured all vision. Then came a sound unlike anything he had ever heard before. It was a creaking and snapping and a moan that was eerily human. A sudden upward gust cleared the smoke for a brief instant, showing the bright blue Nevada sky.

Then the roof collapsed. Mason recoiled and tried to drag the miner with him. A heavy beam crashed smack-dab onto the man. Mason felt him jerk away as he fell to the floor. Before he could move to pull the burning beam away, another, larger one fell amid a shower of sparks. Mason stepped back instinctively, caught his heel and sat heavily. He smashed into a desk.

A quick jerk to the side carried him into the knee well of the desk. The rain of fire and wood from above no longer fell on his head, but he saw his companion stretched out with two large beams pinning his legs down.

Then the rest of the roof gave up the ghost and came thundering down.

RALPH COMPTON

FLAMES OF SILVER

A Ralph Compton Western by
JACKSON LOWRY

BERKLEY
New York

BERKLEY
An imprint of Penguin Random House LLC
penguinrandomhouse.com

Copyright © 2021 by The Estate of Ralph Compton
Penguin Random House supports copyright. Copyright fuels creativity, encourages
diverse voices, promotes free speech, and creates a vibrant culture. Thank you for buying
an authorized edition of this book and for complying with copyright laws by not
reproducing, scanning, or distributing any part of it in any form without permission.
You are supporting writers and allowing Penguin Random House to continue to
publish books for every reader.

BERKLEY and the BERKLEY & B colophon are registered trademarks of
Penguin Random House LLC.

ISBN: 9780593333815

First Edition: May 2021

Printed in the United States of America
1 3 5 7 9 10 8 6 4 2

Book design by George Towne

THE IMMORTAL COWBOY

This is respectfully dedicated to the "American Cowboy." His was the saga sparked by the turmoil that followed the Civil War, and the passing of more than a century has by no means diminished the flame.

———◦◉◦———

True, the old days and the old ways are but treasured memories, and the old trails have grown dim with the ravages of time, but the spirit of the cowboy lives on.

———◦◉◦———

In my travels—to Texas, Oklahoma, Kansas, Nebraska, Colorado, Wyoming, New Mexico, and Arizona—I always find something that reminds me of the Old West. While I am walking these plains and mountains for the first time, there is this feeling that a part of me is eternal, that I have known these old trails before. I believe it is the undying spirit of the frontier calling me, through the mind's eye, to step back into time. What is the appeal of the Old West of the American frontier?

———◦◉◦———

It has been epitomized by some as the dark and bloody period in American history. Its heroes—Crockett, Bowie, Hickok, Earp—have been reviled and criticized. Yet the Old West lives on, larger than life.

———◦◉◦———

It has become a symbol of freedom, when there was always another mountain to climb and another river to cross; when a dispute between two men was settled not with expensive lawyers, but with fists, knives, or guns. Barbaric? Maybe. But some things never change. When the cowboy rode into the pages of American history, he left behind a legacy that lives within the hearts of us all.

—*Ralph Compton*

CHAPTER ONE

Ω

THE BULLET TORE a fist-sized hole in the wood beside Morgan Mason's head. He jerked back and collided with the whiskey salesman crowded close behind him in the stagecoach, anxiously waiting to exit. A strong hand shoved him forward. Mason stumbled and landed on one knee in the dust. He looked around frantically for whoever had taken the shot at him. The Virginia City street was crowded with men and women going about their noontime business. No one paid him any heed.

No one seemed to notice the gunfire. He brushed off his trousers and settled his coat. His vest had ridden up a bit over his paunch. Trying not to be too obvious, he pulled it down and fastened the bottom buttons that had popped open.

"Here. You left this in the stage." The whiskey peddler tossed him his bowler, then lithely jumped to the ground and took a deep breath. "There's that aroma in the air. Isn't it grand?"

Mason sucked in a breath and almost gagged. This was nothing like the sea air blowing off the Pacific Ocean or the Bay in his hometown of San Francisco. Acrid smoke mingled with horse dung and more than a little whiff of alcohol blowing from the three saloons lined up side by side across from the Wells Fargo depot.

"It's awful," he gasped out.

"It's wonderful," the peddler insisted. "That's the smell of thirsty miners wanting just one more shot of my fine whiskey before they return to work." The peddler laughed in delight, hefted his case and left. Mason heard the contents of the leather suitcase gurgle. The salesman carried his wares inside. Without so much as a look back, the whiskey peddler went into the nearest saloon.

"You all right, Mister?" The shotgun guard dropped from the driver's box. "You're looking a mite peaked, but then you got a pale complexion just like most of them miners. Only they don't look fair of skin because they're Irish. They look that way because they spend their lives underground. You thinking on becoming a miner?" The guard looked skeptically at Mason, his bulging waistline, his mussed fiery red hair and then into eyes so blue they rivaled the sky.

"You think I look like a miner?"

"Well, now, ain't my place to say." The guard pushed back the canvas flap on the boot and dragged out Mason's bag. He dumped it to the ground.

Mason cried out and tried to keep it from crashing into the dirt. He failed. The peddler's wares were liquid and alcoholic. His were more specialized and far deadlier. The pints of acids and bases he had in that bag matched anything on the shelves around Virginia City. He had wasted a considerable part of his fortune sending telegrams to inquire about assayers and land agents and then purchasing the chemicals in San Francisco, where there was an abundance of supply off the ships rounding the Horn.

"Don't get so worked up. Whatever you got in there's already survived getting bounced all over on the road coming up the mountain."

"Yeah, there's that," Mason said dubiously. He stood back and waited to see if any of the chemicals leaked out. If they mixed, the least that would happen would be a toxic puddle. The most might be an explosion, followed by a cloud of noxious gas capable of killing a horse. Not seeing any obvious damage, he hefted the case. Then he took out a small bag with his clothing and personal items.

He stood stock-still for a moment and looked around.

"You lose something? You got the look of a man who's not sure of himself." The guard fastened the canvas flap back down and rested his scattergun in the crook of his left arm.

"I was shot at when I got off the stage."

"No, you wasn't."

"There. Look there." Outraged that the man called him a liar, Mason pointed out the huge hole blasted through the dried wood. He shoved his finger through, into the compartment, and wiggled it. "See?"

"I heard the shot. Nobody much cares what happens to these old coaches."

"Somebody *shot* at me!"

"Ain't you the prima donna, thinking anybody cared about a stranger getting off the stage. There's lead flying around all the time. Nobody's aiming at you or likely anyone else. They're just letting off steam."

The driver called to the guard.

"You settle down and you'll find Virginia City a whole lot more welcoming." The guard walked to the front of the team, grabbed a harness on the lead and led the team away, the driver gently snapping the reins to get the other horses pulling.

In seconds Morgan Mason stood all by himself in the middle of Virginia City's main street. He looked around and wondered where to go. The town was built on the side of a steep hill, with three or four levels below him. The streets were extreme enough that ladderlike sidewalks had been installed. Going downhill required a reckless abandon, but climbing up meant a considerable exertion. He had lived most of his life at sea level. Up here in the mountains, breathing was something of a chore for him. Mason rested his hand on his belly. Altitude and being out of shape cut his wind in a hurry.

He chose not to descend but to remain on the street, at least for the time being, until he regained his breath. As far as he could tell, one level was like another, though he thought he saw a tree-shrouded cemetery just off the lowest level.

Warily looking around, not certain the stagecoach guard told the truth about the bullet that had greeted him as he stepped down, Mason walked along the street, taking in the sights. Every other building housed a saloon and did a thriving business. He was almost sorry he had brought hydrochloric acid and sodium hydroxide and all the other chemicals instead of whiskey. The peddler had a distinct edge on him and was likely to do a land office business.

At that thought, he stopped and stared. The city surveyor shared a building with an assayer. The surveyor had a CLOSED sign on the door, but the assay office was still open. Mason hitched up his trousers and smoothed wrinkles in his coat and vest. His starched collar and tie were a complete loss after the long trip here. From the dishabille of most Virginia City citizens around him, he doubted anyone would think him out of place. Stride sure and confident, he crossed the street, adjusted his bowler and tucked a shock of red hair under the brim, then entered the office.

"Leave your sample on the counter. Fill out your name on the form. I'll get it done by the end of next week." The clerk hunched over his desk, his face only inches from a newspaper.

"I'm not here to have an ore sample analyzed," Mason said.

"Ain't got money to give to a beggar."

"It's not that."

"I don't buy into mining claims or grubstake prospectors." The clerk looked up, pushed his glasses back with an acid-stained finger and peered hard at Mason. "You don't look like any of those. Whatever you're selling, I'm not buying."

Such a negative attitude irritated Mason. He drew himself up to his full five-foot-eight height and tried to sound as authoritative as possible.

"I am a chemist and have my own laboratory equipment to aid you in your work." He looked around the room. The chemical odors were whisked away by a strong breeze gusting through two open windows at the rear of the room. Tattered linen curtains stood out, caught in the wind blowing up the slope from Virginia City's lower levels.

"Not hiring any assistants. Not hiring anyone. I'm the town's only assayer, and I intend to keep it that way."

"That sounds a mite threatening," Mason said.

"Good. That means there's nothing wrong with your ears." The clerk looked back at the newspaper in obvious dismissal.

"How much do you pay to restock your reagents?"

The assayer looked up, adjusted his glasses, then said in measured tones, "You got some to sell?"

Mason patted his pockets. He had spent virtually every penny he had buying the ticket for the Wells Fargo coach. Rumor had it that Virginia City streets were paved with silver and they weren't able to find enough workers for the mines. That meant to him that considerable talent was required to support the assay and smelting. He had experience as a chemist as well as geologist. Two such skills must be in demand if Virginia City was the boomtown everyone in San Francisco claimed.

"I'm thinking another assayer might offer more."

The clerk laughed harshly. He pushed back in his chair and hiked his feet to the desktop. One sole had a hole in it. A piece of cardboard in the shoe did little to patch the damage.

"I'm the only one in town."

"Perhaps it's time for competition to move in," Mason said. The clerk's expression warned that something about this fine ambition was flawed.

"You got to pay the license fees. You got a thousand

dollars? The mayor's talking about increasing business fees to a hundred a week, in addition." The assayer laced his fingers behind his head. His smile was pure evil. "Me and the town clerk're cousins. Even if you had the money, getting a business license might take . . . months. You willing to wait around?"

Mason worked to keep his Irish temper in check. His pa had spent more than one night in the calaboose for failing to keep his choler under control. Mason had long ago vowed not to follow in his old man's footsteps. The last time he'd been thrown in jail, it had been with a drunk sailor who'd killed a man on the Barbary Coast. Whatever had happened between the men, the sailor had claimed another life before morning by hanging himself in the cell.

"I have everything you need." Mason cast a quick look at the beakers and bottles on the shelves. "You're running low on what you need to precipitate silver chloride."

The assayer unlaced his fingers, dropped his feet to the floor with a thud and came around the counter.

"Let's see what you got."

The clerk tried to steal the chemicals with a lowball offer. Mason stood his ground. He'd sooner pour the acids out onto the plank floor than be cheated. After a long back-and-forth, he got more than twice what he'd paid for the chemicals in San Francisco, and had the feeling the clerk only paid half what ordering from the bigger city would have cost him. In a way, they both profited.

As he wandered about after the transaction, Mason found that prices in Virginia City were outrageous, even by San Francisco standards.

He settled down in a chair at the rear of a saloon that hadn't bothered thinking up a name, nursing a fifty-cent warm beer. When it had been drawn, it didn't even build a decent head. Flat, warm and ten times what it ought to have cost. He sipped at the bitter brew and had never tasted better despite its warmth. It had been a very long day for him.

"You got the look of a newcomer to town." A giant of a man peered down at Mason. "Mind if I pull up a chair?"

Mason pointed to the chair across the table. The man settled in. Wood creaked under the weight. Mason felt better about his own girth, only his new companion was pure muscle and gristle. If there was an ounce of fat anywhere on his body, it was hidden under the flannel shirt stretched to the breaking point. He wore canvas trousers that had seen better days and folded his hands on the table. From the calluses and nicked skin, those hands had seen a powerful lot of hard work recently.

"You a miner?" Mason watched the man's reaction.

"How'd you guess?" The miner laughed heartily, deep and resonant and carrying real mirth.

"I'm a chemist and I've seen plenty of gold hunters. You have the look." And Mason spoke the truth. There was a hint of eagerness to get into the hills and begin tearing away at the rock to find riches that turned all these men into a secret society. Or not so secret. It was more than greed. It was the need to prove themselves and become someone special.

"I didn't peg you to be a miner. You're dressed all wrong for it."

"Having been rejected by the clerk over at the assay

office, where, by damn, I could double the productivity with some tricks I learned in San Francisco, I find myself without employment and with very little money. Is there any job opening in town?"

"I got to hand it to you, Mister. You don't mince words. No howdy, weather's nice, you see the new gal over at the Crazy Eights, and how about that new strike up along Calabasas Creek. No, sir, you get right to the heart of the matter."

Mason found himself taking to the man. He motioned for the barkeep to bring over two beers. They were dropped on the table and his silver dollar taken. When the man didn't immediately reach for the second beer, Mason pointed.

"Much obliged." The giant of a man picked up the mug and drained it in one heroic gulp. He wiped his lips with his sleeve and put the empty down on the table. Mason vowed to never get into a drinking contest with him.

"My big-city manners need to be honed, it seems. Weather's nice, not a cloud to be seen. So, no rain anytime soon. Since I just breezed into town, I haven't seen that pretty filly, but if you say so, I'm sure she's quite a looker. Now, are there jobs to be had?"

The man laughed again and said, "You didn't mention the new strike."

"I don't know where this Calabasas Creek is, but if you're commenting on it, it must be spectacular." Mason nursed his second beer and studied the man over the rim. "I'm sure I'd have been of real help. Besides being a chemist, I'm a fair geologist."

"Do tell." The giant returned his appraising gaze. "Now it just might be I have need of a geologist. I got a rich strike to work, but the ore's all scattered about inside the mine. Never seen the like before."

"So it'd be a good thing if a man knowledgeable about rock formations and how gold and silver form took a gander, it might just be possible to go straight for the metal and leave the dross for less capable miners?"

"Something like that. I'd be willing to hire you, but I ain't got much in the way of money."

"So paying me to look around won't bring me much. Is that what you're saying?" Mason hesitated, then asked, "How is it you came over, never asked about the weather or the new gal at the Crazy Eights and all the rest and assumed I'm the one to find you a mother lode?"

"Some folks claim I'm gifted with second sight and just know things. Others say I got it from my first wife. She was Paiute. Or maybe Shoshone. She never was too specific about which, but she claimed her pa was a medicine man of great power. Some of that she inherited and maybe it rubbed off on me."

"First wife?"

"She died of the flu in the winter of '70. Been a cold seven years since, it has." The man got a distant look in his eyes. "Never found her like again." He snorted and spat inaccurately at a brass cuspidor by the bar. "Truth is, never found anyone else who'd have me. Not since. She was mostly blind, half-deaf and she'd got her nose cut off, so she couldn't smell me. It's hard to find a woman with all those qualities, believe you me."

Mason had to laugh. He had no idea if any of that was true, but the miner spun a good story.

"I take it you're the owner of the mine over on Calabasas Creek."

"I never said that I was. But that's a decent strike. There's going to be nigh on a million dollars in gold and silver clawed out of the ground around here this year. Might be the richest strike what ever was."

Mason caught his breath. Those numbers far exceeded the ones he'd heard in San Francisco that moved him to pull up stakes and come to Virginia City. Such wealth always left crumbs here and there. If he licked up just a few, he'd be rich.

"Why did you come over to me like a fly to honey?" Mason wanted an honest answer.

"Honey? You got a real high opinion of yourself, now, don't you? When you've been in Virginia City longer, you won't think honey at all but a pile of—"

"Why?" Mason got the idea.

"I picked up a report from Johnny Wilson and he was proud as punch that he had a couple shelves loaded with new chemicals for his assay work. It took some prodding, but you got mentioned along the way."

"Johnny? With spectacles? The assayer?"

"News travels fast in a boomtown. Johnny Four-Eyes, I call him. But he spoke highly of you and your skills."

"I doubt that. What'd he say?"

"You were a lowdown, no-account, thievin' big-city skunk thinkin' on cheatin' honest folks."

"That was a recommendation?"

The man chuckled. "You got a lot to learn. Whatever Johnny Four-Eyes says, is opposite to the truth. He's always the odd man out at a square dance, he can't hold his liquor and he thinks he's about the smartest man in all of Virginia City. Two of them's the Gospel truth."

"I can figure out which isn't," Mason said. "How much are you willing to spend on having a top-notch geologist like myself poke around Calabasas Creek and map out the veins?"

The giant started to answer but was interrupted by the loud clanging of a bell. Every man in the saloon stiffened, then downed their drinks and ran for the door, knocking one another over in their rush to get outside.

"What's going on?" Mason half stood in reaction.

"You come on, if you want to see. There's a fire." That was all the miner said as he kicked over his chair and ran for the street. He bowled over the men still in the doorway like they were skittles. Mason followed in his wake and burst outside. The smoky smell of metals being smelted was shrouded in cloying wood smoke. From the next layer of town downslope rose flames the like of which Morgan Mason had never seen in all his born days.

CHAPTER TWO

THE STRIDENT FIRE bells deafened him. Morgan Mason turned from side to side and the alarms came from every direction. More than this, miners ran past, yelling at the top of their lungs. He followed one knot of men as they ran down the street. The doors to what he had thought was a barn were thrown open, revealing a fire engine. The men struggled into red shirts and pulled on leather helmets as they hitched up a team and pushed the engine into the street.

It had been stark chaos up to this point. With a half-dozen uniformed firemen hanging on to the engine, the driver guided the team expertly past Mason to a crossing street. They slewed dangerously, took the corner and rolled downhill toward the fire. Behind them came a dozen more red-clad men carrying fire axes. Mason had seen cavalry troopers at the Presidio parade ground, moving in unison. Again the chaos evaporated. These men might not have been astride horses or even marching like troopers, but they moved as a single unit as they followed the fire engine down the slope.

The flames licked upward and were hot enough to cause Mason discomfort. He protected his face from the rising conflagration and lit out after the firemen. He skidded and slipped as he went down the steep hill to the next level of Virginia City. A crowd had formed a bucket line to fill the fire engine's tank. Two firemen worked feverishly on a boiler to build a head of steam. The tank filled about the time they got the steam engine coughing and choking out its fumes.

Four firemen unfurled the hose from a large roller, hooked it into the pump and dragged the end forward. They braced themselves as the fire captain counted to five. When he shouted, "Five!" the valves were turned and spigots opened. At first a tiny trickle of water dripped from the end of the hose. Then pressure built and all four men struggled to hold the bucking snake. They fought it around so the water sprayed onto the ever-growing fire.

From downhill, on the next lower level of Virginia City, came new fire alarms. The bells quieted as another fire engine struggled up the hill and pulled in beside the first.

Mason thought the two fire captains would come to blows. They shoved and pushed and bumped bellies. The one arriving first pointed down the street to a lesser fire working to devour a structure that once had held a hardware store. He couldn't hear over the roar of the fire but thought the two men were arguing over who got to extinguish the main fire.

All the while, the bucket brigade continued to pass along water to fill the fire engine's tank. Newly arriving men pushed him aside and took their place in the line. Mason considered doing the same, but the second fire crew gave up trying to horn in on the main fire and rolled away to tackle the hardware store fire. He followed them, thinking they needed his help more than the better-organized engine company valiantly advancing, using their spewing hose as a shield.

The crowd dwindled as he trailed the second engine company. He marveled that they, too, were outfitted in uniforms like the first firemen. The only distinctive difference he saw was the large brass belt buckle each man sported. He couldn't read the inscription but thought it spelled out *Virginia City*, possibly with the number of the engine company emblazoned on the center. Also, these firemen had brass studs pinned onto their suspenders. Some men had more, and two showed only a single large button. These had to be insignia or awards of some kind. The fire captain shouted out, "Put your back into it, men. Earn your medallion. Let's whip that fire before it eats the whole town!"

Mason stood back and watched. This company lacked the coordination of the first, but they still worked their hose into position and started spraying the flames. They either had filled their water tank before arriving or perhaps left it filled in case of such an emergency. Mason doubted that, because even the strong plow horses hitched to the engine would struggle hauling an already-filled tank engine up the slope from the lower part of the city.

The fire built in intensity and drove him back. He shielded his face with his arm to keep his skin from blistering. How the firemen endured the heat was a mystery, but they did. The spray from the hose nozzle might partly protect them. He didn't know.

"Water. We need more water. Form a bucket brigade!" The fire captain exhorted the crowd watching to begin refilling the tank on the fire engine.

Mason looked around for a bucket but saw none. A heavy hand pushed him forward. He stumbled, then regained his balance.

"On the back of the engine. That's where Fire Brigade No. 2 keeps the buckets. Grab one. The water's back down the street."

The giant who had been on the point of offering him a job as geologist herded him forward, then reached a long arm past and took a bucket from the rear of the engine. A spotted dog barked and tried to herd them. The man behind Mason growled and returned the dog's barks. The dalmatian backed off, tail between its legs, chastened.

"That ole dog's more bark than bite. Get on back." The dog obeyed. He grabbed two buckets and handed one to Mason. "Get to it, old son, or the whole town'll go up."

With that, the huge man spun and ran back down the street. Mason followed more slowly until he saw the pump and trough where the bucket brigade formed. He scooped up a full bucket and passed it along to the next man in time to turn and take another full bucket from his would-be employer. A dozen buckets were passed before a youngster ran back from the fire carrying three empty buckets.

These were filled quickly but not before another towheaded boy of about ten ran past with more empty buckets. The two urchins provided the return buckets for the men to fill and pass along. Mason fell into the rhythm of taking the full bucket and twisting at the waist to pass his load along to the next man, then rotate back and do it all again. The fire roared, the steam engine huffed and puffed as it spewed forth extinguishing water and the normal sounds of a vibrant boomtown all faded away. Mason became part of a machine whose only purpose was to put out the dangerous fire.

He passed along one bucket and turned back, only to find his potential benefactor was gone. No bucket waited for him. Rather than stop the line, Mason edged closer to the trough. At the other end a boy hardly old enough to shave worked the pump handle to keep the trough overflowing. Mason had buckets shoved into his hands by one of the young couriers. He took over the end of the line since the miner had disappeared. Mason didn't begrudge him a momentary rest, but he had made himself scarce in the face of real danger from the fire.

The smoke made it hard to see more than a few yards down the street, but Mason saw no trace of the man. Feeling deserted made Mason aware of how dog-tired he was. His arms ached and his belly muscles protested from the constant strain of hefting the heavy water-filled bucket and twisting around. He was used to more sedentary work. His hands were blistered, and tears ran down his cheeks from the smoke. He reached up to brush one away and his finger turned black from soot. For the first time he saw how the others around him looked. They were blackened and moved as if every muscle in their bodies hurt, too.

That made him feel a mite better. But where had the miner gone?

As he looked around, a cold knot formed in his stomach. The hardware store was a loss. Only blackened studs remained where once there had been walls. The roof had collapsed, and the only possible salvage from the store would be metallic. He knew heat did bad things to even tempered steel, sometimes turning it brittle. But sparks from the fire had flown through the air in both directions, not only back up the street toward the major blaze still raging in spite of the other engine company's best effort, and farther along this street.

He saw the miner in the door of an office where tiny fires danced on the roof. Other than this, the building was untouched.

"Look out!" Mason called. His voice came out cracked and weak. He had inhaled too much smoke to be in full throat. He stepped out of the bucket brigade line toward the distant office. Squinting, rubbing his eyes clear of smoke and tears, he saw the miner hesitate to enter, then plunge forward just as the roof exploded in fierce flames.

Mason tried to attract the attention of someone in the fire brigade. They were too occupied with the last traces in the hardware store. He heard the captain and two of his lieutenants arguing over moving to the building next to the hardware store or joining forces with the firemen from the street above. Seeing it wasn't possible to get their attention, Mason grabbed a fire axe and ran to the law office where the miner had entered, not knowing the danger.

The entire roof was ablaze when he reached the door. It stood ajar. Mason poked at it with his axe and called, "Roof! The roof's on fire. Get out!" His voice squeaked, a parody of his usual baritone. He spat. The cottony, gummy blob told him he should have taken a drink of water. Before, he had been so intent on moving water from the trough to the engine's tank to fight the fire, he hadn't thought to take even a small sip.

"Out. Get out!"

He saw the miner moving about inside, rummaging through a file cabinet. Papers flew everywhere as the man searched for something. The roof gave a small moan and then fell in. For a brief instant, Mason saw the miner perfectly. The look of exaltation on the man's face told he had found whatever he sought. Then the triumph turned to fear as fiery timbers crashed down all around him.

Mason summoned all his strength and shouted for the firemen. One glanced in his direction, then turned away. The fire company was too far off for him to explain. Using the axe handle to push the door open wider, he hunted for the miner. The giant man was nowhere to be seen through the smoke and dancing fire. Morgan Mason considered himself a sensible man, one who thought first and acted only when every possible outcome had been carefully calculated.

He swung his axe in a wide arc and knocked away a burning chair as he plunged into the inferno. Squinting, coughing, he advanced one step at a time in the face of intense heat. Never in his life had he reacted without thinking, but another man's life depended on what he did now.

"Can you get out? Come toward my voice!" He waited to see if the miner responded. Nothing. Mason swung the axe back and forth to hack a path through the debris.

He quickly saw why there hadn't been an answer.

The miner lay stretched out on the floor by the filing cabinet. A falling roof support had struck him on the top of the head. Mason chopped his way forward and reached the man's side. He poked him with the butt of the axe handle.

"Wha? What's happened?" The miner stirred, then let out a yelp as he flailed about and touched a hot coal. His eyes shot wide open. It took a second for him to understand where he was and the danger he faced. "Got the papers. Got 'em. Let's get out of here. I'm not dead, am I?"

"Why do you ask?" Mason grabbed a handful of the miner's shirt and pulled him upright. He struggled to force the man to his feet.

"Hotter 'n hell. Musta died and gone to the nether regions, it's so hot."

"You broke into a burning building. What were you hunting for? Never mind. Tell me outside." Mason used the axe handle to lever himself to his feet. He bent and got a grip on the miner's hand and heaved. The man groaned but gathered his long legs and got them under him. He stood on shaky feet.

"Where's the way out?"

Mason started to deride the man, then realized the smoke and fire had blocked the way to the door. There wasn't any way through.

"There must be another exit." Mason pointed using the axe. All he did was fan some of the smoke around without finding an escape.

"Back room. There's a back room." The miner stumbled to the files, then worked his way around.

Mason let the miner lead the way. He obviously knew the layout of the office. He'd save them both.

"Hurry up," Mason urged. "My clothes are starting to smolder." He tried beating out the embers landing on his coat sleeve. He failed. Then he realized that was the least of his worries. His feet felt as if he had marched a thousand miles across a burning desert. And every breath he took made him wonder if the miner wasn't right about this being hell and not a simple Virginia City office.

He reached out and put his hand on the other man's shoulder. The smoke billowing about obscured all vision. Then came a sound unlike anything he had ever heard before. It was a creaking and snapping and a moan that was eerily human. A sudden upward gust cleared the smoke for a brief instant, showing the bright blue Nevada sky.

Then the roof collapsed. Mason recoiled and tried to drag the miner with him. A heavy beam crashed smack-dab onto the man. Mason felt him jerk away as he fell to the floor. Before he could move to pull the burning beam away, another, larger one fell amid a shower of sparks. Mason stepped back instinctively, caught his heel and sat heavily. He smashed into a desk.

A quick jerk to the side carried him into the knee well of the desk. The rain of fire and wood from above no longer fell on his head, but he saw his companion stretched out with two large beams pinning his legs down.

Then the rest of the roof gave up the ghost and came thundering down.

CHAPTER THREE

Mason drew his knees up and hugged them. This cut off the blistering heat assaulting him. Breathing through his coat sleeve filtered out some of the paralyzing smoke, but the inferno all around intensified. If he didn't get out of the building fast, he was going to die.

"My legs. My legs got crushed."

He scrubbed away soot from his watery eyes and saw the miner struggling a few feet away. The burning beams held the man firmly to the floor, but that didn't stop him from trying to get free. Every time he tried to push away the parts of the roof holding him down, he yelped. The wood that wasn't outright burning had to be scalding hot.

"Coming," grated out Mason. "I'm coming. Hold on."

He cursed himself for a fool, but he had no choice.

He might die if he stayed much longer, but leaving the miner behind wasn't in the cards. Mason stumbled out from his hidey-hole, got to his feet and lifted the axe. The miner's eyes went wide with fear when he saw Mason raise the fire axe high over his head, then bring it down.

The miner passed out when Mason cut away at the wood pinning down the man's legs. A few chips flew. He tried again. Then he got in a rhythm as if chopping away at a tree trunk. He'd never been a lumberjack and had never even known one. San Francisco was filled with sailors and cardsharps and men from all walks of life, but there was no call for Mason to have ever met a lumberjack.

He put his back into the downward swing. He found the trick to twisting the blade once it bit into the wood. Chips flew into the raging fire. And then the fallen beam parted, freeing the miner's legs. Mason stared at the result of his frantic chopping. He had freed the man. Now what should he do?

Shock wore off that he had accomplished this much. He cast aside the axe, grabbed a double handful of shirt and heaved the miner to a sitting position. The giant of a man outweighed Mason by fifty pounds, but some inner reserve of strength and determination let him heave the man up to his feet. With a lithe twist, Mason got his shoulder under the man's body. The added weight staggered him, then he positioned his legs under the massive miner and lifted.

The added weight caused him to stagger as he headed in the direction of the back room. Stepping over piles of smoking debris kept him moving in what proved to be the right direction. Through the curtain of smoke appeared a closed door. Mason lowered his shoulder and used the miner as a battering ram. Their combined weight sent the back door flying outward. Mason with his human load followed.

He kept his legs pumping until his strength gave out entirely. The miner cushioned his fall to the ground. Mason worried the rescue had been for naught, but then the miner groaned and thrashed about. The movement started strong and then died down. The only sign of life was the shallow rise and fall of the barrel chest.

"Help me," Mason called out when he saw a fireman tramping along the alley behind the row of buildings. The red-shirted man carried an axe balanced on his shoulder.

He gave Mason a quick look. "You got out just fine. I got to find others who need my help more."

"But this fellow. He's unconscious. He needs help." Mason sat up and pointed at the miner.

"He's a goner. And you need to clear out, too. This whole block is lost." He glanced over his shoulder at the inexorable advance of fire jumping from one building to the next. Without any further ado, he stepped over Mason and the miner and hurried on. Here and there he rapped on closed doors with his axe, listening for sounds inside. But in less than a minute, he disappeared into the pall hanging over the alley.

Mason closed his eyes and gasped, trying to suck enough air into his lungs to regain some strength. All he did was gag. When the spasm passed, he rolled onto hands and knees, then began dragging the man he had saved upright again. Getting the miner draped over his shoulders this time took longer and drained Mason more, but he succeeded. Stumbling down a tight space between buildings, he reached the street.

Chaos had reigned before. Now a half-dozen fire engines pumped water onto the blaze. Mason was no expert but thought the firemen were prevailing. The fires hadn't spread any farther, and where the pumpers spewed water into the heart of each inferno, the voracious flames retreated.

Mason staggered to a street leading to a lower level. He almost took a tumble down the steep hill but managed to keep his feet. At the intersection he saw a sign swinging back and forth in the fitful wind caused by the fire on the level now above him. With grim determination, he plodded ahead and tried to open the door he had singled out. Twice he bumped against the door, then started to use the miner as a battering ram again.

"What's all the fuss? Oh, come on in. Set him down on the operating table." A spare man with thinning sandy-colored hair held the door open for Mason to enter the surgery.

"You the doctor?"

"One of 'em," the man said. He pointed to a table against the far wall. "Virginia City has a lot of need. Last I counted, there's three of us practicing." He hesitated, grinned grimly and said, "And there're four undertakers. This is a dangerous place." He sniffed hard. "Caught in the fire, the pair of you?"

Mason brushed the doctor's hand away as he tried to touch the blistered spot on his face.

"He needs you more than I do."

"Does he, now?" The doctor shook his head. "I've

seen worse. I've also seen miners in better shape that upped and died. What's his name?"

Mason swung the miner around and laid him out on the operating table. For the first time he got a good look at the man he had saved. Chances were good that he'd regret it. The miner was in bad shape, really bad shape. Most of his clothing was singed or burned off, and one leg swung off the table in a way no leg was ever designed to bend. Gingerly, he lifted the damaged limb up and put it onto the table. It looked as if it belonged to another patient.

"Got a jar of salve on my desk. I was waiting to see how many burn cases I'd get. You're the first."

Mason collapsed into the chair behind the doctor's desk. From the nameplate he saw he had blundered into Dr. Sinclair's surgery. He pushed it aside to take the ceramic jar with the salve in shaking hands. The lid almost defeated him. When he opened it and dropped the top onto the desk, the smell rising from the yellow, viscous goo made him woozy.

"Smear it on," Dr. Sinclair said. He began slicing off the miner's clothing with a knife, peeling back pieces burned into the man's body. "Just a little bit. I'm going to need most of that jar for your friend."

"Not my friend." Mason settled back and let the ointment work on him. It felt cool when he smeared it on, then it burned like hellfire. Before he cried out, the pain began to fade, and he only felt numb. Numb was good, he decided. "I don't know who he is."

"You mean you risked your life to pull him out of a fire and you weren't expecting a reward?"

"Reward? You mean he's an outlaw with a bounty on his head?"

Sinclair laughed. He began cleaning the burns with carbolic acid. Every drop on the miner's body made the man wince.

"Just about the reverse. Now that I cleaned off his face, I can recognize him. This here's Blue Dirt Duggan, the current holder of the most lucrative strike in the Comstock."

"Blue Dirt?" Mason had to smile at that. *Blue dirt* meant an especially rich vein of silver. "He's the owner of the Calabasas Creek mine?"

"You've heard of it but not him. Figures." Sinclair looked up from his work. "You're no miner. You're dressed all wrong and . . ."

"And it doesn't look as if I've done a day's work in my life. He said the same thing, but he was about to offer me a job. I'm a geologist."

"That and mining engineers are in short supply here. Duggan must have had the idea of hiring you away from the big companies to keep them from gobbling up all the good claims."

"Isn't everything a good claim?"

"You'd be surprised how many holes in the mountain bring out nothing but worthless rock. There are millionaires scattered all over. There're ten times that number who never find so much as an ounce of gold or silver. Oh." Sinclair took a step away from the table.

Blue Dirt Duggan rose up and supported himself on one arm. His brilliant eyes blazed forth from a mask of flesh slathered with yellow salve.

"Howdy, Doc. Pleased to see you and not Saint Peter."

"Mr. Duggan. You are lucky to be alive. Your remarkable constitution has saved you, I would say."

"Ain't just me being too ornery to kick the bucket. It's that I got a good friend willing to risk his own hide to save mine. Thank you kindly, Mister . . ."

"You don't know his name? Don't that beat all," Sinclair said. "Fact is, I don't know his name, either."

Morgan Mason introduced himself, then said, "You were going to hire me on as a geologist. That job still open?"

"It is, but I'm needing help with the real work. In spite of my legs feeling fine, I 'spect I'll be hobbling about on a crutch for a spell. Not the first time I busted a leg, so I know."

Sinclair looked from Duggan to Mason. The skeptical expression warned Mason something wasn't right. Then he saw. The doctor had shoved the knife he'd used to cut away the miner's clothing into the leg that flopped around. Duggan never reacted.

"Nice that we all know each other now," Sinclair said. "Mr. Mason, why don't you get on back to the fire and see if they need more help."

Even as he spoke, steam whistles blasted and almost drowned out his words.

"What's that?" Mason half stood. "Sounds like a train coming into the depot."

"That's the all-clear signal. The fire engines vent their steam when the fire's been put out. You get on out now and have a drink or two. A lot of the saloons serve up free liquor."

"For the fire crews," Duggan said. His voice came out weak now. He sank back to the table and stared up at the ceiling. "You can always cadge a drink or two if you butter up the fire captain. Right about now he's feeling his oats, everyone's slapping him on the back to congratulate him and all the women . . ." His voice trailed off because Sinclair sloshed a liquid on a cloth and held it under his nose.

"Chloroform," Sinclair explained. "It's potent stuff. Why don't you close the door behind you as you go? Do as Mr. Duggan suggested."

"I could use a drink," Mason said. "Food, too. It's been forever since I ate."

"Bring me a bottle of rye whiskey when you come back." Sinclair hesitated, then added, "If you've a mind to come back, that is."

Mason saw the doctor stripping off his coat and pulling on a white jacket. Dried bloodstains showed how he used the jacket to protect his clothing.

Without another word, Mason left the surgery, gently shutting the door behind. Whatever medical procedure went on inside wasn't anything he wanted to know about. He marched out into the street and saw that the fire hadn't been as bad as it might have been. The large warehouse that fed the first blaze was a ruin. Stores on either side were similarly devastated. Then other buildings along the road were either strangely preserved or complete losses. He made his way to the law office where he had saved Duggan. The wall studs were charred and the roof was completely collapsed, as he well knew. Two men stood in the street arguing. One pointed repeatedly at the devastation. The other shook his head.

"What was that place?" Mason stopped a few paces away. Neither man looked all that friendly, but his curiosity got the better of him.

"That was our law office. Ruined! Completely ruined!"

"The file cabinet at the back might be all right. A beam fell on it, but the contents weren't burned."

The men stared at him, openmouthed.

"How do you know?"

"I left my fire axe in there." Mason took perverse pleasure in how both lawyers fell silent. He kicked away debris and found the beam he had chopped up to free Duggan. The axe was half-buried under ash. He pulled it out, brushed it off, hoisted it to his shoulder and returned to the street.

"You went in? You saved our files?"

Mason half smiled, then walked off whistling an off-key tune through chapped lips. He was battered and burned and was feeling his oats. Coming to Virginia City had been uncharacteristic of the way he lived. No risks: Look at ore samples and maybe burn his fingers on reagents. That had been the most thrilling thing that had ever happened to him in San Francisco. Stepping off the stage, he had been shot at and caught up in a raging fire and saved a man's life—by the doctor's account, one of the richest men in Virginia City—and now strutted away with a fire axe over his shoulder, just like the firemen trained for their jobs.

His high spirits faded with every step he took up the street, heading for the top street in town. Mason gasped and every muscle in his body screamed in agony by the time he reached this elevated position looking back over the town. The saloon with no name beckoned. He saw the Crazy Eights Saloon a dozen buildings down the street and wondered at the new girl working there. Blue Dirt Duggan had thought she was something special, but the huge crowd trying to enter that establishment kept him headed for the unnamed gin mill.

It was almost filled to capacity, too, because a half-dozen red-shirted men lined up along the bar, accepting drinks from a grateful citizenry.

He tried to get to the long bar but found the crowd too thick and unwilling to part. From what he overheard, most of the men wanted to heap praise on their heroes and thank them for saving the town. Mason drifted back and pressed his back against the far wall. The crowd had to thin out enough for him to get a drink eventually.

"Won't do you any good waiting there. This can go on till dawn," said a man seated in a rickety chair. "Here. Take a pull. You look like you were caught up in the middle of the firestorm."

Mason hesitated. The bottle was a quarter full. The way his thirst exploded, he would have to restrain himself from downing it all in a single swallow. He took the bottle, licked his lips, then sampled the whiskey. It about tore his throat out.

"Good rotgut, ain't it? Old Smitty, he's the barkeep, makes it up himself. You should see the still in the back room."

"There's more 'n alcohol in this."

"That's his brandy. He puts a drop or two of nitric acid in to give it the kick of a mule."

"Brandy?" Mason held up the bottle. The label plainly read BOURBON.

"Most all his concoctions taste the same. That's because he don't change his formula from one batch to the next." The man pried the bottle from Mason's fingers. He reluctantly surrendered. "Set yourself down before you fall down." The man pointed to the chair across the table. "I don't need to hear them jackasses tell me about how they saved every last soul. You tell me a new story. You got the look of a man itching to spill his guts."

"You really want to hear?"

"I don't like drinking alone. I can do that out on the mountain. I come to town to socialize."

"I hear tell there's a new gal down the street at the Crazy Eights."

"Now *that's* the kind of jawing I appreciate. Tell me about her."

Mason took the chance to swallow another jolt of the acid-laced "brandy" before going on.

"A friend of mine says she's really something. She just blew into town not long ago and—"

"Hold up, Mister. Captain Delahunt is fixin' to say his piece. From the way he's teetering around, he'll pass out drunk 'fore he gets to the part where he's about the bravest fire eater in all of the Comstock Lode."

The fireman jumped to sit on the bar, then stood. Mason's drinking companion wasn't far wrong about the captain's condition.

"Fellow citizens of this here fine town of Virginia City, me and Fire Brigade No. 1 put out the goldangest, most re-cal-see-trant fire ever in the history of this town. It took all our skill and daring, but we got there first. Them pretenders from Fire Brigade No. 2 had to clean up the ashes after us. We . . ."

Mason sat bolt upright, all weariness gone. The alarm bells were clanging out their warning once more.

Silence fell on the crowd, then Delahunt and the rest of his firefighting company ran for the door. Another fire threatened Virginia City.

CHAPTER FOUR

MORGAN MASON MOVED as if he had been dipped in molasses. The world flowed around him in strange eddies, but the one thing that brought him back to the here and now was the choking smoke filling the air once more. The first fire had been directly in front of the no-name saloon but on the next level down. The new fire was on the lower level but farther to the north, past where the law office had gone up in flames.

The fire bell clanging deafened him and the firemen stumbled along, returning to their fire engine, now parked on the street. Two youngsters helped bring the horses out and hitch them to the wagon. By the time they'd finished, the entire fire crew had climbed up and held on for dear life. The driver lashed the team and got the wagon with the steam engine and water tank rolling. The spotted dog ran alongside, yelping to get on. The dog was left behind as the driver once more took the turn and rolled down the steep incline, standing on the brake to keep the engine from running over the horses.

"Come on," Mason said to the dog. "Let's go see what we can do."

The dog looked up at him, turned its head skeptically and then let out a single bark, as if saying, *What are you waiting for?*

Only then did he realize he still clung to the fire axe. The dog might think he was one of the firemen. The dog ran ahead, but Mason had to follow more slowly. His body was one giant ache, and muscles he hadn't known he had protested every move. He slipped and slid down the street to the lower intersection. The dog barked at him, waiting impatiently.

"Go on. Find your master," Mason urged. The dalmatian only barked louder. He gave in and walked past the site of the first fire. Smoke curls rose from the wreckage. A quarter mile down the street the fire company started working to build a head of steam in the pump engine and once more refill the water tank. The helpers were fewer now, exhausted from earlier efforts.

From what Mason saw, this might be more threatening than the first fire. If it jumped from the single building already fully ablaze, it had a considerable ways to spread. A half mile or more of tinderbox buildings could go up in flames.

"You, get to work. Chop out walls that might let the fire spread."

Mason looked around, wondering who the fire captain had called to. The barking dog woke him to the situation. Captain Delahunt was giving him the order. He raised his axe in response, but the fire captain had already turned back to getting the stream of water gushing from the hose onto the right parts of the fire. Mason saw that Delahunt fought places that looked less dangerous but that afforded spots for rapid spread. The man knew his job.

Without any further instruction, Mason hiked down the street looking for spots where the fire might jump from one building to the next. He found one office that, if it caught fire, gave an easy conduit in several directions for the voracious flames. Putting his back to it, he started chopping at the wall closest to the fire. Sweat poured off him, and breathing became more difficult as new clouds of smoke blew down the street, but he made progress. The wall began to lean, then toppled from his effort.

He stepped away and studied his handiwork. A decent fire break had formed because of his effort. If any of the wood from the downed wall caught fire, it only spread along the ground. The real danger came from jumping roof to roof. He remembered a friend in San Francisco telling of a fire across the Bay where the crowns of treetops had caught fire and then the flames had jumped from tree to tree without ever touching the ground.

The barking dog drew his attention. He went back into the street. The sight a few doors farther down the street made him catch his breath. A quick pat on the dog's head to thank the dalmatian and he rushed to look inside.

A small fire burned in the middle of the floor of what looked to be another lawyer's office. He wasted no time using the broad side of the axe head to scatter the papers and then stamp them out. He finished and sank into a chair to rest. The charred sheets haunted him. It was as if someone had piled up the loose sheets and then set them on fire.

"Arson?" Mason found that hard to believe. In a town so prone to fire, such a crime deserved hanging. He leaned forward and poked through the papers with the axe head, then bent over and picked up a piece of wood. He had been skeptical before. Now anger burned in him as fierce as the fire.

This fire had been started by someone dropping a lucifer into a carefully prepared pile of paper. A quick flick sent the matchstick flying. Mason got to his feet and looked around to be sure other heaps of paper hadn't been lit. When he went back into the street, the dog barked loudly and ran this way and that. Sure that it had his attention, the dog ran for a store across the street.

Mason wasted no time to see what the dog had found in the tailor shop. A quick look around showed nothing. The dog crowded past and ran for the back room. Mason went to see what the dog already had.

Two small children huddled together under a table.

"Come on out," Mason said. "You shouldn't stay here with the fire so close. It's only a few stores away."

The children clutched each other. The boy looked to be four or five, and he was the older of the pair. The little girl wasn't much older than three. From their matching dark hair and green eyes, they had to be siblings.

"Is this your pa's tailor store?" Mason looked around, wondering why a parent had abandoned his children.

"Mama's," the boy said. "She told us to stay."

"Where'd she go?" Mason didn't expect an answer and got none. He changed his tactics. Trying to grab the children if they tried to get away from him would only delay them going to safety. In the distance, he heard the roar of the fire, the chugging steam engine powering the pump and commands shouted by the fire captain. If he understood Delahunt's orders, the fire was marching along the street in this direction.

"I need your help. Can you help me?" Mason saw he had the boy's attention. The girl buried her face in her brother's chest. "Someone needs to take care of the dog. The spotted dog."

"Smudge?"

"Yeah, Smudge. He'd like you to see that he got back to Captain Delahunt."

"He's a hero. My mama says so."

Mason whistled. The well-trained dog came to him and sat at his feet.

"Smudge wants you to look after him. Both of you." Mason motioned for the children to come out from under the table. For a second, he thought they'd argue. Instead, the boy led his sister out, both of them crawling on hands and knees. To Mason's relief, the dog went and licked the little girl's face until she giggled.

Mason backed away. The dog and his two charges came out. Mason did everything not to spook the kids until he got them out of the shop.

"Smudge will stay with you until you find your ma." He saw this wasn't the right thing to say now. The children threw their arms around the dalmatian's neck and clung to him. In spite of his training, the dog didn't cotton to such attention and tried to pull away.

"Tommy, Iris!" The shrill voice cut through the general hubbub. "You're safe!" A tall woman stumbled along from the direction of the fire, arms reaching out. "My babies!"

The two children looked up at the woman. The boy—

Tommy—called, "See, Mama, I got to pet Smudge." The dog barked in response. The woman ignored the dalmatian and scooped up the boy. Iris crawled over and used her mother's skirts to pull herself up so she could hug a leg.

"You found them," she said, turning to Mason. "Thank you. I got cut off by the fire. There's a barricade. It took me—"

"They're safe, ma'am," Mason said. "You'd better take them as far as you can from this street, though it looks like the fire's almost under control." He saw Captain Delahunt waving off the bucket brigade filling the engine's water tank in spite of the fire still licking at exposed walls.

"My brother's place is outside town. We'll go there." The woman gathered her young-uns and hurried off. Mason watched until he was sure they were safely on their way, then frowned. What did he care? He wasn't a fireman. There wasn't any reason for him to risk his life the way he had, though he felt good about rescuing the children.

Thinking about Blue Dirt Duggan sobered him up. He had saved the man's life, too, but that might not have been any favor, from the look of his injuries.

Smudge barked and trotted away, circled and came back, barked again, then ran off to where the fire captain supervised a length of water hose being rolled up and properly stored. Mason took his time approaching Delahunt. He wasn't sure what he should say about the pile of papers and the lucifer that had been dropped onto them.

"That's our axe." Captain Delahunt grabbed it from Mason's hands.

Mason almost protested. He had saved lives with that axe—then he realized how loco that sounded.

"Glad to be of help." He pointed to the distant figures of the woman and her children. "Got them to safety and made a fire break out of the office three or four doors down the street."

Delahunt fixed him with a hard look. Before he said anything, Smudge barked and jumped up on Mason. He had to pet the dog.

"Well-trained fire dog, here," he said.

"Smudge doesn't take kindly to that. People petting him," Delahunt said. He whistled twice and the dog tore off, jumped and landed on the seat beside the driver of the fire engine. "Is the tank drained? Then get on back to the firehouse. We've got some *more* serious drinking to do."

"Did you miss a coal from the first fire?" Mason asked.

"We got them all. This was another fire," Delahunt said. He stalked off, angry at the criticism of his firemen's abilities.

Mason started to ask some more questions, but the fire captain stepped up and grabbed a handhold. The engine rattled and clanked as it headed back to its firehouse on the level above. It was all well and good having confidence in men he had undoubtedly trained, but Delahunt hadn't given any reason for the new fire. For all that, the first was something of a mystery.

Rather than following the fire company back into their saloon, Mason began poking through the ashes of the first building. The side toward the crossing street was in the worst shape, as if the fire started on that wall and spread. Mason slowly walked the perimeter, not sure what he sought. The next building down had suffered some serious damage, but as he neared the site of the second fire, he saw less trace of fire. Wood had been scorched, but it hadn't ignited. When he came to the far wall of the second building, he saw how the flames had reared up and fanned out.

The source of the fire was a huge burned spot.

"Whatcha doin'?"

Mason looked up. A fireman wobbled about and finally tried to keep himself upright by leaning against a burned stud in the front wall. It gave way and he stumbled about. When he came closer, Mason realized the man would go up in a bright blue flame if he got too near heat. He had been drinking, and he wasn't one of Delahunt's crew. His brass buckle proclaimed him to be a member of the other fire brigade. The numeral 2 was smudged with soot, and other parts of his uniform showed he wasn't part of the current firefighting effort. Suspenders were marked with yellow stripes, not brass buttons, and he wore a curious insignia on his right sleeve.

"What's that mean?" Mason pointed to the insignia.

The man came closer, bent and stared at the source of the second fire.

"Somebody got real careless, that's what it means. Why'd anyone miss the fireplace that much?"

"No fireplace," Mason said. "There's a Franklin stove." The iron, potbellied stove stood forlornly at the middle of what had been the main room. Everything around it had been turned to charcoal. "But I meant your insignia."

"This? We're the Fire Drake Brigade. Best damn firemen in Virginia City. They may have started 'fore us and call us Fire Brigade No. 2, that's why they got number one on their buckles. But we're better. Finley's Fire Drakes." He braced himself against the wall and peered at the fire pit. "Somebody set the fire. Why'd they go and do a thing like that?"

"You know about this?"

"Been with ole Donald Finley goin' on three years. I'm the best he has. Course I know. I teach the green-horns what it takes to get a fire going. Fuel, fire and . . . and . . ."

"Air," Mason finished for him. "I'm a chemist. I know some of what it takes to smelt ore."

"Air. You're right. I'll tell Captain Finley to recruit you."

"That's good," Mason said, "but we should tell some-body about this. If it's arson, he has to be stopped before he sets more fires."

"Arrest him! That's the ticket!" The fireman waved his arm around. "The marshal's off over there. Let's go tell him."

Mason considered what the lawman might think if a newcomer to Virginia City reported a crime. He wasn't sure having a drunk fireman telling of arson was much better. The two of them might carry some weight.

"Lead on. I don't know where the marshal's office is since I just arrived this afternoon."

"New to town? Well, you can't just join any of the brigades. No, sir. You got to be recommended. You got to be upstanding and then you can volunteer. We're the town's royalty, we are. Common folks, they look up to us."

"There's rivalry between the two brigades?" Mason steered the man into the street and waited to see which direction he took. He was drawn back past the steep cross street.

"Two? Rivalry between *two* of us? There's seven other brigades. Sometimes we get into fights over who can put out a fire."

"The victors are heroes, at least for the day?" Mason shook his head sadly. The "winning" fire crew was feted, given free drinks and probably a lot more.

"We got traditions to uphold. The Fire Drakes are the oldest."

"Why's Captain Delahunt get to put 'one' on his belt buckle, then?"

"Finley never thought of it, that's why. One day we saw Delahunt's boys show up with those buckles. They stole a march on us, but we were first in town. We're the best. Ask anybody. The honest ones'll tell you that."

Mason had to support the man the more they walked, but when he saw the jailhouse, the drunk seemed to sober up. He stopped in the middle of the street and pointed at two deputies coming from the office.

With a roar like a lion, the drunk pushed Mason aside and charged. He crashed into the two lawmen, fists swinging wildly. The trio went down in a writhing, fighting, clawing pile. Mason stared, not having any notion what to do.

CHAPTER FIVE

MORGAN MASON'S FIRST instinct was to run. The three men rolled over and over in the dirt, kicking up a small dust storm. He backed off a step or two, then remembered why he had brought the fireman here. The idea of someone sneaking around town setting deadly fires had to be addressed. Whoever did it hadn't killed anyone yet—that he knew of. If both fires had been set by the same varmint, there might have been others set earlier. From the look of the town, the smallest fire could turn deadly if more were set in the future.

He stepped forward, saw a flash of suspenders marked with stripes, grabbed and yanked as hard as he could. His feet shot out from under him, but he clung to the fireman's suspenders long enough to pull him off the two struggling deputies. They rolled away and came to their knees, both reaching for their six-shooters.

"Wait, stop, don't shoot!" Mason's voice cracked with strain. "We came here to report a crime."

"Jasper Jessup's the only criminal I see," snarled one deputy. He cocked his six-gun and pointed it at the fireman, who sat cross-legged in the dirt.

"Don't!" Mason stepped around the seated fireman. He held his hands out to stop the lawman from firing. The look in the man's eyes told him a second dead body in the street wouldn't cause him to lose any sleep.

"What's the ruckus? Put that hogleg away, John. You know better 'n to shoot an unarmed suspect." A tall, thin man made of piano wire and cured leather strode from the jailhouse. "You, too, Luther. You know what I told you boys."

"He's the one, Marshal. He's the one what gave me a hotfoot over at the Crazy Eights. The whole danged bar laughed at me." John thrust his six-gun out and wove about to get a shot at Jasper Jessup around Mason.

"I don't know what he's done, but him and me have something important to tell you, Marshal. Real important." Mason stood his ground.

The marshal stepped forward, grabbed his deputy's collar and pulled him to his feet. He whispered something in John's ear that made the deputy turn fiery red in the face. Grinding his teeth, the deputy lowered the hammer and shoved his gun back into his holster.

"Come on, Luther. We got a patrol to do." John stepped around Mason, shot him daggers in a look that cut deep and hurt hard, then stormed off. Luther slid his six-shooter back into his holster. His glare was reserved for Jasper Jessup.

"I just saved you from getting ventilated," the marshal said. "This had better be worth my while. Otherwise, I'll call my boys back and let them use you both for target practice."

"John started it, Marshal Benteen. You know how he is when he gets a snootful of whiskey. He was downright disrespectful and needed to be shown what for. He had the gall to say the Fire Drakes were slackers and that Delahunt's scoundrels were the best in town. Them's fighting words!"

"Jessup, you cause more trouble than any three others. I don't care if you're Finley's pet. The townsfolk might look at you like you're some kind of god, but to me you're a troublemaker and nothing more." The marshal took Jessup by the shoulders and lifted. For a man who looked like he had one foot in the grave, being so thin and all, he showed considerable strength. Mason vowed not to cross the lawman.

"You still owe us the bounty for putting out the fire last week, too."

"The mayor's got the reward money all tied up. Finley will get it when I do. And after today's fires, Delahunt will demand to be paid first. Those were big fires compared to the one you put out."

"Marshal Benteen, we have proof the fires today were set on purpose." Mason had no desire to get caught up in the city's politics. From what he had seen, the fire brigades were the first and foremost cause of gossip. For a boomtown floating on a sea of gold and silver, that made some sense. The miners who had struck it rich weren't inclined to do anything but work their claims, and who wanted to hear the sad stories of prospectors unable to find a decent vein to work?

"That's a mighty serious charge. How do you know?"

Benteen looked him over from head to toe. He obviously did not approve.

"I can show you what I found."

"What *you* found? Not him?" Benteen shook Jasper Jessup like a terrier with a rat. The fireman's teeth clacked.

"He agreed with me when I pointed it out." Mason shifted nervously from foot to foot. This wasn't going the way he'd expected. "Come with us and I'll show you."

"Wait here." Benteen yanked Jessup around and shoved him into the jailhouse. Mason heard loud protests followed by the iron clang of a cell door closing. He flinched at the click of a key turning in the lock. The marshal came stomping out a few seconds later. "Get moving. Show me what you found."

"Why'd you lock him up? He's only trying to help."

"Public drunkenness."

"If you threw everyone who got drunk in Virginia City into the clink you'd need a jail ten times this size."

"There's still an empty cage right next to his." Benteen's meaning was clear. Mason clamped his mouth shut and walked a little faster.

He got to the office where he had found the evidence of arson and pointed it out. The sun was sinking behind Gold Hill, the tall hill to the west.

"Sure does get dark here early in the day," Mason said. "But then dawn must come fast, since there's nothing but open space to the east."

"This it? A scorched spot on the wall?"

Mason explained what he had found and how this had to be deliberately set. The lawman grunted, spat

and walked around, kicking at piles and finally returning to the street.

"The other fellow, Jessup, seemed to know all about
setting a fire. He'll agree that this was an attempted
arson." Mason expected some reply. He didn't get it.

Marshal Benteen said nothing. With a shrug of his
shoulders, he walked off with his eyes straight ahead.
If he had shouted that he wanted to be elsewhere, anywhere else, he couldn't have made it more obvious.
Mason ran to keep up, his shorter legs pumping hard.
He realized the marshal returned to the jailhouse and
slowed, finally stopping. He watched Benteen's back as
he left him behind. He had no clear idea what went
through the man's mind, but he doubted it had anything to do with finding someone who had tried intentionally to burn the town down.

"Sir. Sir!"

Mason looked around, realizing he had stopped in
front of the tailor shop where he had found the children. That seemed an eternity in the past. The woman
beckoned to him to come over.

"What can I do for you, ma'am?" He glanced back
in the direction taken by the marshal. The lawman had
disappeared into the twilight. "Are your children all
right? Tommy and Iris, wasn't it?"

"They are fine, thanks to you. I can't repay you, not
with money, but you look as if you could use a new set
of clothes. Those rags you've got on have seen better
days."

Mason laughed at that. "That better day was this
morning, before I stepped off the stagecoach."

"Do let me outfit you. I can't give you anything
fancy, but I have a few things that might fit you."

"You don't have to, ma'am."

"Come inside now, young man." She took his arm and pulled him into her shop. "I'd rather give you a set of durable clothes than have it all go up in smoke if there's another fire along this street."

"It was pretty grim today. Twice," he said.

"Nothing like the fire back in 1875. That burned most of the town to ground. I came from Kansas City right after that terrible fire with my husband. He's gone now, may he rest in peace. He's down in the Silver Terrace Cemetery." She smiled sadly but proudly. "He was a Knight of Pythias and has a fine grave site in their reserved section. You aren't a Knight, are you? No, of course not. Maybe you should consider joining. You have the moral character." She moved him around closer to a coal oil lamp. "Now, let's see what we can do."

A half hour later, Morgan Mason stepped out of the tailor shop with decent clothing that would be in style in San Francisco, as well as a brown paper package wrapped in twine with heavier work clothes.

The heavy smoke hung in the air as a reminder of the day's disasters. He stopped at the big street coming down from higher up on the hill. For the first time he saw street signs. He walked along C Street and had almost tumbled down Union more than once that day. Getting the lay of the land was important. He felt better with the fancy duds. That would give him confidence and improve his chance of finding a job the next day.

The clerk at the assayer wasn't likely to be any more agreeable, so he had to find a job that made use of his skills without making every day one filled with sore muscles and cuts and bruises. He stretched a little and stared uphill toward B Street. Laughter, loud music and the sounds of gaiety drew him. But he had only climbed a dozen steps when he knew he had to do something about Jasper Jessup. While he wasn't responsible for the bad blood between him and the entire Virginia City police force, letting Jessup rot in the jail wasn't the responsible thing to do.

He returned to the jailhouse. The door stood open and light spilled out from inside. He tucked his bundle of clothing under his arm and stepped inside. The marshal sat at his desk with a carpet of WANTED posters spread in front of him.

"What do you want?" Even as he spoke, Benteen lifted one of the posters and compared it to Mason's face. He scowled, put down the poster and chose another. Disgusted, he dropped this to his desk, too, and stared at Mason.

Mason wasn't going to be intimidated. He had endured too much during the day for that.

"I want to talk to your prisoner."

"You got bail for him? Ten dollars will spring him." Marshal Benteen glowered even harder. "You got fine duds there. Miz Logan fixed you up nice."

"How can you tell?" This startled Mason. While adequate, he saw nothing distinctive in the clothing the woman had given him. He hadn't even thought to ask her name, in spite of knowing her children's.

"She's the best seamstress for a hundred miles." Benteen coughed and added, "She sews mighty fine shrouds for the undertakers, too. For all of them."

"All four?"

Mason was pleased to finally shock the marshal out of his glaring choler.

"Some things are general knowledge," Benteen said.

"I suspect that's one of them, but nothing a prospector or miner wants to think on too much. But you're not either of them, not with clothes like you wore before."

"Jasper Jessup. Can I exchange a few words with him?"

"No reason why not." Benteen grabbed a key ring and rose, towering over Mason. The marshal moved like a coiled snake, lithe and dangerously ready to unwind in a strike. He went to a door at the rear of his small office and unlocked it. He silently opened the door and waited.

Mason suspected he wanted to tell how easy it would be to add a prisoner in the cell next to Jessup, but he held his tongue. The dozen cells in the back were all empty, save for the one holding the drunken fireman.

"Stay as long as you like." Benteen closed the door behind Mason with a loud bang. The lock made a metallic rasping sound like the peal of doom.

In spite of the marshal's attitude, Mason considered the offer in a different light. He had nowhere to stay. The cells were clean and the cots, while not feather beds, looked more comfortable than many of the beds he'd slept in on his way here from San Francisco.

"You came to spring me? You're a prince!" Jasper Jessup leaped to his feet and clung to the bars. His breath was fierce enough to bowl over a charging bull, and his bloodshot eyes matched many a topographical map Mason had seen in his day.

"You're about the only person I know in town," Mason started.

Jessup laughed and pointed at his new clothes.

"You're all decked out in mighty fine duds. Did you

sweet-talk Miz Logan? That's quite an accomplishment since she's not paid the least attention to any man since her husband died."

"How'd he die?" Mason wasn't sure he wanted to know, but the question slipped out.

"A fire down in the mines. There's nothing as deadly as a fire burning five hundred feet underground. He wasn't a miner and he wasn't even a fireman. When the call went out, he came running. He worked a hand pump like a demon." Jessup shook his head sadly. "Never real sure what happened. The pump handle broke, and it bucked back like a mule. He was impaled on the sharp end. It kept goin' up and down a few times like they do." Jessup made a face. "Real messy. I'm not sure anybody ever told his wife the full story since it turned so bloody and there was pieces of him all over the mine opening."

"That's gruesome."

"Not as gruesome as what happened to the miners trapped in the mine. They—"

"I don't need to know the details."

"Reckon not. Just that it's sorta ironic and all." Jessup saw Mason's expression. "She sewed up all the shrouds, including the one for her hubby."

"I think it's worth your time to help stop the arsonist, if one did start both fires today." Mason pulled up a chair and sank into it. His legs turned to butter, and keeping from falling asleep became increasingly difficult.

"Solving one problem like that's not out of the question." Jessup took a couple steps back and fell onto the cot. The alcohol in his veins still held him in thrall. "If I was you, though, I'd look in other directions for problems to solve. Don't concern yourself with any firebug.

I've been sittin' and thinkin' on it and maybe I was wrong about that fire bein' set. Folks get careless. That'd be my judgment in this case, yes, sir."

"Will you just tell the marshal who you think's the culprit?" Mason said, not budging.

"Culprit?"

"Name the one who set the fires today. If he gets too bold, he might set so many that the fire brigades cannot possibly snuff them all out."

"Back in '75 was a big fire."

"I've heard. It burned down almost the entire town."

"I almost wish that'd happen again. A man fighting a fire that big could make quite a reputation for himself. As I opined before, I'm not so sure today's fire was set."

Mason shot to his feet, angered at such a callous wish.

"How many would die in such a fire? Think of the destruction." He hesitated. "Even the Fire Drake Brigade headquarters would be burned to the ground. Such devastation could spell the end of the town."

"Never happen, not with so much silver in the ground. Don't know how, but miners would figure a way of making suits to walk right through the flames to get to that metal. Why, look at my shirt." Jasper Jessup pinched a bit and pulled it out. "This here's got asbestos in it to keep from catchin' fire. Real smart, ain't it?"

"Will you talk to the marshal?" He stopped by the locked door, his fist raised to knock on the panel.

"Be my pleasure," Jessup said.

Mason rapped sharply. He expected to wait while the marshal took his own sweet time to open, but the door opened almost immediately. For all Mason knew, the marshal had listened to their conversation with his ear pressed to the wood.

"He has something to tell you, Marshal."

"Go on, Jessup. Spill your guts, and I don't mean puke on my floor again. You do, you clean it up."

"I am quite under control, sir," Jessup said with dignity fueled by the booze in his bloodstream. "My good friend here has asked me to tell you something of great importance."

Mason heaved a sigh of relief. Jessup naming a potential arsonist gave the lawman somewhere to start investigating. He felt he'd accomplished more with this than all the work he had done fighting the fires. If he had learned of the arsonist earlier, Blue Dirt Duggan wouldn't have been trapped and injured. The Logan children would—

"I am proposing my friend for membership in the Fire Drake Brigade, and will present his case directly to Captain Finley. After all his fine work today, even if he helped that scalawag Delahunt, makes him a worthy addition."

"That's what you wanted to tell me?" Benteen stared at Mason in disbelief.

"No, no, Jessup said he knew who the arsonist might be. He—"

"I'm turning you loose, Jessup. Get out of here before I figure out real charges against you." Benteen opened the cell door.

"But there's someone setting fires. The entire town is in danger!" Mason was outraged at the marshal's indifference to such a crime.

"I told you I'd look into it, but there's other lawbreaking going on that requires a more immediate response."

As if to emphasize his duties, gunshots suddenly echoed down the street. "Clear out. Both of you."

Mason and Jessup stood in the street outside the jailhouse, listening to volley after volley of gunfire. A Civil War battle couldn't have sent so much lead flying. Marshal Benteen locked the jailhouse door and hurried off, bellowing for his deputies to follow him.

"You come with me," Jessup said, tugging on Mason's sleeve. "I wasn't joshing when I said I'd propose you for membership. That's about the biggest honor you can get in this here town. The rest of the brigade has to vote on you, but we got a couple spots open. Them boys lit out and were never seen or heard from again."

Morgan Mason let the still-half-drunk fireman steer him to Union Street and then downhill to D Street and the volunteer fire company's sumptuous headquarters. At least he'd have a place to sleep for the night.

CHAPTER SIX

"WAKE UP. YOU got to wake up."

Strong hands shook Morgan Mason and rolled him off the bed. He hit the floor hard. His eyes popped open and panic seized him. He had no idea where he was. Then he took a deep whiff and inhaled heavy smoke. With a reflexive shove, he came to hands and knees and began crawling around. He bumped his head against the side of the bed. With a quick twist he rolled over and sat up, looking around frantically.

He saw legs and worked his way up to Jasper Jessup's frightened face. Everything flooded back. Jessup had brought him to the Fire Drake Brigade headquarters after he had gotten out of jail. The place had been empty and he had chosen a bed to stretch out on. He hadn't intended to fall asleep for very long. All he wanted was a quick catnap before going on his way.

Sunlight slanted in through an east-facing window and warned him it was well past dawn.

"Is there a fire?" Mason used the bed to lever himself to his feet. Axes were racked in the wall opposite. Red shirts and canvas trousers hung on hooks, each hook marked with a different number. Those had to belong to the individual firemen.

"There will be if Captain Finley catches you sleeping here. Nobody but brigade members are allowed in."

"But you said it'd be all right, and you're a member. Aren't you?" Mason's sleep-muzzy brain worked through everything he'd heard. Even Marshal Benteen had named Jessup a member of this brigade. He'd said something about him being the fire captain's favorite.

"I'm allowed, you're not. They'll string you up if they find you here." Jessup made a motion like a noose had been dropped over his head and then tightened.

"It's a crime punishable by death?" Mason hardly believed that.

"By my sacred honor, it is." Jessup's answer carried no hint of lie or joke. "There aren't many things as honored as membership in a volunteer company. This might as well be a cathedral." He waved his arms about like a windmill in a stiff breeze. "Hurry up. They've spent the night getting drunk and won't be in any mood to fool around. They'll not think twice about stringing you up."

Mason went to the window and looked out. A dozen men, arms locked, marched down the street toward the firehouse. From the noise they made, they all sang a different song. Each tried to drown out his partner. Mason backed off and looked around. He didn't see how to get out. If he went down the stairs, he'd run smack-dab into the returning firemen. If he tried to drop out the second-story window, they'd catch him for sure.

"What am I going to do?" He looked around, scooped up the bundle of work clothes that constituted his only possessions and prepared to bluff his way out. Some lie had to do, but his brain churned, and nothing came to him.

"There. In there. Can you climb?" Jasper Jessup pointed to a door in an alcove that Mason had overlooked.

He threw open the door and let out a yelp of surprise. Jessup pushed him forward as he took a startled step back.

"Grab hold and climb. You can get to the roof."

"What are they? Th-they're snakes!"

"That's where we dry out the hoses. We let them dangle down from hooks at the top of the shaft. Go on. Hurry!"

The sound of boots clacking on the steps as the firemen came up to the dormitory gave wings to Mason's feet. He stuffed the brown paper wrapped parcel under his vest and launched himself into the air. Rough canvas hose slid past his fingers. He grabbed and clung for dear life. He swung to and fro like a clock pendulum. For a second he wanted nothing but to swing back to the door and stop.

Jessup slammed the door shut, blocking his retreat. Mason closed his eyes, settled himself, then craned his neck around and looked upward. Jessup had been right. The hoses were looped around hooks fastened into the four-story-high ceiling. He wrapped his legs around the hose, then began climbing. He got to the third floor before his strength began to run out of him like sand from an hourglass. He was rested, but his muscles hadn't recovered from the previous day's exertion.

Mason looked down. He might escape that way. The hoses shed water into what looked like a French drain. But the lower floor was open and the returning firemen might not all have gone to bed on the second floor. With grim determination, he summoned up what power remained in his arms and began climbing again. Inch by inch, he made it to the top. A final frantic grab brought an iron hook into his grip.

For a heart-stopping moment he hung, holding on to the hook. He kicked hard, swung and let loose. He landed on a ledge where men used a pulley system to lift the hoses. Hands on his knees, he regained his strength, found a small door that led out onto a railed balcony around the top of the tower. The breathtaking sight of sun lighting Virginia City for a new day was lost on him. Edging around until he faced the center of town, he made out the two burned areas from the day before.

There'd be more unless the arsonist was stopped. All he could hope for was that Marshal Benteen believed him and found the culprit before more damage was done. Having someone burn the town down before he made his mark here outraged him.

He edged further around the balcony to the rear overlooking the sheer drop-off. He paused.

"Silver Terrace Cemetery," he muttered. A large area dotted with trees glowed in the morning sun, probably reflections off grave markers.

More important, a ladder from the balcony all the way to the ground let him get away from the firehouse. He descended slowly, making as little noise as he could. He passed a window and chanced a look inside. The firemen were either stretched out and asleep or sitting and staring into the distance, comatose. When one stirred and looked right at him, he abandoned his spying and slid down the rest of the way to the ground. He lit out running until he climbed up to C Street.

The doctor's surgery was the last place he wanted to go, but he felt an obligation to see how Duggan fared. He knocked timidly on the door. If he didn't make too much noise, Dr. Sinclair might not hear, and he could lie to himself that he'd met his obligation.

Mason had no such luck. His second tentative tap brought the doctor to the door.

"I wondered if I'd see you again. Come on in." The doctor opened the door and waited for Mason to enter. With great reluctance, he did.

"I just wanted to see how Mr. Duggan was getting on," Mason said. The smallest hint that all was well and he could bolt and run.

"You've got new clothes." The doctor sniffed hard. "You still smell like smoke. Then again, after what the whole town went through yesterday, who doesn't?"

"If there's nothing I can do . . ."

"He's taking it pretty hard, not that I blame him. Duggan's always been cantankerous and independent. That's the way most prospectors are. Even fewer make the change from hunting for silver to mining it. Two different ways of looking at the world."

Mason remained silent. He had no idea what the doctor was going on about.

"Go in and talk to him."

"Isn't he sleeping?" Mason looked toward the back room, hidden by a dangling curtain.

"He claims he'll never sleep again. There's nothing you can say that'll upset him further." Sinclair smiled ruefully. "He may be permanently upset."

If Mason had a lick of sense, he should have left Duggan to his own devices. He pushed the curtains aside and went into the small room where a bed had been pushed against the far wall to make room for a chair in the middle where Blue Dirt Duggan sat slumped over. A blanket covered his legs, and he wrapped his arms around his barrel-like body. Somehow the giant of a man seemed diminished.

"You come to see the sideshow freak?"

"What do you mean?"

Duggan whipped the blanket away. Mason blinked but made no other sign he saw anything amiss. The miner's right leg had been amputated above his knee.

"That beam crushed all the bones in my leg. The doc said infection was setting in. It was either my leg or my life." Duggan growled like a mad dog. "He made the wrong choice. I'd be better off dead."

"Can I have your claim, then? If you don't want to go on living, let me have it."

Duggan opened his mouth, then clamped it shut.

"I never took you for a thief."

"Dead men can't own mines. My granny used to tell me that shrouds don't have pockets."

"Nasty woman, your granny." Duggan sat a little straighter. "I think I'd've liked her."

"She's still alive and kicking. Going on seventy years old, she is. It's just been a while since I made the trip away from San Francisco to see her. She's in Eureka, up the coast."

Duggan countered with a story of how his pa lived to be a hundred. Mason didn't believe a word of it, but the miner's mood improved with his tall tale-telling. Dr. Sinclair looked in a few times but never interrupted. After an hour of increasingly outrageous stories, Duggan stopped in midsentence and fixed a gimlet eye on Mason.

He finally said, "They'll be coming for me."

Mason thought this was part of a story and asked what the miner meant. He went cold when he realized Duggan wasn't spinning a campfire story but meant it.

"Claim jumpers, old son, claim jumpers. Virginia City is filthy with them. Why break your back mining or spend long, lonely hours where a mule's your only companion hunting for blue dirt? They understand a bullet gets them out of all that work." Duggan lifted his stump. "This keeps me from properly fighting them off." He snorted. "It keeps me from working my claim."

"I haven't been in town long, but from a couple drinks in the saloon I saw more out-of-work miners than you can shake a stick at. Hire one or two of them."

"Thieves, the lot of them. Why do you think they're not underground with pick and shovel but sucking up beer suds or knocking back whiskey that'll burn out their intestines? They're crooked, that's why. Crooked and lazy."

"There must be an honest man somewhere."

"I'll have to watch like a hawk to find him. Or I can hire you."

"What makes you think I'm honest?" Mason didn't know if he should be flattered or skeptical.

"Don't much matter, does it? You risked your life to save me. And a couple fellows came in to see the doc with burns from the fire. They were jealous of you for getting so close to Miz Logan."

"I didn't do anything but get her kids back to her. They were too little to know what to do and . . ."

"And?" Duggan smirked. "Not many men in this godforsaken town would have bothered. You're her knight in shining armor. Or if not armor, then some of the fancy vesture she sells for a pretty penny." He pointedly stared at Mason's clothes.

"She had this laying around. She—"

"Stop arguing, will you? I do declare, I never before saw a man who'd argue over whether he was honest and take the side of being a lying scoundrel."

"I'm not, Duggan. I . . ." Mason cut off his protest and grinned. "All right. I'm honest. It comes from me working assay for so long. Mine owners want honest reports, and I always gave it to them. But I'm not cut out to be a miner." Mason stretched a little and kept from moaning. His muscles had tightened up over-night. His paunch had shrunk a mite since it'd been so long since he'd had a decent meal, but he wasn't in any condition to do more than walk around hunting for a decent restaurant.

"That's an outright fib, and you know it. A prospector doesn't want an honest assay. He wants to be told he's struck the mother lode and is going to be setting pretty up on Russian Hill in San Francisco, hobnobbing with all them fancy-dressing railroad and banking tycoons."

"There is that," Mason admitted. He got to his feet and started for the door. "I'll check in on you . . . later."

"Now, old son, that has the ring of a lie to it. See? You come to Virginia City and you start acting like everyone else."

"I need a square meal." Mason rubbed his belly. It dutifully growled to let Duggan know this wasn't a lie.

"I wanted to hire you before. Still do."

"As a geologist? I can do that, whenever you're up to it." He stared at the man's leg—or where it had been. It was downright rude, but he couldn't help himself.

"Get your equipment and come on out to the Mira Nell this afternoon. I'm out in Calabasas Creek and the road's marked real good." Duggan smiled, a bit grimly Mason thought. "There's so much silver coming out of that mine, the road's got decent ruts in it and the dirt's all packed down hard as rock."

"You'll be there? Dr. Sinclair will let you go?"

"The doc wants me out of his hair—what he's got left, at least. You run along and feed your face. Let me take care of my own business. Now go, go!"

Mason pushed through the curtain and went to stand at the doctor's desk. Sinclair looked up from a magazine he was reading.

"I heard what he said. I'll be glad to be rid of him."

"Is his mine that easy to find?"

"The Mira Nell is about the richest in the area. You won't have any trouble." Sinclair went back to reading, but called out as Mason reached the door. "Thanks."

"What for?" Mason half turned.

"He was close to suicidal before you came. You're getting him out of my hair." Sinclair ran his fingers through his thinning hair. "What I have left. If Duggan had stayed much longer, I'd've been tearing this out."

Mason left and looked around, then started his hike up Union Street. He considered seeing if the Crazy Eights Saloon really had a new gal worth all the gossip, but he had started with the no-named saloon and figured it was as good as any to find a meal. He pushed through the swinging doors, let his eyes adjust to the dim light and went over to the bar. The barkeep never looked up from wiping glasses clean and said, "Beef sandwich, ten cents. With a small beer and a pickle, twenty-five. That's my lunch special."

"Sold." Mason fished around in his pocket for change. The search felt odd since the only other time he had reached into these pockets was to transfer his money from the old, ruined clothes. He dropped two bits on the bar.

The bartender looked up, then smiled broadly.

"It's you!"

Mason looked over his shoulder, thinking the barkeep meant someone else.

"You're the one that left a bag here yesterday. In all the confusion it got kicked around, but I stashed it behind the bar." The man dragged out Mason's small bag with his spare clothes and picks and hammers.

Mason reached for it, but the barkeep pulled it back. He cleared his throat and said, "It might be nice if a reward for finding this was being offered. After all, I can't be real sure this is yours. It could belong to about anybody."

"What? My clothes wouldn't fit you?" Mason stared up at the man, who topped him by a goodly six inches.

"That's a nasty insinuation, Mister. Why, them hammers and rock picks are valuable. And them's the sort of equipment just about any miner would carry."

Mason silently went fishing. He hadn't made that much off selling the chemicals to the assayer, but he had a few dollars. Nimble fingers found a cartwheel and brought it out. He set it spinning brightly. The bartender snared it, deftly flipped it into the air and made it disappear into a pocket hidden by his canvas apron. He made no effort to stop Mason from pulling the carpet bag to him and hugging it.

"My food and beer."

"Coming right up." The barkeep produced a sad-looking sandwich with a drooping pickle tucked beneath it. He was more expert drawing the beer into a mug that was hardly larger than a shot glass.

Mason wrestled the food, beer and bag to a table at the rear of the saloon and sat down to eat. He wolfed down the sandwich. The beef was tougher than shoe leather, the bread was moldy and the pickle burned his lips. He washed it all down with the warm beer and tried to remember when food had ever tasted better.

A second beer, this one the full fifty cents, made him feel mellow and at peace with the world. Only then did he tuck his brown paper and string-tied bundle into the carpet bag and leave the saloon to look around town. The afternoon slipped away as he sought more proof that an arsonist was loose in Virginia City. Finding nothing Marshal Benteen would consider as evidence, he hiked back down the hill and headed out of town.

Blue Dirt Duggan hadn't exaggerated about the traffic along the road leading to the Mira Nell Mine. He had no trouble hitching a ride on an ore wagon all the way to the northern base of Gold Hill. Signs sprouted up all around proclaiming this to be Calabasas Creek, and the road leading to Duggan's mine had a gate across it.

Mason had to laugh. The gate was locked, and there wasn't a fence on either side of the fence posts holding it up. He walked around and then started the long climb to the mine. He had a job to do before he returned to Virginia City and was anxious to get to it.

CHAPTER SEVEN

MASON WAS DRENCHED in sweat by the time he got to the top of the road. To his right, a line shack that had seen better days leaned into the wind whipping down from the top of Gold Hill. Just beyond it, a shed housed a horse, chewing diligently at hay in the feeding trough. And even farther uphill to his left opened the Mira Nell Mine. Tailings dribbled down the side of the mountain. Mason tried to judge how much ore had been removed. His estimate wasn't anywhere near accurate, he decided, since so much of the dross had been shoved even farther downhill, leaving a black tongue sticking out of the mine's mouth for a quarter mile or more.

He caught his breath and went to the shack. He rapped on the door, worrying that he might knock it off its hinges. When he got no answer, he cautiously opened the rickety door and peered inside. No sign of

Blue Dirt Duggan. He dropped his bag with his clothing and equipment and turned back to the path leading to the mine. How a man without a leg could scale this incline was quite a question. Mason had had trouble making it uphill, and he had two perfectly good working legs to propel him.

At the mouth, he cocked his head to one side and listened hard. Tiny scratching noises like rats picking clean a bony carcass made him shiver. He preferred working as a chemist because he had spent enough time examining mine geology to be wary of such noises.

"Mr. Duggan? You in there? I've come to do an analysis of your mine like you asked. Hello?"

The scratching noise became more of a scraping sound. He recoiled when Duggan suddenly appeared from a side drift and loomed before him, not five feet away.

"Are you expecting a revolution?" Mason rubbed his sweaty hands on the sides of his coat as he gave the miner a once-over.

Duggan wore crossed bandoliers filled with cartridges. A heavy leather gun belt supported a pair of six-shooters, and Duggan had slung a rifle over his shoulder held by a piece of dusty rope. He carried enough weaponry to make a man's knees buckle. He worked along painfully on a pair of crutches.

"You bet I am. Being away from the Mira Nell for even a day draws claim jumpers like flies to cow flop. A man's got to be ready to defend his property."

Duggan slowly edged out toward the open air. The scraping and scratching sounds Mason had heard were caused by the tips of the crutches dragging along the mine floor. Even hunched over the crutches, Duggan

was tall enough to bang his head on the roof. He filled
up the entrance as he finally reached daylight.

"That the way you dress to poke around in a mine?"

"I didn't have a chance to change," Mason said defen-
sively. "My work clothes are back at your cabin, along
with my equipment."

"Then go change into sensible duds and get to work.
I ain't paying you to lollygag."

"We've never settled on what you *are* paying me."
Mason pressed his hand against his vest pocket. He
had less than twenty dollars from the sale of his chemicals. If he hadn't been in such dire need of money, he
should have sold the chemicals over a week or two and
gotten a better price. Still, he wasn't in such bad shape.
He had two new suits of clothing and retained his geology equipment.

"Depends on what you find. Make me richer and I'll
be real generous."

"It doesn't work that way, Mr. Duggan. What if
there's no more silver to be found?" He bent and examined some of the ore chunks scattered around the
mouth of the mine. Using his thumbnail he scratched
a streak of black. "Silver chloride," he said. "This is
from your main lode?"

"You tell me." When Mason didn't say anything,
Duggan growled like a dog deep in his throat and said,
"Ten dollars for a survey. That's generous."

"That's a steal—for you."

"So walk back to town without earning a dime."

"You've gotten to be a cranky old geezer. It's a good
thing you didn't lose both legs or you'd be completely
unbearable." Mason flushed when the words came out

of his mouth. This was a cruel thing to say to a man who had just lost a limb. The thought flashed through his mind that Duggan, armed to the teeth as he was, might start throwing lead in his direction. Nobody would ever look for his body, and even if they did, the hills had a thousand places for a shallow grave that'd never be found.

But to his relief, his words calmed Duggan rather than infuriating him.

"Twelve and not a penny more. Get on back to the cabin and collect your pick. I don't have all day."

Mason gratefully retreated to the cabin, hefted his bag and went inside. He opened the paper-wrapped bundle for the first time. Mrs. Logan had said it held work clothes. To his relief they were simple, rough and exactly what he needed to poke around in a dusty, dirty mine. The denim shirt and canvas pants fit poorly, and he needed boots to replace his shoes. He vowed to make that his first purchase when he got his money from Duggan and returned to Virginia City.

He carefully folded and packed away his fancy suit of clothing, took a rock hammer from the bag and rummaged about until he found a chisel. The hammer might be all he needed, but a chisel was useful for leveraging out larger pieces of ore. The blunt edge even provided a way to scrape softer mineral deposits away from walls.

Feeling plucky, he hiked back uphill where Duggan sat on a rock outside the mine. Using a stick, the miner drew a map in the dust.

"This here's the layout of the Mira Nell. You don't need to go down this side stope," he said, poking at part of the map with the stick. "That vein's all played out. I have real high hopes for this section. If I'm right, it'll go all the way through the mountain and make me a millionaire."

"Don't let your expectations run away with your reality. Just because you want the silver to be there doesn't mean it is. You know how fickle deposits can be." Mason hefted his pick hammer and chisel and went into the mine. The roof was just an inch above his head. He glanced at the rock there, expecting to see bits and pieces of Duggan's scalp left behind. Somehow the miner had avoided banging his head as he carved the mine out of the mountainside.

Another five yards in, Mason found the shelf with a supply of miner's candles and a helmet with a mounted reflector. He positioned a fresh candle, stuck another two in his pocket, carefully lit the one that ought to last him for the entire exploration. The wick sputtered a couple times, then decided to burn with a bright yellow light. He settled the helmet on his head, adjusted it to shine light directly in front of him, then started following the twin iron rails of the ore cart deeper into the mountain.

The air became close, and sweat poured off him by the time he reached the end of the tracks. An ore cart waited, half-full. Carefully crowding past it, Mason examined the walls and area on the wall where Duggan had worked most diligently. Humming as he worked, he picked away samples from floor to roof and examined them carefully.

"You've got one whale of a strike here, old man. No wonder they call you Blue Dirt Duggan," he muttered to himself. He edged through a crevice and began working down a long galley barely large enough to let him pass. More than once he regretted having so much belly. The denim shirt began to fray when he rubbed more and more against the narrow passage.

Then he came out into a larger natural chamber. The light barely lit up the ceiling, close to five feet over his head. But the way it sparkled gave him hope. A slow circuit of the cavern allowed him to collect a dozen samples and place them in a pyramid. When the stack reached waist-high, he settled down cross-legged and began a real examination. Using the hammer to pound on the chisel produced dust. He rubbed it between his fingers and examined the smudges closely. After a half hour, he got to his feet and walked the perimeter of the cavern one final time.

It wasn't often he saw enough silver in the walls to make a man a millionaire ten times over. He regretted not bringing a knapsack. Getting a real assay on the richest samples would confirm his guess about the metallic wealth buried in this single cavern.

"Blast along this part, open it up and you might even find more silver than you can imagine," Mason said to himself.

He squeezed back into the channel leading to the developed part of the mine. It seemed an even tighter fit returning. For once he was glad he hadn't brought more tools or tried to carry out a few pounds of ore. Getting stuck in the passage would be the end of him. Mason grinned as he popped back into the main shaft. The ore farther on was so rich he would have relived the parable about the bear getting his paw stuck in the honey jar.

Open the paw and escape, but the honey was so tempting. Dropping a sack filled with almost pure pieces of silver would be the same. Mason knew how rare a find like this was, and parting with even a flake of it required discipline.

He edged around the ore cart and knew Duggan needed to blast a better path to the silver cavern if he wanted to lay tracks. That was a better method for getting the ore out than hauling it by hand.

He trudged along the tracks until he reached the ledge, where he replaced the two candles he hadn't used, blew out the stub remaining on the one on his helmet and then put the helmet aside. He would use it again soon enough. His mind raced to what tests needed to be done and more legal work to be certain Duggan owned rights. And—

Gunshots froze him in his tracks. He was only a few paces away from emerging from the Mira Nell when another shot echoed back to him. Then the echo turned into a whine as lead scored a long gouge in the wall at eye level.

He flopped forward and began wiggling to find what went on. Duggan had no reason to use him for target practice, though odd suspicions rose in his head.

What if the miner was determined to keep the richness of the find secret? Mason wasn't going to gossip about the find, but Duggan had turned a bit loco. That was only to be expected. It wasn't every day a man lost his leg. But shooting his geologist now made no sense. If Duggan had any such intent he'd hear the report before pulling the trigger.

"Keep your fool head down, boy." The snarled warning came from just outside the mine as Mason tried to get free of the rocky confines.

"What's going on?" Mason cringed as more bullets spanged off the rock above his head. Part of the timber supporting the mouth of the mine had been blasted away. Someone threw a whole lot more lead than necessary, unless they intended to collapse the mouth.

"You know how to use a six-gun?"

Mason sat with his back to the wall so he caught sight of Duggan huddled behind an overturned, rusted-out ore cart on the far side of the mouth. He used his rifle and had one six-shooter on the ground beside him where he could grab it when his rifle magazine came up empty.

"I've never . . ." That was as far as Mason got before Duggan clumsily tossed him the six-gun. He fumbled and caught it with both hands.

"It's easy. Aim it at one of those claim-jumping varmints and pull the trigger. If Lady Luck's riding on your shoulder, you'll kill him. Then you find another varmint and plug him, too."

"How many are there?"

"Too many. I hit one. Winged him. He's still throwing lead in my direction. There's two more, maybe three. Can't tell." Duggan used a crutch to push himself to the far side of the ore cart. He thrust his rifle barrel out and fired several times, as fast as he could lever in fresh rounds.

"Dang," he grumbled. "Missed all of them again. They're slimy ones, they are. Slippery and sneaky."

"Sneaky," Mason repeated. He held the six-shooter in both hands, cocked it and then rolled from the mine, ending up on his back and facing the slope above the Mira Nell's mouth, he spotted a man wearing a red bandanna and carrying a six-gun edging down the slope. He fired. His first shot hit the man square in the chest. His next four rounds went wild.

"I got one!"

"Fat lot of good that's gonna do us. I never saw that one to count. There's four of them, not three. Three are still coming up the hill after us." Blue Dirt Duggan cast his rifle aside and drew his second six-shooter. He shot at a man darting from one pile of tailings to the next. As far as Mason could see, Duggan missed every time.

Mason flopped on his belly and braced the pistol against a rock. His hand shook so hard that was the only way he could draw a bead. He jerked back on the trigger. The round went high over the head of a claim jumper trying to rush them. Instinctively, he pulled the trigger again.

"I got one! Another one," he quickly amended. Mason tried to fire again when the owlhoot limped back downhill. This time his hammer fell on an empty chamber.

His mind went blank. No more bullets. What was he supposed to do?

"Duggan, throw me some more ammo. I'm out." He thumbed open the gate and began ejecting spent brass. He had seen men do this enough times to know the process. When all six empties bounced away on the ground, he looked over at Duggan to see if the request for more ammo was being honored.

The miner pulled himself up on his stump to peer over the ore cart. With great deliberation he loaded his rifle from the rounds thrust into the bandoliers then he used the cart as a support to climb to his feet.

"You mangy cayuses! I'll bury the lot of you where even the worms can't find you!" He began shooting steadily.

"Duggan, more ammo. I need more for the gun you gave me!" Mason saw the bloodlust had taken Duggan in its firm jaws. Nothing got through to him.

Getting his feet under him, Mason scrambled across to skid behind the protective cart. A bullet tore through rusted metal just over his head. He flinched and wished he could curl up in a ball until this all blew over. Only the claim jumpers weren't going to simply walk away. They had attacked thinking to make short work of a crippled man. Mason blinked hard to get dirt from his watery eyes. The revelation hit him that they probably thought Duggan was here alone. Only the presence of a second gunman had thrown their murderous plans onto the scrap heap.

"Bullets. Give me bullets!"

He clawed at the bandoliers over Duggan's shoulder, then saw the size of the cartridges was different. He used another caliber in the rifle from that in his six-shooters. The rounds thrust into loops on his gun belt were what Mason needed. Daring to work cartridges from those loops, he got enough to reload both six-guns.

Mason held them in his hands. The weight somehow erased his nerves. But he wasn't going to fire both at the same time. He had twelve rounds. How was the best way to use it?

Morgan Mason stood, all nerves gone. He thrust one pistol into the waistband of his trousers and gripped the other with both hands. Then he held it in his right hand, elbow stiff.

He stepped around the tipped-over ore cart and began walking downhill. A claim jumper popped up like a prairie dog. Mason shot. He grazed his target. Walking at a steady clip down the steep hill, he fired until the gun came up empty. He switched weapons and kept walking, kept firing.

At the bottom of the hill he pulled the empty six-gun from his waistband and, a pistol steady in each hand, yelled, "Come on, you yellow bellies! Come on and try to steal the Mira Nell Mine!"

Mason let out a shriek that curdled blood and curled toes as he ran straight for the nearest claim jumper. The man's eyes went wide in fright. Mason saw the whites all around and then was on top of the outlaw. He swung first with one six-gun and then the other. Both blows collided with exposed temples. The would-be claim jumper collapsed like a bag of wet oats.

Bending, Mason scooped up the man's fallen gun and homed in on another of the claim jumpers. This time his cry bounced off the mountains and echoed all the way into Virginia City. The claim jumper let out a yelp and lit out, running like a scalded dog. Mason kept after him, even when the man vaulted into the saddle of a waiting horse and galloped off. Slowing his pace, Mason took time to aim the captured six-gun. Yanking the trigger before had ruined his shot. This time he drew back slowly on the trigger. The hammer fell with a metallic click.

Empty.

He stared at the gun, then tried firing it again and again. Each time the hammer fell on a spent round. Three guns, three with completely empty cylinders.

Mason laughed hysterically until tears ran down his

cheeks. Then he dropped to a stump beside the path leading to the shed where Duggan's horses continued to munch away at their hay, unfazed by the gunfight.

It took him several minutes to regain control and realize he had driven off the claim jumpers. With empty six-shooters.

CHAPTER EIGHT

Ɔ

MASON HIKED BACK uphill, every step like dead men clung to his legs. Blue Dirt Duggan sat on an overturned powder keg, his crutches drawn up beside him. He eyed Mason closely, then said, "You need to wear a hat."

"What?" Mason had expected the miner to say something, but this made no sense. "What do you mean?" He swiped sweat off his forehead, then sank down onto another powder keg beside Duggan. Both of the Giant Powder kegs were empty.

"Sunstroke's the only explanation for why a man like you'd go plumb loco and go charging killers like them." He jerked his thumb over his shoulder to show the first man on the hillside that Mason had plugged. "Them six-shooters are empty, aren't they?"

Mason grinned sheepishly. He handed Duggan's back and kept the third pistol he'd picked up after buffaloing the claim jumper. At that memory he jumped to his feet and tried to find the man's carcass downhill where he'd laid him out.

"I saw him get up and stumble away. Except for the two you shot, they hightailed it."

Shock hit Mason now.

"Do you think they'll come back?"

"For revenge?" Duggan laughed. It was a nasty sound. "If they have a whit of sense, they're already in Mexico by now. Who dares rob a man who fights like you did with empty pistols?"

Mason was glad the two surviving claim jumpers had left. He wasn't sure he'd ever be up for another skirmish like this. He twisted around and stared at the man sprawled on the hillside above the mine. It finally hit him like a sledgehammer that he had killed a man. Men! He had shot two outlaws dead. The notion of self-defense hardly soothed his heaving emotions. He had never thought he'd have the guts to kill another man, yet he hadn't even considered it when faced with his own possible death. He had done the deed and moved on, without giving it a second thought.

Until now.

"This ain't a civilized place like San Francisco," Duggan said. "Men die out here. And men kill, if they want to stay alive."

"San Francisco's not that peaceable a place. The Barbary Coast. I've seen men strung up on lampposts by vigilance committees. And . . . and I saw the police beat a man to death once right at Union Square. Nobody ever said what he was supposed to have done. They—"

"I ain't paying you a dime more."

Mason shook his head to clear it. His chaotic thoughts settled as he struggled to understand what Duggan meant.

"Are you offering to pay me to kill? I'm not a hired gunman."

"To do the survey. You're a geologist. It's as plain as the nose on my face, and that I'm missing this"—Duggan reared back and thrust out his stump—"that you're about as poor a mine guard as I could find in this godforsaken place."

Mason settled himself and said, "In my role as a geologist, I have some bad news for you."

"Bad? You mean there's not any more silver in the old Mira Nell?"

"I mean you're sitting on a heap so pure that you can pull it out with your fingers. And it's all piled up so that you're going to need a lot of timber to shore up the mine. Otherwise, the whole mine will collapse on you."

"It's that rich? Huge pure walls of nothing but silver?"

"More than that," Mason said solemnly. "You won't even have to blast to get the silver out, but you will have to if you want to reach it and shore up the walls and roof."

Blue Dirt Duggan let out a whoop, threw his hands into the air and lost his balance. He toppled over backward and landed hard on his back. His good leg kicked and his stump moved around in circles.

"I'm so rich now I can hire somebody to do my walking for me!"

"So is this worth twelve dollars?"

"Don't get greedy, old son. I said ten and you agreed."

Mason helped Duggan back onto his powder keg seat.

"You said you'd make it worth my while if I found more. I've found a whole mountain of silver. That ought to be worth a bonus of two dollars."

"I knew I should have put it in writing. You're a citified crook come out to Virginia City to fleece poor old miners like me."

Mason wasn't sure if Duggan was having him on or if he really begrudged the extra two dollars when he had hit a strike bigger than the Ophir Mine. He'd always heard the richer the man, the stingier he became.

"One dollar. I'll give you a one-dollar bonus."

"Done," Mason said. "Now we've got another problem to address."

"The assay," Duggan said. "There's got to be proof of how rich the mine is. If it's as good as you say, claw out a fist-sized nugget and let that worthless assayer in town write up the report."

"You'll need an army to keep away the claim jumpers if I do that," Mason said. "Why don't I hire myself out to several other mines, then take in a half dozen or so samples for assay?"

"Clever," Duggan said. "Very clever. There won't be an easy way to trace back who's got the big strike."

"You'll have time to hire that army to guard the mine," Mason said. "And work it. There's no way you can keep working the mine by yourself." He looked significantly at the missing leg. "You might blast or load ore, but moving it to the smelter is too difficult for you."

"You make me out to be an invalid. I'm just missing a leg, no thanks to you!"

"I saved your life!"

"You didn't get me out from under that beam soon enough."

The two of them continued to argue, but Mason figured out this was Duggan's way and that he didn't mean a bit of it. When the argument began to die down, he helped the miner downhill to his cabin, then hiked back up for the disagreeable chore of taking care of the two bodies.

Digging graves in the rocky mountainside was out of the question. He rolled the corpses downhill to the road and considered what to do then. There was a grassy meadow not too far off where digging would be easy, but such desperadoes must have rewards on their heads. If he took the bodies into Virginia City, he might collect a few dollars for his trouble.

"For my trouble," Mason whispered. He shuddered. The fight had been fair and he had prevailed, but taking the outlaws into town was too onerous for him. Even if a hundred dollars apiece might be in the offing, he decided it wasn't worth it. Explaining to Marshal Benteen what had happened might not be easy, either. The lawman already pegged him as being a troublemaker hanging out with the likes of drunken firemen and causing public disturbances.

Moreover, the marshal hadn't believed the evidence Mason had shown him about an arsonist at work. With only corpses giving mute testimony, believing a newcomer to town about how lead happened to end those lives might be stretching the limit of his credulousness.

Finding one of the outlaw's horses proved easy. Mason heard it protesting being tethered in a cottonwood grove not too far from the cabin. He led the horse back and heaved both bodies belly down over its back. The smell of blood and death made the horse skittish, but Mason kept a strong hand on the bridle.

He led the horse past the toolshed where Duggan kept his equipment, grabbed a shovel and then headed for the meadow. The grassy green expanse was so different from the mountain where the killings had occurred. Peaceful, green, with soft winds, it was a world apart from death. Mason began digging, but his aching muscles convinced him to put the two bodies in a single grave. He had no idea as to who they were. A quick search of their pockets didn't give him anything definite. Their names were probably as loose and easy as their morals.

He finished mounding the dirt and sat under a tree, staring at the fresh grave. Never when he came to Virginia City had he thought life would take the turns it had. Two major fires and maybe an arsonist, saving little children and a cranky old prospector and now a pitched gun battle.

He had killed two men. Growing up in San Francisco had been a cakewalk in comparison. He had shot down two claim jumpers and discovered a silver strike that put others in the Comstock to shame. Using the shovel as a crutch, he stood. The horse came to him and nuzzled him. His contact with animals in San Francisco had been limited, but he patted the horse's nose and realized he no longer had to walk.

"To the victor belongs the spoils," he said. "So what's your name, old girl?" The horse jerked her head about and tried to rear. He held the mare down. "You think you're a queen, eh? I'll call you Victoria. How's that?"

The horse settled down, as if the name was satisfactory. It took some work to adjust the stirrups. The original owner had been quite a bit taller than Mason. He finally figured out the cinches and buckles, then mounted. While he had never owned a horse before, he wasn't a total novice riding. Still, keeping control proved difficult. Victoria had a mind of her own.

He rode back to Duggan's cabin and found the man asleep inside. Mason had been forced to do things he had never considered himself capable of doing, but compared to all Duggan had endured the past couple days, he was in clover. Unsure what to do, Mason decided to start around the mountain and visit other miners. The claim jumpers weren't likely to return, and the chance of another gang descending on the Mira Nell was small.

Mason continued up Calabasas Creek to the next mine. A pair of men sunned themselves rather than working what their sign said was the Lost Cause Mine. Mason drew rein a dozen yards away from them and waited to be noticed. He was aware that he still carried the outlaw's six-gun in his belt—and that he didn't have any ammunition to reload it. Coming up on a pair of miners like this wasn't too smart, but he made no move for the gun.

That might set them off, since one had a shotgun leaning against the tree to his right.

"Hello," Mason called. "How're you boys doing?"

The one with the shotgun climbed to his feet and grabbed it. The other didn't pay a whole lot of attention to either Mason or his partner.

"Who are you?" The challenge wasn't hostile. It was a simple question.

"A newcomer to the area. I arrived in Virginia City from San Francisco a couple days ago, and I'm out here looking to ply my trade."

"Which is?" The man rested his shotgun against the tree again, showing he considered Mason to be harmless. "From the look of your clothing, you're a miner. We ain't got need of any help in our mine."

"I saw the name. For a small fee I can explore your mine and see if there's anything you're missing. I'm a geologist. I just looked over the Mira Nell and found some silver chloride worth exploiting for Mr. Duggan. Chances are that I might do the same for you."

"Our mines are only a couple miles apart," spoke up the second miner, showing interest for the first time. "He's been right lucky in how much pay dirt he's pulled from his mine."

"Five dollars, and I can see if that's also true in your mine." Mason considered asking the same of these two that he had of Duggan, but the name of their mine hinted that worthless rock was all he'd find. Them sitting and watching the world go by when they ought to be digging away at the ore in that mine warned him of two men on the brink of giving up.

"All we got between us is two dollars, but if you find a decent nugget in the mine, you can keep it."

"Even if it's worth more than three dollars?" Mason dismounted, tucked his pistol into the saddlebags and hesitated, wondering what else might be there in the dangling leather pouches. He hadn't bothered to look. He had just picked up his bag with his clothing and tools and strapped it down.

"It'd have to be a mighty big nugget," said the second miner. The first elbowed him to silence. A final grumble and he once more ignored everything in the world except whatever he stared at in the distance.

"I'm willing to take the risk," Mason said. He fished out his chisel and pick hammer. "You hear any gunfire earlier? Say, an hour or two back?"

They exchanged looks, the talkative one shook his head and said, "Ain't heard much but the birds chirping. We haven't even felt any of the tremors lately."

"Tremors? What do you mean?"

"Me and a few of the others have felt the ground shaking like an earthquake trying to cut loose."

"Somebody's blasting, that's what it is," said the second miner. "I was in a quake once and this is nothing like it."

"I'd have to look at a special map, a topographical map, to see if there are fault lines here. I don't think so," Mason said. "In San Francisco we get quakes all the time because of the cracks in the ground. The sides of the break in the ground shift back and forth. That's an earthquake."

"Blasting," insisted the second miner.

"Let me get to exploring the Lost Cause," Mason said. He felt an argument building between the partners over earthquake or blasting just as he and Duggan had argued over a two-dollar fee. It didn't amount to a hill of beans but relieved tension and gave them something to do since they weren't inclined to swing a pick or heft a shovel in their mine.

Mason rode as close to the mine as he could. He found a patch of grass for Victoria to occupy herself while he ducked into the mine. The miner's candles were all less than an inch long, and there were only a couple of them. A tin lantern rather than a helmet proved to be the only way to carry the lighted candles. Holding the lantern high, he slowly made his way down the main mine shaft.

Branching both left and right, other tunnels looked even less promising than the main drift. When the air began to get stuffy, he stopped to examine the walls. What little ore had ever been here was picked out. Creeping inch by inch, he went deeper into the mine, then stopped. Little work had been done on a section of wall. He began chiseling until a hole the size of his head revealed a dark flash. More work cut out a yard of rock. Mason fumbled through the pieces and held the lantern close.

His heart beat a little faster. Using his chisel, he scored the rock above the hole so the two miners could find it. He dropped to his knees and scrabbled out even more of the ore, then measured the width of the vein. Mason swung around and examined the wall opposite the hole he'd created. More than a half hour brought out the continuation of the large vein he had initially found.

A few more measurements confirmed his guess. The miners had driven their main shaft through the vein, not along it. Some few pounds of ore had been taken out, but they had missed the real strike. Mason stuffed the samples he took into a gunnysack. He considered going farther into the existing mine, but the stubs of candle were about gone. When he stepped out into the late afternoon air, he took a deep, cleansing breath. Sharp odors made him choke, but compared with the feeling of constant suffocation in the mine, he was pleased to be free of the rocky coffin.

He secured the gunny sack above the saddlebags and opposite his carpetbag of clothing and rode back down to where the miners still argued. The subject had changed, but the idle good feeling told him this wasn't a serious misunderstanding. Chances were good they could switch sides and continue the argument unabated.

"I've got some good news, gents." Mason dismounted,

showed them what he'd found and said, "If you pay for the assay, I can let you know how big that strike is. My guess is you won't get rich but you'll be richer than you are now."

"Ain't hard to do that," the first miner said. "We hardly have a pair of nickels to rub together."

"What's it to be? I marked the spot. You don't need an assay, but if you want to figure how much more you can take out of the Lost Cause, it's a good idea."

The two looked at each other.

"We'd need an assay to sell the Lost Cause, wouldn't we?"

Mason caught his breath. He'd wondered what business he'd find once the assayer had turned him down for a job. An idea blossomed.

"If you want to sell, I can act as agent. I know about deeds and rights, and I can sign a notarized statement about the silver still in the ground." The two said nothing. "I'd take a percentage of the sale price so you wouldn't have to pay me anything up front and I'd tend to all the details with the land office."

"We're talkin' 'bout going our separate ways. Him, he wants to go back to Boise, and me, I miss ole San Antone, down Texas way. You just can't get decent tequila this far north."

"With the ore samples in this sack I'm sure I can get a good price for you," Mason said confidently.

"Soon?"

He looked from one miner to the other and nodded. "Soon enough. Before the weather turns cold again."

"I don't mind the snow. Kinda like it," said the one intent on Idaho. The other man shivered at the thought.

"I'll start asking around," Mason said. He shook

hands with the two partners. He was going to make quite a mark for himself in Virginia City. Once word of one successful sale got out, he'd have dozens of other miners begging him to sell their claims.

He mounted, waved and headed back toward the Mira Nell Mine. As he rode, he realized Duggan might be the fly in the ointment. That additional strike was going to be on every man's lips. Who'd want to sell if they had a ghost of a chance to be as rich as Croesus? Or Blue Dirt Duggan?

CHAPTER NINE

M ORGAN MASON SAT astride his new horse and looked into the darkness. Miles away he saw lights from Virginia City. The road was long, and he was bone-tired. He had put in a day unlike any other in his life. His fingers lightly touched the butt of the six-shooter shoved into his waistband. A quick look over his shoulder assured him that the gunnysacks holding samples from both the Mira Nell and the Lost Cause Mines were secured.

Victoria stirred under him, as if telling him it was time to turn in for the night. He was hungry and thirsty and tired, and it was a long, dark road back to Virginia City. And once there he wasn't going to find a bed as nice as the one he'd slept in the night before. The few dollars he had might not put him up even in a flophouse.

"Should have demanded Duggan pay me," he muttered. Victoria whinnied agreement. He patted the mare's neck and answered, "You should have insisted. What kind of horse are you, not telling me these things?"

The mare looked back at him, and he knew she disapproved. Riding back to town would bring even greater disapproval. He turned the horse uphill toward the Mira Nell Mine. The going was rough, but he finally arrived at Duggan's falling-down old cabin. The man would be rolling in the dough soon enough and able to build a decent house. If Mason was even half-right about the silver in the mine, Duggan could build a house in San Francisco up on Russian Hill, buy himself a membership in the Union Club and hobnob with the upper crust.

He stepped down and secured Victoria's reins to a nearby tree limb. He ached all over, not only from earlier exertion putting out fires and rolling around on the mountain shooting claim jumpers but from riding. Mason rubbed his aching posterior, then knocked.

"Duggan, you there? It's me, Morgan Mason."

"Whadya want?"

"A place to rest my weary bones for a few hours. I'll be off for town at first light."

"I only got one bed."

"I'll sleep on some straw in your shed. I just can't keep going. I'm close to dead on my feet."

Blue Dirt Duggan growled and made his way to the door. At least Mason guessed that was the sound made by crutches and a foot scraping along the first floor. With a screech like a nail being pulled from dried wood, the door opened.

Mason recoiled and held up his hands.

"Don't shoot me. You know me! I'm harmless!"

"Harmless, my eye. I saw you kill two men this very day. Get your carcass in here. You can sleep on the floor. It's not cold enough for me to use my second blanket. You can use it to wrap yourself up."

"Much obliged." Mason edged in past the muzzle of the six-shooter Duggan brandished. Even knowing who his guest was didn't make the miner relax one whit.

Duggan muttered constantly as he hobbled back to his bed. He flopped down hard. The bed groaned under the strain. Then Duggan stretched out and snored loudly within minutes. Mason found the threadbare blanket and spread it on the dirt floor under the table. That was about the only spot inside where even a man as short as he was might stretch out.

He half turned and pulled the blanket up over his shoulder. Uncomfortable, he took the unfamiliar six-gun from his waistband and laid it beside him on the floor. This made his bed comfortable enough to let him fall into a deep sleep almost instantly, only to sit bolt upright when the ground shook. He banged his head on the table and sank back, rubbing his forehead and wondering how long he'd been asleep for.

The two miners at the Lost Cause had argued over whether the ground shakes were due to an earthquake or blasting. Mason pressed his hand onto the dirt floor. There weren't any further temblors. More than one quake in San Francisco had rattled his teeth for long seconds. One had endured for close to a minute. This had to be a single blast.

But such an explosion had to be the talk of Virginia City for days or weeks. He had no idea how much dynamite had been detonated, but it was more than a stick to bring down another few feet of rock inside a mine.

He rubbed his eyes, then realized the sun was slanting through the crevices in the eastern wall. Although he felt as if he had slept only a few minutes, the truth was shown by the bright sunlight. Moving stiff muscles made him all too aware of having spent the night on the cold ground with only a single blanket beneath him. He came to hands and knees, then was buffeted around with another explosion. Reacting in surprise, he rose and banged his shoulders against the underside of the table.

Mason flopped down, then regained his composure. For a terrifying instant he had thought this was an earthquake. They were notorious for giving a strong shake, pausing, then following with a secondary buffeting around. But the secondary quaking had been too similar to the initial one.

"Another blast?" He rubbed his shoulder, used the table to pull himself to his feet and looked around. The cabin's disarray gave no hint as to the magnitude of the seismic activity. Duggan wasn't much of a housekeeper. "No, not a blast. That one felt . . . different."

Mason tried to put his finger on how it differed from the first and couldn't. He wasn't too well versed in the effects of dynamite and other explosives, but the second quake had been deeper, more prolonged. It seemed more like a pain in the gut rather than being punched in the belly. Slow and enduring rather than sharp and then over.

"Duggan! Mr. Duggan? Where'd you get off to?"

Finding the miner wasn't all that important. He might have headed for the outhouse. Mason opened the door and watched a dust cloud sweep past.

"Duggan! Are you in the mine?" He rushed outside and looked uphill. On his way to Virginia City he had seen more than one dust storm. The wind whipped up enough sand and debris to pull a nasty brown veil over the land. What he saw now was the same—and different. Roiling clouds gusted downslope from the mouth of the mine.

It had collapsed!

"Duggan! Where'd you get off to?" Mason rushed around hunting for the miner but found no trace of the man. His horses were still in the shed, nervously pawing at the ground and trying to back out past their restraining ropes.

Mason soothed his own horse, then began the climb up the hill to the mouth of the mine. He shook his head when he saw how the timbers supporting the opening had given way. The roof had collapsed, sealing the mine. Not sure what to do, he began pulling away what rocks he could. The task was harder than dipping water from the Pacific Ocean with a teaspoon. Too much rock, so little he could do to reopen the Mira Nell.

He stepped away and coughed. The dust from the collapse was finally settling. He reconstructed what he had seen and used his knowledge of geology to guess how far the collapse extended. He doubted it was more than ten or twenty feet.

Still, a plug of rock twenty feet long presented an insurmountable barrier to opening the mine using only his two hands. He felt desolate thinking that Duggan had been inside when the collapse occurred. The miner had been a potential millionaire the day before and now he had a silver-lined coffin.

Legs turning to rubber, he sat on a rock and stared at the mine mouth. He wondered who Duggan's next of kin was. Whoever it was had become immensely wealthy all because some careless blasting had shaken the entire mountain. Head in his hands, Mason tried to get his churning emotions under control.

"*. . . get me out!*"

"I don't reckon there's much hurry," Mason muttered, answering the voice in his head. "It might be best to put a marker here and whoever gets the mine can drive a shaft parallel."

"Out! Get me out!"

Mason looked around, frowning. The voice wasn't in his head. It came from the mountainside. Slowly rising, he turned back and forth, straining to hear. Nothing. He was imagining it. Voices in the head. A ringing about drowned out real sounds of the world.

"Help!"

He jerked around and rushed to the mine. Scrambling up the slope of broken rock he flopped belly down at the top and found a tiny hole going back into the mine. It was hardly the size of his arm and somehow had remained open in spite of the tons of cascading rock from the mine roof.

"Is that you, Duggan? Are you in the mine shaft?"

"Unless the sky's turned black, of course I'm in the mine. Rescue me!"

Mason let out a whoop of glee. Blue Dirt Duggan was still alive! Then the exhilaration faded. How could he ever dig out the rocks to save Duggan before he died of thirst? As tiny as the opening was, he might suffocate. If he wasn't careful as he tunneled back, he might cause the air vent to cave in and doom the miner. Mason saw more ways of killing Duggan than saving him.

He wasn't a miner. He was a geologist, and nothing like this had ever been mentioned during any of the classes he'd taken.

"I should have been a mining engineer," he moaned.

"You talkin' to yourself or is somebody caught in the mine?"

The voice from behind caused him to jump, startled. Mason half slid down the pile of rock and faced the two miners from the Lost Cause.

"Duggan caught in there?" One miner scratched his stubbled chin, pursed his lips and walked about slowly. "Getting that varmint out will be a real chore. Suppose we could leave him in there." He grinned broadly, then shouted, "What do you think of that, Duggan? You think we ought to spend the time and dig you out or can we just leave you in there?"

Mason would have laughed if the situation hadn't been so serious. Duggan launched into a sulfurous string of curses that should have melted the rock separating him from the outside.

"There's a tiny hole going straight back," Mason said. "I don't know how far, but it's how he's getting air."

The second miner climbed up and looked in, then slid back.

"There's plenty of air in the mine, even if we do collapse that itsy-bitsy tunnel. I'm thinking we got to be quick, though, since he probably not got anything to drink in there."

"No whiskey? That's enough to make a man kill himself," said the first.

Mason had to grin at their joking, then he sobered. There were other dangers, and pulling Duggan out as fast as possible was vital.

"There might be damp inside," he said. "Those explosions might have been gas blowing up and not dynamite. This whole mountain might be ready to collapse on itself if there's enough methane caught in pockets."

"You said you was a geologist. There's not been any trouble like that, not in these shallow mines. Now, the Ophir goes down twenty levels. They have damp. They also have flooding. Hot water, it is, too."

The two began arguing over the best way of getting Duggan out while Mason climbed back and yelled down the hole, "You hurt? We're working on getting you out."

"Of course I'm hurt. I ain't got a leg, thanks to you. You planning on doing me out of my other leg?"

"Be glad I didn't leave you in that burning building," Mason said.

"You wanted to save me for this torture. That's the way you are. If you don't get me out, I ain't ever going to pay you your five dollars!"

"Ten," Mason yelled back at him. "Or was it twelve? I might start adding to your bill. How's fifteen sound?" He realized he and Duggan were barking at each other like the other two miners from the Lost Cause.

"You want to let us get up there or do you want to do some shoveling?" The two miners worked their way up the slope. They pointed to parts of the cave-in and shook their heads and otherwise silently argued.

"Do what you can. Is it going to take long?" Mason looked around anxiously.

"From what I can see, we got ten feet of rock to burrow through. If we use them timbers to shore up the sides as we go, we can pull Duggan out in an hour or two."

The second miner said, "And if we're real lucky, we can get him out in four or five. No reason to dig out a man and have him bad-mouth us 'fore we're all prepared for his sharp tongue-lashing."

The pair began working at the hole, moving timbers in to support the sides and shoveling steadily. From where Mason stood, they might have been prairie dogs digging their burrow. A constant stream of dirt and rock cascaded down.

"I'm going to do some exploring," Mason said. "Unless you need me."

"You'd be in the way, geologist fellow. Go do what you need to do."

A new flurry of rock rocketed from the hole, driving Mason a few steps away. He left the pair to their work. They knew what they were doing, and he wanted to see if more damage had been done by the first explosion. He spent a few minutes calming Victoria, then mounted and rode along the road until he came to a fork. The lower trail led to the Lost Cause. He took the upper road. As he slowly circled the mountain, he saw a few abandoned mines.

None was in the sorry condition of the Mira Nell Mine. And they had been abandoned for some time, if he was any judge. Several miles farther, he came to another fork. The smaller trail petered out fast, but the larger came around to the west side of the mountain where Virginia City clung to the eastern slope. The road was well maintained. Mason tried to remember if this was the main way into Virginia City and if he had traveled it in the stagecoach.

He shook his head in wonder. It seemed like a lifetime ago when he'd arrived in Virginia City. But it hadn't been. So much had happened in such a short time. Riding a mile along the road took him along a curving path that narrowed into a stretch hardly wide enough for a heavy wagon or stage. He looked down the precipice and shuddered. If a blast happened here, it was a hundred-foot drop into a ravine filled with jagged rocks.

He drew rein and looked ahead. The way was deserted. He was sure now this was the road from Carson City going into Virginia City. There wasn't any reason for him to stay on the western slope when Duggan and his mine and the two from the Lost Cause were on the far side. He wheeled Victoria about and retraced his way.

The exploration had taken him the better part of four hours, and there hadn't been any sign of what caused the explosion—or explosions. They'd been occurring for some time. He thought on the possibility of gas pockets blowing up. That was always a danger for mines, but usually only those burrowing far into the ground like the Ophir and other gold and silver mines run by the big companies. If there had been any trouble at them, the whole town would be abuzz.

He reached Duggan's cabin and dismounted, making sure his mare had fodder and enough to drink. His own belly quaked and growled. It had been too long since he'd had anything to eat. While it seemed like stealing, he rummaged through Duggan's larder, found a couple sourdough biscuits that almost broke his teeth, and gnawed on them.

Trooping back uphill, he saw the two miners crouched down. As was usual with them, they argued, but this time they did so in muted tones. That made Mason curious. He stopped a few feet away.

Blue Dirt Duggan lay stretched out on the ground between the men. They looked up. Joking now was out of the question.

One said, "We got him out, but just as we was pulling him free, he smashed his head on a rock."

"The roof caved in," said the other. "You make it sound like it was something Duggan did wrong. There wasn't any way to keep him from getting his skull bashed in. There wasn't."

Mason dropped to his knees beside the unconscious miner. Duggan had a long gash in his temple. It had clotted over, but part of his hair had peeled back as if he'd been scalped. White bone stuck out from the gash.

"His skull's been broken," Mason said. "He's still alive, but I don't know why."

Duggan's chest rose and fell as he sucked in ragged breaths. A cursory examination showed the head wound was the worst he'd suffered. Mason kept looking at the pants leg tied in a knot just below where his knee once had been. The miner had gone through hell. A fire, getting his leg amputated, now this. All the silver in the world meant nothing to him if he died.

"I can't do anything for him." Mason looked at the other two. The expressions on their faces told of utter helplessness. They had no more idea what to do for the miner than he did. "I'll try to get him into town and see if Dr. Sinclair can patch him up again."

"You think that's a smart thing to do, move him now?" The first miner looked skeptical.

"It might be the dumbest thing I ever did," Mason said, "but I don't know what else to do."

The three of them took Duggan down the hill, rigged a travois and Mason set out for town, pointedly not looking at the man behind the horse. He didn't want to see when Duggan actually died.

CHAPTER TEN

H E'S ABOUT THE unluckiest man I ever did see," Dr.
Sinclair said, pressing his stethoscope over Blue
Dirt Duggan's chest. "Or maybe he's the luckiest. He's
still alive, and he's got you for his guardian angel."

Morgan Mason looked up, startled. He sat in a chair
across the surgery from where the doctor examined
Duggan. The long road into town had taken every
ounce of energy he had. What should have been a few
hours' worth of riding had turned into a nightlong ex-
cursion. The slower he went, the less Duggan had been
jostled in the travois, but somewhere around two in the
morning Mason had realized he had to move faster.
The miner was slipping away. His horse had found a
compromise between speed and throwing the wounded
man from side to side.

"Me? An angel? You've got that wrong, Doc. If anything, I'm a jinx. Duggan never had troubles like he does now before I came to town."

"It all depends on how you look at it. Duggan's not dead. You saved him. I can't see you had much to do with the predicaments that lost him a leg or came crashing down on him in his very own mine. Was there a demon bringing it? I see you as being his angel."

Sinclair motioned for Mason to help him move the miner into the back room. It was all Mason could do to lift the man. He started to make a joke about Duggan being lighter because of his missing leg, then he shut his mouth. That wasn't proper, not when Duggan's next bed was likely to be the inside of a coffin.

"You got him here. He's got a nasty head wound, but the bleeding's stopped."

"His skull's showing through his scalp."

"It looks worse than it is." Sinclair raised his eyebrows at Mason's disbelief. "Wait and see. His chest injuries will lay him up longer. I am sure one rib's broken, maybe two, but even then he's lucky. He didn't puncture a lung."

Mason stepped away and let the sawbones splash carbolic acid over his hands. He felt woozy, as much from his exhaustion as the sight of so much blood and exposed bone.

"Get out of here. I don't need a second patient."

As Mason turned to go, Sinclair called after him, "The Mira Nell's still spitting out silver, isn't she?"

"You won't operate unless he can pay?"

"I'll do my best to save him, no matter what, but if he can pay, I'll put the stitches closer together. Otherwise, I'll save on the thread and use big sutures." The doctor smiled. Mason wasn't sure if this was some sort of gallows humor.

"The mine's spilling out silver," Mason said. "He's a rich man."

"More than before? Never mind. Clear out and let me get to work." The doctor began cutting away the coat and vest to gently peel off the blood-soaked shirt.

Mason cast one last look at Duggan's head and wondered at the doctor's priorities. But he was the medical expert. Let him patch up what looked to be the worst injuries. But the exposed skull . . .

He stepped out into the dawn and squinted. Victoria neighed to get his attention. He went to the horse and patted her nose.

"You need to eat. So do I, but you've saved a man's life tonight, so you first." He led the mare away until he found a livery stable on D Street. Mason fished through the coins in his pocket and paid in advance, to be sure he didn't squander what little he had and then find the stable owner keeping the horse until he did pay.

The benches along the boardwalk drew him. All he wanted was to stretch out for a bit, get a few minutes' sleep, but as he veered in the direction of one he saw a deputy grab a down-on-his-luck miner by the collar, yank him to his feet and frog-march him along. From what he overheard, the man was being arrested for loitering and would spend time in the town jail until he paid a fine. Mason didn't hear the named sum, but he knew it was more than he had in his pocket. Not wishing to join the derelict in the calaboose, he trudged up Union Street's steep incline until he reached Howard Street above A Street, where the saloons still served miners and townsmen like it was Saturday night.

"I ought to forget looking for a job as geologist," he grumbled. "Being a saloon owner's the best job in this whole town."

He wandered about until his legs turned to rubber under him. It took both hands pulling at the railing to get up the steps into the Crazy Eights Saloon. His mind was wooly with fatigue, but he remembered coming into Virginia City and hearing the name of this establishment.

"A lovely lass," he said as he pushed through the double doors. The gin mill did a brisk business but didn't seem as crowded as other saloons along the street. It wasn't that the Crazy Eights wasn't doing as brisk a business. It was only that it was three times the size of most others.

"Where's the most beautiful girl in all Virginia City?" He looked around for a woman but didn't see any. The working girls had all returned to their cribs to rest up for another evening's business.

"What can I get you?"

Mason looked up to a stocky man wearing a canvas apron. He might have seen bigger handlebar mustaches in his day, but he couldn't remember when. Before he said anything, the barkeep spoke up.

"I'm from Texas, and they used to say my mustaches were wider than any longhorn on the range." He made a big show of twirling the tips into sharp points imitating a bull's fearsome weapons.

"They call you Tex, right?"

"Texas Jack. Now how'd you guess that?" He grinned and the tips of his mustaches wriggled about. "You don't look like you're ready to start drinking. Coffee, breakfast? Ain't much, but it's cheaper than the restaurant down the street." Texas Jack proved how jolly he was by venting a deep-bellied laugh. "Ain't as likely to pizzen you, neither."

Mason counted out his change on the table and looked up.

"That's good enough." Texas Jack snatched the money and went off, whistling "Yellow Rose of Texas." Mason leaned back and started to close his eyes. Just for a minute. Then he forced them open again. If he let sleep overtake him, he wasn't likely to get any food. Texas Jack had the look of a man who'd eat a customer's breakfast, then lie about how much the patron enjoyed it once he awoke.

The coffee was bitter and black and what Mason needed to perk up. The fried eggs and slab of ham weren't the best he'd ever eaten, but they filled a hollow spot in the pit of his stomach. Only after he'd wiped the plate clean with a slice of sourdough bread did he lean back and let his eyelids droop. The barkeep would chase him out sooner or later, but he wasn't as likely to call a deputy and have him dragged off to the jail.

Mason came bolt upright, hand going to the six-shooter slid into his waistband when alarm bells rang loud enough to raise the dead. From outside he heard the cry, "Fire! We got another fire. Big one! Captain Delahunt's already assembling the brigade!"

Mason went to the doors and peered out. Texas Jack crowded close behind.

"Them fires are getting worse every week. It won't be long until the whole danged town burns down again."

"I heard about the earlier fire. Wiped out everything down to D Street," Mason said.

"If you stick around and throw water on the front of

the Crazy Eights, I'll see you get a decent meal out of it."

"Why me?"

"The rest of the town's rushing down to the fire. If they catch Delahunt's attention, they think they might be asked to join the brigade. You don't look like the kind wanting fame as much as you'd prefer another plate of food."

Mason considered the offer. The coffee had brought him back to the land of the living, but its potent effect would wear off soon enough. He balanced food versus the notion he'd become famous.

"Maybe that pretty gal you're supposed to have here would give me the time of day if I belonged to a fire company."

Texas Jack muttered something under his breath about social diseases, and Mason didn't think he was talking about the kind transmitted between the sheets. Fame wasn't something he sought, but keeping Virginia City from burning to a cinder motivated him. There wasn't any reason for him to spend his last dime coming to Virginia City, only to find nothing here because it had burned to the ground.

He tipped his hat, smiled regretfully, then ran into the street. Smoke billowed up from B Street. A quick dash down Howard to Taylor Street set him on the proper track. He came out on B Street at the edge of the fire. Remembered heat bathed his face. He closed his eyes and took a step back. He had blistered before going after Duggan.

Memory of fire made him remember something more. Duggan had been rooting through the files in the lawyer's office, hunting for something. He had meant to ask what the miner sought at such risk to his life, but events had always cropped up that made such questions irrelevant. Now the miner might not even live after having the Mira Nell Mine fall in on his head.

Mason dropped to one knee and shoved his hand against the dirt in the street. He burrowed down to the solid roadbed and felt a new shock. Only the roar of the fire drowned out his warning of "Earthquake!" Then the shivering turned back to its usual unmoving bedrock.

Which would be worse? Temblor or conflagration? The answer burned a little closer to him. The fire brigade shot through a wall of flames with a hand pumper truck and skidded to a halt a few yards in front of him. The firemen jumped down, deployed hoses and two of their number began pumping hard, like rail workers on a handcar.

"Water! You! Find us water for the pumps!" Delahunt himself bellowed at Mason.

He jumped to obey. Across the street in an alley stretched a line of a dozen rain barrels. Mason peered into the first one. Empty. He had better luck with the next four. All his effort failed to budge the full barrel. Water sloshed about. The next thing he knew Delahunt worked beside him. Somehow, the fireman brought the barrel onto its edge and began rolling it into the street by himself. Mason tried on a second barrel and failed to even tip it. As Delahunt took his filled barrel to the pump, another man dressed in his red shirt, fancy brass buckle and helmet took the barrel from Mason.

"I'll be damned," Mason said, watching this man work his heavy barrel as easily as Delahunt had. He tried to tell himself a bigger meal and a good night's sleep would have let him wrestle the barrel like the others did, but he was only kidding himself. They had done this before. They knew the proper leverage and way to twist and turn at the precise instant.

He trailed them into the street and watched the pumped water arch upward in a wide spray onto the fire. The man working the nozzle changed the way the water spewed forth. From a spray to a torrent and then back, he varied the water so the fire vanished as if by magic.

Captain Delahunt came over and slapped Mason on the back.

"Thanks for your help, citizen. You're a part of Fire Brigade No. 1's success today."

"I . . ." Mason had nothing to say. He had located the water and nothing more.

"We're having a social this weekend. It's a private affair but consider yourself invited. At our firehouse. Just tell the gent at the door 'salamander' and he'll let you in. Bring a lady friend or two, if you want!" Delahunt slapped him again on the back, laughed and went to congratulate the rest of the pumper crew on their swift, decisive action.

"A private party and I'm invited?" Mason swelled with pride, then deflated a mite. He hadn't done anything to deserve such a reward. But he'd been given a secret password to get in. If only he had a lady friend to take.

Movement at the corner of his vision made him spin about. Fires proved devilishly hard to extinguish, especially with wood buildings like those in Virginia City to feed upon. Sparks flew on the wind and set roofs ablaze dozens of yards—more!—away from the main blaze. What he saw was a flare, a leap of voracious fire.

Only nothing was there when he faced the direction

of the untouched candle store. He started to call to Delahunt and tell him of his concern, then saw the fire captain hoisted onto the shoulders of his men and carried away amid great cheers. A crowd called out to Delahunt, offering him drinks and, if Mason heard aright, the cluster of women at the front of the crowd offered far more than that. The life of a fireman in Virginia City was certainly special.

He started to join the crowd. When he had first come to town he had gotten caught up in the celebration. After all that had happened to him and those around him, a bit of celebration appealed to lift his spirits. But he pivoted and went to the candle store's front door. He rapped on it.

"Hello? Anybody here?" It seemed unlikely since the fire down the street had forced an evacuation. Nobody in this town ignored such warnings as had been given by the ringing fire bell.

Mason tried the door. Open. He pushed inside and looked around. The wax scents from hundreds of candles made his nose wrinkle. Stacked along the rear wall were dozens of crates of miner's candles. This store did a land office business, he suspected. The idea of doing a "land office business" made him smile, just a little. Maybe he could learn to be a surveyor if freelance geologist didn't work out for him.

A door at the rear of the store slammed.

"Who's there? I won't hurt you!" He touched the six-gun tucked into his waistband. Throwing lead wasn't going to happen. But why would anyone run from him? If he had come across the proprietor, the man would have braced him for entering his store. Or more likely in this town, tried to sell him a crate of candles piled high.

Mason crossed the store and sidled past the mountain of miner's candles. He burst into the back room where the candlemaker plied his trade. But not now. The room stood empty. The rear door swung to and fro in a gentle morning breeze. Mason stuck his head out and looked around. He let out a yelp of surprise and burst out in the alley. A pile of garbage smoldered with a few tentative flames poking up, trying to find enough oxygen to become a real fire.

He kicked at the pile and spread it out so he could scoop up dirt and throw it on the smoking mass. A broken broom handle gave him the means to scatter the debris used as fuel.

He wiped sweat from his forehead and realized he smeared soot all over his face. He had been close enough to the real fire to catch a snootful of carbon black.

"Maybe not the same as Captain Delahunt and his crew, but I did a good job." He poked a little more at the garbage pile and made sure not so much as a single ember remained.

Mason jumped when he caught a flash of fire once more out of the corner of his eye. Moving faster this time, he spun and looked eastward into the sun. The flare wasn't caused by the rising sun. It was a man thrusting a torch into another pile of debris. The bright light hid the man's face in shadow. All Mason saw was a dark outline.

"Stop! Don't! You'll set the store on fire!"

The man turned toward him, shook the torch, then leaned it against the wall before running off. Mason wasn't up to it but found the strength to run flat-out to the new fire. He kicked the torch away so it no longer fed on the wooden store wall. Then he stomped and kicked and used his broken broom handle to scatter this potential town-killer fire.

"You miserable cur," he grated out. If only he had caught a better look at the man! Whatever he thought he was doing might have brought out all the fire brigades. Mason poked and pushed and even felt the garbage to be sure it was cool and didn't hide any embers waiting to burst into full-blown fire.

When he finished, he looked up into the sun again, but something blocked the light. Just as his eyes adjusted and saw a man's body, a rock came crashing down into his head.

CHAPTER ELEVEN

MORGAN MASON JERKED to the side but the rock cut deep into his forehead, just over his left eye. Blood spurted and blinded him in that eye. Rolling back, he flopped onto his back. His vision was gone in his left eye and blurred in his right from the concussion. He saw shadows and movement and the flash of sunlight off a brass belt buckle. Hardly knowing what he did, he pulled the six-shooter from his waistband and shoved it out. His elbow locked, and his hand shook. Somehow he cocked the pistol.

The sound was loud enough to sound like a death peal. The shadow towering above him held a sputtering torch in one hand and the rock in the other. Mason tried to cry out that he'd shoot, but his voice clogged in his throat.

Then he was blinded by the full force of the rising sun. He was alone in the alley.

He sagged back. His arm trembled, and the heavy six-shooter turned into a ten-ton anvil. Unable to support it any longer, he collapsed.

"Where'd you go?" His voice sounded dim and distant. He spat blood and said in a stronger voice, "Who are you?" Mason forced himself back against the wall and slipped about in the garbage pile like a pig in a wallow. The stench caused him to choke and start breathing naturally again. This revived him.

Using both hands, he lifted the pistol and looked around. The specter with the rock and torch was gone. It took a few seconds using the wall as a support to get his feet under him. By the time he stood and looked around, the world of Virginia City was perfectly normal once more. No one else prowled the alley. The heavy pall from the earlier fire blew away, and the sounds of a town coming alive again told him there was no way to track down the arsonist.

He took a few tentative steps and found what might have been a burned torch. Or it might have been nothing more than a stick with a rag caught on the end. He poked at it with his toe and knew it wasn't any kind of evidence.

"He wore a fancy belt buckle. It reflected the sun." With more than a hint of bitterness, he added, "And it blinded me." There was no way to tell who had tried to set more fires. Or who had tried to kill him.

He thrust his six-gun back into his waistband and made his way out onto B Street. Other than the scorched buildings down the street, everything was as it should be. Trudging along, he made his way to Union and then climbed back up the hill to Howard Street.

The Crazy Eights Saloon was doing a brisk business. The firemen had gone there with their adoring crowd to knock back shot after shot of whiskey and to boast of their exploits fighting yet another blaze. He sank into a chair outside the saloon and closed his eyes. Just for a minute. He came awake with a start when someone kicked at the chair leg and almost tipped him over.

"There's not many laws they enforce in this town, but loitering and vagrancy are two of them. Marshal Benteen thinks it reflects poorly on him if drunks sleep it off out in public." Texas Jack wiped his mouth with his sleeve. "Can't rightly think of many other laws he enforces with as much gusto. I've even known him to let killers go, if he thought their victim deserved it. Said it saved the town the cost of a trial." The barkeep settled down on a rail and swung his feet back and forth as he took in the sun.

Mason saw it was almost mid-sky. He had slept longer than he thought.

"Don't you have customers?"

Howard Street bustled with life, men and even a few women carrying parcels and going into stores and advancing the commerce of the mining town.

"The brigade left an hour back when most of their admirers returned to work. Miners have to work their claims to make enough money to buy their favorite fireman a drink, you know."

"That sounds like men I've known back in San Francisco who follow showgirls from saloon to saloon."

"Same idea, I reckon. Bask in the reflected glory. Those fellows want the chanteuses and dancers for a different reason, unless I miss my guess. The miners and shopkeepers in Virginia City butter up the firemen to get voted into the fire companies themselves. There's nothing more admired in these parts."

"Not even politicians?"

Texas Jack laughed until tears ran down his cheeks.

"You city boys got strange ideas. That's not where the power lies in a town like this. Adulation lies at the top of the heap. And the richest miners, the bankers, the ones who handle and move the silver and gold. They control purty near everything. They buy and sell politicians. But even they can't buy their way into the top fire brigades."

"What about Marshal Benteen?"

"Every man's got his price. I just never heard what his might be, leastwise not yet." The barkeep jumped down from the railing. "I'm figuring what your price might be. You already ate. The way you drink beer tells me you're not a slave to demon rum. You make my fine draft beer look like you was sucking down pizzen. No, your price is . . . ten cents an hour to clean up the place. I can promise you five hours today, if you sweep up, wash the beer mugs and otherwise do the tedious work I don't want to."

"Ten cents an hour and dinner." Mason stood and thrust out his hand. Texas Jack looked at it, then shook his head.

"I don't know if you think this is binding me to some sort of contract or something you need to tell yourself you're actually doing a job that amounts to a hill of beans." The barkeep shook.

Mason started sweeping out the saloon, moving all the sawdust on the floor to the back and picking through it to remove broken glass and less identifiable objects before sweeping it back to soak up more spills and blood. As he worked he tried to find out more about Virginia City from Texas Jack. When he asked about firebugs, the bartender turned sullen and even downright uncivil.

"You hush your mouth about that," the barkeep said, glaring. "Talk about it and it happens. Everyone knows it's bad luck."

"I saw a man setting fires."

Texas Jack turned his back and stalked into the back room. From the pop of a cork and the clink of glass, he poured himself some of his own stock. Mason worked on the front of the bar, polishing it the best he could before cleaning glasses and wiping them spotless with a rag dropped into a bucket of water behind the bar. When the barkeep didn't appear, Mason fixed himself another meal. He considered the beer and instead worked on a glass of water. That sat better in the pit of his stomach.

He looked up when the double doors banged open. It took a few seconds for him to recognize the customer.

"Jasper," he called. "Jasper Jessup. You're all cleaned up and looking downright civilized."

"It's a woman, old son, a woman. Why else would I put sweet smell'um on my hair?" The fireman took off his hat and showed Mason how he'd slicked it down until it gleamed like polished metal.

"She's not here. Texas Jack's in the back room, getting drunk, I reckon. But no ladies here at all."

"What'd you say to get him all het up? Never mind. And I know she's not here. She'd be at the better establishments in town."

"Better than the Crazy Eights? Where'd that be?"

Jessup sidled up as if sharing a secret.

"She'll be at Captain Delahunt's shindig tonight. That's the finest social of the year, or so his men keep telling me."

"But surely Finley's Fire Drakes put on a better one?" Mason was joshing. Jessup took it seriously.

"We're not competing with Delahunt on that score. He's got the money, even if his brigade's nowhere near as good."

"His men have number one on their buckles because they were here first," Mason said, remembering the tidbit of history Jessup had passed along before. He reared back and got a look. Jessup wore his brass buckle emblazoned with the numeral two.

"Do all the fire companies wear the same belt buckles?" He remembered the sunlight shining off such a buckle. This suggested that his attacker—the firebug?— might well be a fireman. He frowned, wondering if he had it all wrong. If the man was in one of the brigades, he would have been looking for fires, not starting them.

Mason touched the deep cut on his forehead and winced. It was one of those wounds serious enough to have a doctor look at it but not so serious it required stitches. Or so he told himself.

"Each has their own special design. That's what makes Captain Finley's stand out." Jessup thrust out his belly so Mason got a better look. In addition to the number, lettering etched around the large oval buckle carried more information than Mason could read. "Tells our history, each one does. Yes, sir." Jessup pursed his lips and looked toward the backroom. "You think you could fetch me a beer? Jack's not likely to come out for me."

"Because I made him mad?"

"Because Captain Delahunt carouses here. It's not like Finley's Fire Drakes aren't allowed in, it's just that folks ignore us when we come in. We hold court at other places."

"Better places?" Mason circled the bar and drew a brew. He considered asking for Jessup to pay, then decided if Texas Jack got sore about it, losing a half hour's pay was small enough price to talk to about the only friend he'd made in town.

"Not better as long as that sweet little filly's here." Jessup looked around the empty saloon. "I reckon she'll be at Delahunt's party tonight."

"Are you going? You might have some competition for her attention, but she's obviously not here right now."

"I . . . I haven't been invited."

Jasper Jessup sounded so forlorn Mason blurted, "I've been asked."

"Get on with you," Jessup said. "How? You're joshing me, aren't you?"

Mason shook his head, not sure what to answer.

"What's the password? They always have a password. You don't know it, do you?"

"Salamander." Mason worried he'd have to pick Jessup up off the floor. The fireman looked as if he'd been punched in the breadbasket.

"One of Delahunt's crew invited you? Told you?"

"I helped them find water to fight the fire down on B Street. Is this supposed to be a secret? Nobody told me that."

"That's 'cuz everyone in Virginia City *knows*. Otherwise, their firehouse would have every last living soul in the whole danged county elbowing his way in." Jessup drained his beer, licked his lips, then whispered,

"Can I go with you? If they only invited you, maybe I could tag along."

"They did say for me to bring friends." Again Mason thought Jessup was going to swallow his own tongue. "Of course, they specified *lady* friends."

"To get a chance to see her, I'll put on a dress!"

Mason laughed. He took Jessup's glass and cleaned it before Texas Jack noticed there'd been a customer and no extra money had been dropped into the till.

"I can use a guide. When's it start?"

Jessup looked up at the Regulator clock on the far wall and said, "About an hour from now. Sundown. I'll come back by and show you the way." He slapped Mason on the back, turned and left, mumbling to himself. Mason heard *salamander* several times before Jessup left the saloon.

Mason worked steadily and cleaned as much of the large saloon as he could before Texas Jack returned from the back room. The barkeep glared at him, cast a cursory look around at Mason's work and went behind the bar. He leaned on it, one bloodshot eye fixed on Mason, the other closed. There was no telling how much of his own witch's brew he had sampled in the hours since he had retreated to his storeroom.

"You've done all right," he said. "Here's your pay." He dropped two bits on the bar.

Mason made no effort to pick it up. His heart beat faster as he silently engaged the bartender. They both knew what he was owed. For a few seconds, Texas Jack glowered. Then he fished around in his till and dropped another two bits onto the bar.

"Thanks," Mason said. He slid the two quarters off the bar and tucked them into his vest pocket. He started for the door, hesitated and half turned to say, "There's a firebug out there, no matter what you think." The barkeep reared back, as if he could throw a punch from such a distance, then seemed to melt into himself.

Morgan Mason stepped into the late afternoon and sucked in a breath of air. The smoke from the early morning fire was gone, leaving only the stench coming from the smelter and general town odors. Compared to the acrid smoke of a burning building, it was perfume to his nose. He considered occupying the chair outside the Crazy Eights and decided against it. Texas Jack had turned against him just because he brought up the possibility of an arsonist setting fires. As he wandered along Howard Street, he tried to figure out why.

If he was right, Virginia City was in danger. If he was wrong, all he did was run in small circles and no one was hurt. He wondered if the Crazy Eights barkeep worried he would accuse an innocent citizen. If that was it, what did it matter to Texas Jack? Mason had never so much as hinted that he thought Texas Jack was the firebug.

Did someone the bartender know well go around setting fires? Why not stop him rather than let him endanger everyone, including the Crazy Eights Saloon? Nothing fit together. Further thought on the matter was derailed when Jasper Jessup shouted his name.

He turned and waved to the fireman. Jessup hurried down the street.

"You're all gussied up. Even more than earlier," Mason said, aware he needed a bath and clean clothes. To match Jessup he'd need finery more appropriate for the Union Club back in San Francisco.

"Naw, I just threw on the first thing I found." Jasper

Jessup looked down shyly. Then he grinned and said, "If she's there, I want to make a good impression. Since it's not a good idea to wear a Fire Drake uniform when Captain Delahunt's throwing the bash, this was the best I could do."

"I'm sure she'll take notice of you," Mason said. He started to protest when Jessup steered him around so they headed down the street toward Fire Brigade No. 1's firehouse. Then he let the man lead him. Jessup was like a horse ready to start a race. There was no reason to deny him his anticipation.

He and Jasper Jessup found the end of the long line to enter. The sun had barely set, but the music blaring from inside and the crowd pressing to enter brought a brightness that Mason had not felt since coming to Virginia City.

CHAPTER TWELVE

J ASPER JESSUP CROWDED behind Mason when they
reached the door into the firehouse.

"You know the password?" The fireman moved
closer to Mason and turned his ear to better hear over
the ruckus coming from inside.

Mason spoke in a low voice, feeling this was similar
to secret meetings of the Masons and Elks, only he was
part of it. He cupped his hand and said, "Salamander."
For a heart-stopping second, he worried this wasn't the
right word, that he had misheard, that he would be turned
away. The fireman reached out and slapped him on the
shoulder.

"Enjoy yourself." The hand moved him along. He
was officially part of the upper crust in Virginia City.
He was accepted to join Fire Brigade No. 1's festivity!

The whirl of dancers inside momentarily dazzled
him. He looked around when he realized Jessup wasn't

right behind him. Jessup stood exchanging words with the fireman acting as the gatekeeper. Fearing an altercation because a rival fireman tried to enter, Mason started to go to Jessup's aid when the fireman thrust out his hand and shook. Delahunt's man slapped Jessup the way he had Mason and let him in. Jessup grinned ear to ear.

"Thanks, my friend, thank you. He recognized me, but because I was with you, he let me in." Jessup stood on tiptoe and looked past Mason. He dropped back and started to say something more, then clamped his mouth shut.

Mason looked around, wondering what caused Jessup's sudden silence. It took him a few seconds, then he saw her.

"She's the one you're always going on about?" Mason watched the lovely woman working her way through a Texas star. Everything Jessup and others had said about the woman at the Crazy Eights was right, if this was her. And why wouldn't it be? There wasn't a man inside the firehouse who wasn't watching her as she spun and whirled and do-si-do'd around the square. She passed within a few feet of him.

"I can die happy now," Jessup said. "I've just seen a bit of heaven come to earth. Ain't she an angel, just as I said?"

Mason nodded. The brunette's hair swung out long and glistening in the light as she whirled about. The tanned oval face showed fine bones and a straight nose and brown eyes that danced with as much enjoyment as the woman did herself. She wore a crisp white blouse boldly unbuttoned so the swell of her breasts showed just enough to be daring but not enough to provoke even the strictest pastor's wrath. A trim waist was cinched with a wide tooled-leather belt. A Mexican embroidered skirt flared and flashed in the light and made it seem that Jessup was right. This was an angel come to grace them with her presence.

"I need to wet my whistle," Mason said. He started to repeat it, but Jessup was mesmerized. Without any further thought, he made his way through the crowd to a bar set up along the back of the firehouse. The bartender wore a full fireman's outfit, red shirt and helmet. The brass belt buckle reflected and reminded Mason of his encounter in the alley. The suspicion he had been attacked by a fireman haunted him.

He took the beer shoved across at him. He started to fish out one of the quarters he had earned that day, but a lilting voice stopped him.

"It's free. Captain Delahunt is a very charitable man."

He looked over his shoulder and smiled. "Then can I offer you a drink?"

The brunette started to say something, stopped, then laughed. Her brown eyes glowed with merriment.

"Aren't you the generous one? Very clever, sir." She reached past him to take a drink pushed across by the barkeep. She raised it in a toast and knocked back the shot in a single quick move. Then she was caught up in a hug from Captain Delahunt himself. They pressed close together and whispered.

Jessup would be jealous if Mason ever told him of his brief encounter with the object of his desire. He inhaled deeply and thought he caught just a hint of her perfume, but the air inside the firehouse was close, filled with coal oil smoke from the lamps, sweat from so many bodies crowded in and even the beer already spilled on the bar. He signaled he wanted another drink. The bartender obliged, but his eyes were fixed on the woman a few feet behind Mason.

He turned and leaned back so he got a better look at her. She was an eyeful, and she was Delahunt's exclusive property tonight. Again the respect and social status of the firemen was driven home.

"You just came to town?" The fireman barkeep set up Mason again. "I saw the captain invite you this morning. You ever work as a fireman?"

"Can't say that I have," Mason said, turning to face the barkeep. "I just came in from San Francisco. Now and again I'd see the firemen there going to a fire. Fires along the Embarcadero were always the worst. I saw a China Clipper catch fire. It burned the masts and sails like they were trees and branches in a dry forest. It's hard to forget the sight."

"If you're not a fireman, you come to make your fortune in the mines?"

Mason laughed as he considered that.

"I heard of the silver strikes and came because of that, but I'm a chemist."

"Like what works in an assay office?"

"I tried," Mason said, "but that's a closed shop. I've been out along Calabasas Creek gathering ore samples to find richer veins. I worked as a chemist, but I'm also a geologist."

Something warm and yielding pressed against his back. Slender arms reached around him on either side so he was pinned to the bar. Delightfully so when he saw the lovely woman was the one doing the pinning.

Her hot breath gusted into his ear.

"You're a geologist? How fascinating."

"I've worked as both chemist and geologist in San Francisco for years," Mason told her. He twisted around in her embrace. She made no effort to let him go free.

"So many miners have no idea what they're doing. Learning to look for only one or two types of ore limits them," she said. Her ruby lips parted slightly. Her tongue darted out to wet those enticing lips, then she said in a husky voice, "Emma Longview."

It took him a second to understand this was her name. He started to touch the brim of his hat, but she still held him captive. He introduced himself.

"So, Mr. Mason, why don't we find a quieter spot to talk? I am *fascinated* by your expertise as a . . . geologist."

"I have to admit, Miss Longview, you are the first person ever to say that to me."

She laughed delightedly and said, "You are so droll. I am sure the San Francisco ladies flocked around you to hear your marvelous stories." She looped her arm in his and steered him away.

Mason caught sight of Captain Delahunt being inundated by his own ocean of local ladies, all wanting to dance with him as the band swung into "Turkey in the Straw."

"That's supposed to be William Bonney's favorite song," he said. Mason found himself as tongue-tied as Jasper Jessup when it came to this lovely lady.

"Do you know much about notorious outlaws such as Billy the Kid? There's more to you than meets the eye, Mr. Mason." She rubbed against him and any comeback he had died in a mental jumble. For the moment he was content enough to step out into the cool night with her. He tried to hang back, not wanting to go too far from the gaiety inside, but she would have none of it. Emma Longview kept him moving along until they reached an especially dark area in front of a bookstore.

He gallantly brushed off a bench for her, then sat next to her at what he considered an appropriate distance. Emma Longview slid closer and clung to his arm as if he might run away at any instant.

"Tell me about your practice in San Francisco. As a geologist?" She made him forget what clever reply he had thought up.

"There's not much work in the city itself, so I worked across the Bay and in the hills. Mostly, miners wanted to know if they'd struck it rich."

"Had they?"

He shook his head sadly. In the years he had worked in San Francisco, there hadn't been a single strike rich enough to justify sinking a hole. But he doubted she wanted to hear that.

"I did some work for a hydraulic mining company, but there wasn't much geology required. They tear down entire mountains and sift through the debris. There's not a great deal of useful work."

"Any work on building roads? Analyses that required you to look at granite and how to deal with it?"

"Some," he said, not sure where she was going with this. This hardly seemed a fitting way to court. He felt as if he had become a witness to some crime and the prosecutor grilled him. "Are you thinking to enlist my aid in some project? I am sure we can come to some . . . consideration."

"That fool in the assay office refuses to look at my

specimens," Emma Longview said with a touch of anger at such mistreatment.

"He is a fool not to look at your specimens," Mason said, trying to shift back to less mining business and more monkey business. After all, she had sought him out. That showed she had some interest in him.

"Do you know anything about blasting through granite reefs?"

"I'm not a blasting engineer, but I have watched a few at work." The words hardly slipped from his mouth than he felt a change in her attitude. She didn't move away, but her pliancy turned into something less appealing. "I am sure there are plenty of men working these hills with such experience."

"They're all hidden away in their own claims. Silver is a great lure." She sounded a tad bitter about that, for some reason.

"Why are you here in Virginia City? Are you a singer or other performer? I am sure—"

A sudden noise from farther down the street caused Emma Longview to jump to her feet. One hand vanished into the folds of her skirt, then came out. She looked down at him, a wan smile on her lips.

"Excuse me a moment." She started off. He caught her arm, which showed surprising muscle. With a slight twist, she pulled free. "Excuse me," she repeated. This time her tone brooked no argument. Mason sank back as she hurried away.

A dark figure stepped from the shadows farther down the street. Emma Longview showed no hesitation going to him. She pressed one palm against the shrouded chest to hold him at bay. From the way she acted and her new companion moved, Mason had no doubt her tryst was with a man. They spoke in voices too low to overhear.

He felt the exchange become heated when the man took Emma Longview by the shoulders. Mason stood, hand resting on the six-shooter in his waistband, but there was no call for him to go to the woman's assistance. She shoved the man hard enough to force him to release her and step back a pace. Again he failed to make out the words, but she read the man the riot act. She stepped forward and shoved the man again. This time he spun away and faded into the shadows without saying another word.

Emma Longview stood, hands on her hips for a moment. Mason imagined her stamping her foot angrily. Then she turned back toward him, hesitated as if composing herself, then returned.

"I must get back to the social."

"Do you think Captain Delahunt misses you? If he hasn't, he's a fool." The small compliment fell on deaf ears. She strode off for the firehouse, letting Mason rush to keep up.

"If you need my services . . ." he began, speaking to her back.

"I am sure I can find you." She looked over her shoulder. Her expression was unreadable. "You aren't working for Wilson?"

"Wilson?"

"The four-eyed fool assayist. Oh, there's the captain. You were right. He has missed me!" With that, Emma Longview rushed off and melted into the fireman's arms, letting him twirl her about and out onto the dance floor to share the "Cotton-Eyed Joe" dance Mason had heard described as "heel and toe poker."

From what he could tell, Delahunt was as adept a dancer as he was at fighting fires. He had no idea about Emma Longview's terpsichorean skills. He was too engrossed watching her lithe body swaying about.

And how she looked at Delahunt.

Mason decided the fire captain had skills beyond fighting fires and dancing that drew the lovely woman. He indulged in another free beer, then departed, leaving the festivities behind to find fresh straw in the stall where Victoria awaited him. He trusted the mare not to step on him as he curled up to one side and drifted to sleep thinking of firebugs and Texas Jack . . . and the beguiling Emma Longview.

CHAPTER THIRTEEN

Y OU MIGHT AS well rent the back room," Morgan
Mason said. "Spend enough time here and a
monthly rental will be cheaper than the day rate."

"I'll die first!" Blue Dirt Duggan tried to sit up in
bed and couldn't. His head was wrapped in clean white
bandages, and his face and exposed skin were smeared
with bright red antiseptic, which made him look as if
he still bled from a dozen cuts. "This dye you're using
makes me look like I'm on the warpath!" Duggan
thrashed about a bit more and then sank to the bed. In
seconds he was snoring loudly.

"What is it you've painted him with?" Mason asked.
"I've never seen anything like it."

Dr. Sinclair held up a bottle of the fluid.

"A colleague of mine at Johns Hopkins when I was
a student fiddled about looking for a way to treat mi-
nor cuts. This is merbromin. It's not safe since it blows

up easily." He held out his hand to forestall Mason's objections. "It's safe enough if I keep it away from ether. My friend refuses to put it on the market until he can claim it to be safe." Sinclair smiled ruefully. "Out here on the frontier, nothing is quite safe, and healing wounds is more important."

"You mix that witch's brew up yourself?"

"When I can. The ingredients are hard to get. If I'd known you were arriving from San Francisco, I'd have placed an order with you and let you act as courier."

Mason hesitated, then asked, "Would you have paid well for this?"

Sinclair motioned Mason out of the room into the office. He drew the curtains behind them. That did nothing to muffle Duggan's loud snores.

"Are you thinking of returning to San Francisco?"

"Before this moment, the notion hadn't entered my head, but I'm not making any money, and the price of everything is high here."

"Virginia City is a boomtown, and no, I couldn't pay you that much. Too many of my patients don't pay at all."

"You mean they die?" Mason saw this was the case.

"Mining is a hazardous profession. Mr. Duggan is one of the few who's shown his determination to remain among the living."

"He doesn't sound loony," Mason said. "Head wounds can sometimes turn a man around. An acquaintance in San Francisco was hit over the head with a belaying pin during a fight at the Embarcadero. He was never quite right again, but at least he avoided being shanghaied to China."

"Mr. Duggan is renowned for being mule-headed. Indeed, if a mule kicked him in the head, I'd have to treat the mule's hoof rather than a cracked head." Sinclair settled at his desk.

"I'm afraid I am unable to pay for your services," Mason said.

"You're hurt? You look fine to me."

"Oh, there's nothing wrong with me, except possibly a broken heart." The way Emma Longview had brushed him off the night before caused a flash of both pain and loss. "Rather, I brought in Duggan, so I assume I'm responsible for his bill." Mason fished about in his pocket. He had a few coins more than the fifty cents he'd earned at the Crazy Eights the day before, but not much. Finding a meal for less than a dollar presented a challenge. Better to find a saloon serving a lunch special, though from the way he and Texas Jack had parted, another drinking establishment beckoned. Perhaps the one with no name.

"Duggan is quite able to pay his own way," Dr. Sinclair said. "You are a man out of place in this town, sir. Taking on another's obligation is honorable, but there is no reason in this case." He shuffled a few papers, then looked up. "From your reaction when I suggested you act as my courier, your employment as a chemist must not be bringing you much money."

"I brought in samples from the Mira Nell and the Lost Cause for analysis, but I don't have enough to pay for the work at the assayer's, and I lack the chemicals and equipment to do it myself."

"Getting Mr. Wilson to advance credit isn't likely to happen. For one so young, he is quite hard-nosed."

"A product of being politically connected. He detailed the license fees and other obstacles in my path to starting a competing business."

"His uncle, I think. Or his cousin? I don't remember. Yes, that is true." Sinclair rubbed his chin as he thought, then said, "How long would such analysis take, given the wherewithal to perform the work?"

"An hour, perhaps longer."

"A pity. If Mr. Wilson was waylaid, one might say lured from his office, with the promise of free liquor, a clever scoundrel might sneak in and use the supplies and equipment in that office. Though I am thinking aloud and would never suggest such a dishonest thing, mind you."

"The idea is clever, but lack of money again keeps me from even beginning the scheme. How much whiskey can he put away in an hour or even two? Paying for a half bottle is beyond my means."

"It was just a thought. Mr. Duggan ought to pay you in advance for your work. That would be enough to honestly engage Wilson."

Mason made his way to the door.

"I have been told he has quite a backlog of work. A . . . a friend told me of being unable to get analysis done in a timely fashion."

"All the more reason for competition, but that's for you to figure out. Either close the door or leave, sir. You're letting in the horseflies. They are demons to kill once they get inside."

Being shooed out by the doctor gave Mason the reason to begin his search for work. There ought to have been jobs going begging in such a boomtown, but too many of the men flooding into Virginia City failed to find blue dirt and were as broke as he was. After a half-dozen failures to find decent work, he started thinking about selling Victoria. His fingers slipped over the butt of the six-gun thrust into his waistband. The iron ought to fetch a few dollars. He had seen a similar weapon for sale at the gunsmith's for ten dollars. Half that would get him through another day.

And a fine mare like Victoria was worth a hundred dollars. Somehow parting with the six-shooter was one thing, but selling the horse caused him to rebel. Better to mount and ride away, living off the land as he returned to San Francisco, where he knew people willing to offer him a job. Perhaps not as a chemist or geologist, but clerking was an honorable profession, even if it paid little.

His hunt took him uphill even farther, to the Wells Fargo office. A small crowd gathered in front of the main office building, next to the bank. Mason worked his way through the crowd to see a sheet of paper nailed to the front door.

"I can't read it. What's it say?" A down-and-out man next to him stood on tiptoe, trying to see. Mason wondered if the man lacked eyesight to see or if he simply could not read. He moved a little closer and worked his way down the page.

"They're hiring guards for a big shipment of silver," Mason said. "In a couple weeks, from the way it's written. You need your own horse and six-gun or rifle."

"I heard rumors they wanted a hundred men to guard the shipment," said a man on Mason's other side.

"Why so many?"

The man snorted and pointed to the bank.

"There's a vault in there that'll hold a ton or more of silver, all going to the San Francisco banks. It's close to a year's silver from the richest mines. The Ophir alone's shipping three hundred pounds, or so the chin-wagging goes."

"How much they pay?" The man unable to read the notice tugged at Mason's sleeve. "What're they paying?"

"Not enough," said the other man, turning away.

Mason scanned to the bottom of the page to find the answer.

"A hundred dollars for the entire trip to San Francisco. They're offering food along with the hundred dollars."

Mason considered the numbers. A hundred dollars, a posse of a hundred men. That was more than many army posts boasted in strength. And what cavalry unit had a payroll of ten thousand dollars for a single month? He touched his pistol and considered the chance of signing on. Wells Fargo would pay him to return to San Francisco, and feed him along the way, in addition to a decent wage for his time. What could go wrong with that many guards?

A hundred men were enough to scare off any gang of road agents he'd ever heard of. Sometimes companies like Wells Fargo hired Pinkertons for such work, but he doubted there were that many Pinks anywhere in the country, much less in Nevada.

"No way, no sir, not for me, not at all." The man backed away. "If they're hiring that many men, they expect trouble."

Mason had a different idea and told the man, "The idea's to scare off anybody thinking of hijacking the shipment. That's got to be four or five freight wagons filled with silver. Twenty guards on each wagon have to make any outlaw take pause."

"How many road agents will hire on, looking to push one of those wagons over a cliff and pillage it later? They don't have to steal it all. Just one wagonload's enough to make twenty men plenty rich."

Mason watched the man walk away, muttering to himself. As much as he hated to admit it, the man had a point. Like a wolf pack separated out a cow from an elk herd, so, too, could that many desperadoes rob a single wagon. Wells Fargo might consider that an acceptable loss. One wagon failing to reach the financial center while the others arrived. Woe to an honest man trying to guard the wagon the road agents chose as their prey.

More than this, Mason wasn't a gun handler. He had used this weapon and the results still shook him. It had been self-defense. He had saved his own life and Duggan's, but killing another human being wasn't something to do lightly. Mason wasn't sure he could bring himself to do it again, even in self-defense.

Steps slow and leaden, he left the Wells Fargo office and passed the telegraph office a few storefronts down the street. The door stood open. He was almost bowled over when a smallish man boiled from the office, pushed Mason out of the way and stormed off. A dozen paces away, the angry man turned and shook his fist at a man standing at the door.

"He seems to be a mite irked," Mason said when he reached the door. "Did he get bad news in a telegram?"

"I fired him. He was stealing from the company."

"He was the telegrapher?" Mason had no idea how a telegrapher stole, unless he dipped into the till or sent 'grams and pocketed the fee. Such seemed petty larceny, unless the telegrapher did this over a long period of time, and then not catching him rested on the manager's shoulders. Such thievery had to be noticeable from simple accounting.

"I'm the telegrapher. And the manager."

"It sounds as if you need to hire a bookkeeper. I've some experience." Mason had little notion what it took to be an accountant, but the job was being handed to him on a silver platter.

As fast as his hopes soared, they were crushed.

"I keep the books. I send and receive the telegrams. I'm the regional manager," the man said. He turned to go back inside. Mason stopped him.

"You said you fired him. What was his job?"

"Lineman. I caught him stealing rolls of wire and selling it. Copper wire's hard to get out here, and miners use it for who knows what. Not sending 'grams, that's for sure."

"He repaired the lines? I can do that." Mason tried to keep desperation from his voice. "I've got my own horse. All it takes is climbing a pole and pulling up wire to splice into the circuit, right?"

"You know about impedance matching on the lines? You ever do this kind of work before?"

"If it pays, I can do it. I know some physics. More chemistry, but if you tell me what you need I can do it."

"Sometimes the wires come loose. Wind will do that. Sunlight, too."

"Thermal expansion," Mason said hurriedly to show he understood. The telegraph station manager nodded and rubbed his chin in thought.

"I'll give you a tryout. If you don't screw up, you're hired. Otherwise, you can take a hike. Like *him*." The manager spat. "Get your horse and come around back in an hour. I have a stack of traffic to send along the way."

"Traffic. Telegrams, right," Mason said. "Thanks. I'm Morgan Mason." He thrust out his hand.

The manager took it and shook, in a way showing how tentative he considered Mason's job. "Bernard Ammer. Now git."

Mason was completely out of breath even running downhill to the stables. Victoria was hardly pleased with him when he tried to gallop her uphill. He didn't want to miss the chance at a job after spending most of the day being turned down. The mare was lathered from the climb by the time he reached the telegraph office and dismounted.

Inside, Ammer still hunched over his key, pounding out code and sending one telegram after another along the wires.

"Wait outside. I'll call you when I have a moment."

Going into the street, he paced restlessly until Ammer finished his work. To kill time, Mason took a good look at the Wells Fargo office and the bank next to it. The bank was isolated, away from the steep mountainside, while the stagecoach office's back wall braced against the rock. Of the two, the bank looked as if it had been constructed to withstand anything man or nature could throw at it. The brick walls were sturdier than the wood-frame construction of the Wells Fargo office, and the roof showed signs of being metal sheet, topped with shingles. The wood shake shingles might burn, but the roof itself could endure any of the fires so prevalent in Virginia City.

Mason doubted the Wells Fargo office stood a chance against even a single spark.

"You done daydreaming?" Ammer motioned him back to the telegraph office. "Here's your tool kit. Take twenty feet of wire with you and ride the line. If you see any sag, check it out. If it's pulling free from the insulators on the poles, replace it."

"Splice in a section and—"

"Of course, splice it in. Be aware that every time there's a break in the wire, no 'grams come in. Do what you can to keep the disconnect short and sweet. Also, though we haven't had this problem lately, keep an eye out for places where wire might get replaced by rawhide."

"I don't understand."

"I worked a station out of El Paso a few years back. The Apaches would cinch up a section with a rawhide strip, then cut away the wire. It stopped transmission, but anyone riding the line wouldn't see a dangling wire. As I said, that's not been a problem here, but you can never tell. Now get out there and repair what you can. I'm getting a lot of static on the line going south, so start that way."

Mason hesitated.

"That's south." Ammer pointed. He left grumbling to himself about regretting hiring his newest employee.

"I could have figured it out," Mason said to his mare. He secured the spare wire, put the tools in the saddlebags and mounted. He looked around. "I could have figured out which way's south. All I have to do is follow the wires."

He put his heels to the horse's flanks and started out, the telegraph wires humming in the wind overhead. He had landed a job! Now all he had to do was figure out how to do it.

CHAPTER FOURTEEN

$\curvearrowleft$

Morgan Mason rode along slowly, occasionally studying the telegraph wires swaying above his head. Getting out of Virginia City revived his senses and made him feel better about his decision to come to the Comstock Lode. He had expected to use his skills as a chemist, but if this was an option, he'd accept it. The day was perfect, the wind gentle and even soothing, and the sun bright and warm on his face.

"There's a spot that looks like trouble in the making, Victoria," he said, tugging on the reins to slow the horse's already leisurely walk. A battered pole showed some storm damage, but what caught his eye was how the wire swung to and fro in an uneven arc. How it was fastened to an insulator warned him of a potential break.

He dropped to the ground, dug out his tools and cut off a foot of wire before staking his mare near a patch of fresh grass. Victoria began nibbling daintily, then fell to dining with a will. Mason whipped a leather strap around the pole and began inching upward. He moved carefully, not wanting to slip and fall the distance down to the ground. Held on to the pole by the strap, such a tumble would scrape the skin off his chest and belly. The climb was more difficult than he anticipated. He sweated like a pig by the time he reached the wires.

"Got to get better at climbing," he said to himself. After a few weeks of practice, he was certain he would. With deft fingers, he pushed and prodded the connection and saw how it had come close to failing. A section of wire had worked back and forth in the wind, flexing the copper to the breaking point.

He set to work, peeling insulation and considering how best to make the splice. As a chemist he had scant experience with electrical equipment, but Mason had watched others closely and remembered how they repaired their equipment. More than this, he had been friends with a telegrapher in San Francisco and offered some help with the lead-acid batteries the man used.

Mason wound the new copper wire around the post before doing what he could to bypass the almost-broken wire. He wondered if he ought to leave the old wire in place. The new wire was sturdy and carried the current, but having two wires fastened onto one post seemed wrong. He started to snip the weak connection when something toward town distracted him. He hesitated, looked over his shoulder and tried to figure what troubled him. After all, he was hanging fifteen feet above the world, enjoying superb weather.

Then he saw it.

Across most of Virginia City, smoke rose from cook-

ing fires and other ordinary pursuits. But one tall plume
of black smoke was different. Mason pulled down his
bowler to shield his eyes and got a better look.

"A new fire." He jerked about and almost fell. He
caught himself. Repositioning the strap allowed him
more stability. It was almost impossible to believe the
alarm hadn't gone out to bring the fire brigades to attack the blaze. But he wasn't so far from Virginia City
that he'd not hear the clarion call.

Mason ran his fingers over the spliced wire, then he
acted. He snipped his handiwork and broke the circuit.
That would get Ammer's immediate attention. With
great care, he touched the wire to the post. Having to
support the weight of the wire dangling to the next
telegraph pole caused his hands to cramp. He worked
faster.

He searched his memory for all the times he had
spoken with his telegrapher friend. The man had de-
lighted in lording it over everyone he met that he knew
Morse code and they didn't. Mason had learned some
letters. He couldn't remember F. He tapped the wires
together twice quickly. Two dots for I. Dot dash dot for
an R. And E. That was easy. A single dot. Over and
over he sent his illiterate warning. When his shoulders
began to ache from holding the wire hanging on to the
next pole, he fixed the break he'd made. The repair
work went slower this time, but he finished. He imagined messages zinging back and forth along the wire,
sending warnings and letting others know of the danger facing Virginia City.

He clung to the pole with both arms and watched the
column of smoke begin to sway and break apart. Soon
only sporadic puffs drifted over the town. Whether his

warning had been heeded or others had warned of the fire didn't matter. If the fire had been put out, that was all he could hope for.

Working his way to the ground, he worried what to do next. Continue on his circuit? Return to town? As shaky as his legs were, he decided to abandon his job, at least for the day. It was getting toward dusk and harder to see the wires from horseback. If Ammer fired him, so be it. He needed to know more about the fire. Although fires happened all the time, he wanted to find if this one had been set, just as he suspected the others had been. Marshal Benteen was an honest man and would investigate, if he had evidence of arson. While he wouldn't look for it on his own, Benteen had no choice but to find the firebug if Mason gave him the evidence.

He rode back slowly, letting Victoria take her time so he had a chance to think about the fire and the chance the firebug had struck again. When he reached town, all seemed normal. The telegrapher worked at his key, hunched over and sweating hard. Ammer motioned for Mason to leave. Whether this was *go away, you're fired* or *good work* caused Mason to hesitate. The telegrapher looked up from transcribing his messages and answered the question.

"Got your warning on the fire. Captain Delahunt had already come to the bank."

"The bank?"

"Where the fire started. Get out of here. Be back at six tomorrow morning. I might have you deliver 'grams, too." Ammer made a shooing motion, then dived back into the sea of dots and dashes. Mason thought he recognized a letter here and there but wasn't sure. Some telegraphers handled their "bugs" at more than sixty words a minute. He doubted he was capable of learning the code to ever replace Ammer.

He led his mare away, toward the bank. The Wells Fargo office had sustained some scorching, but the bank hadn't a smudge on it showing the fire had started here. He swelled up, chest puffed out and gut pulled in, when he saw Emma Longview talking earnestly with Captain Delahunt. If he had a lick of sense, he'd go scrape up a cheap meal and then bed down once more in the livery stable until Ammer paid him.

That was if he had any sense and wanted to avoid the humiliation of being ignored by the lovely brunette and the Virginia City hero.

He tried not to look too much in a hurry as he went to the bank. Emma heard Victoria whinny and turned to see him leading the mare. For a moment, her expression was unreadable, then she brightened and rushed to him, not giving the fireman so much as a fare-thee-well.

"Mr. Mason! It's so good to see you again." She took his hands in hers and squeezed with more than casual greeting. He noted how callused her hands were. Most women with Emma Longview's looks were strangers to hard work. She had put in quite a few hours to get those otherwise dainty hands so work-hardened.

"Miss Longview. I heard there was another fire and came to see if there was anything I could do. You weren't harmed, were you?"

"The bank is untouched," she said, looking over her shoulder. Her tone conveyed immense relief. "And the good captain is convinced this was an attempted arson." She started to say something more, but someone behind him caught her attention. She waved. Before

Mason swiveled around to see who merited such a greeting, she took his hands again and tugged him around to face her. "We must talk, but later. Your services might be exactly what I require since that dunderhead Wilson has again refused to examine my rock samples in a timely fashion."

"You mean he won't do yours first?" Mason caught his breath. He set off a flare of anger in her, and he thought it was because he hit the bull's-eye. She was not a woman who failed to get her way.

"Later . . . Morgan," she said in a low, intimate voice. Her smile would have melted all the snow on the Sierras. Then she rushed off.

He tried to see who commanded her presence, but the street leading to the bank was empty. Whoever she had signaled already moved on.

While Delahunt wasn't as intriguing a person as Emma Longview, Mason wanted to have a few words with him.

"Captain, I saw the fire and sent a telegraphic message to Mr. Ammer. Was he able to alert you?"

"Two of the firemen saw the first puffs of smoke and sounded the alarm. Mr. Ammer's warning—yours—wasn't required. But thank you."

"Miss Longview suggested it was set intentionally. Is that so?"

"She was quite upset over that." Delahunt moved closer and put his arm around Mason's shoulders to draw him close. "I remember hearing you say that you tangled with a firebug. Is that so?"

"I tried to convince Marshal Benteen, but he showed no interest in finding out if I was mistaken."

"You don't think you were, do you? You're certain

you saw someone set a fire?" The captain steered Mason toward the bank.

A few discolored spots on the bank walls showed where small fires had been set. If Mason hadn't seen the pristine walls before, he would never have noticed the scorching now.

"More than once. A second time, someone clobbered me with a rock. The first time I fear that a falling beam cost Blue Dirt Duggan his leg."

"The owner of the Mira Nell Mine? I heard that, and that you rescued him. Of course you did. I knew that. This has been a trying time for me, working almost around the clock. Makes it hard to keep up with all the gossip the way I should."

"That is unusual?" Mason tied Victoria to an iron ring mounted at the corner of the bank.

"I try to act as fire marshal, also, but most of my time has been spent putting out fires. We lost several brigade members."

"To the fires?" Mason perked up. "If they are the victims of an arsonist, this must, excuse the expression, light a fire under the marshal."

"No, no, they moved on to another rumored gold strike to the north. Miners are one breed; prospectors are another. I should never have approved them, knowing they weren't likely to stay in town very long."

Mason kicked at the spot where a fire had started and pointed out how the fuel—dried brush—had been stacked. He did his best to let the captain know he understood the chemistry of flame and how to snuff it out. Oxygen, fuel, heat. Remove one and the fire died. Delahunt nodded in agreement with all he said. Mason felt as if he were back in school trying to impress the teacher with his knowledge.

And perhaps he was. Delahunt took him around to the bank's locked front door. The fireman banged on it until a man wearing a fancy suit opened the door a crack and peered out. Mason saw a six-gun in his hand.

"Oh, it's you, Captain Delahunt. Are you ready now for your examination?"

"This is Mr. Bronfeld, the bank president," he introduced. "This is a consultant, sir."

Mason looked around, then realized Delahunt was introducing him as the "consultant." He touched the brim of his bowler and wished he had both bathed and changed his clothing to look more presentable.

"Come in, come in. Hurry." Bronfeld swung the heavy door wide, letting his visitors in. He slammed and bolted it behind them.

"I'm checking the bank in my position as fire marshal," Delahunt said in a confidential tone. Louder, to the banker, "Before examining the walls where the fires were so expertly extinguished by Fire Brigade No. 1, let me examine the vault."

Mason saw how the banker bristled at this. He clutched his six-shooter tighter, and denial started to form on his lips.

"Come now, Mr. Bronfeld, one man cannot jeopardize your vault. Would I bring such an outlaw in with me, working under my personal guarantee?"

"No, no, of course not." Bronfeld's words said one thing, but the tenseness in his body screamed another. Mason had an idea to put the man's mind at rest.

"Sir, please hold my six-gun for me while I crawl

about." He waited to be sure the banker didn't gun him down as he reached for his weapon. Holding the butt by thumb and forefinger, he passed it over. The banker now held two six-shooters. Even then he wasn't entirely at ease, but his suspicion faded. A little.

"You must realize how anxious I am about the forthcoming shipment."

"I saw your advertisement for a hundred guards. That's quite an army," Mason said.

"Quite an army, yes, but even then I'm not confident it will be enough. I am considering sending a request to Fort Halleck, but the army has been notoriously reluctant to provide protection."

"They chase the Paiutes around," said Delahunt, "and have often claimed guarding shipments is the job of Wells Fargo, not the cavalry."

Mason started to relate what the man looking at the broadside asking for guards had said about outlaws signing up to steal only one wagon, then held his tongue. The shipment's protection was Bronfeld's problem. Mason had plenty of his own. The way his belly growled from lack of food was only one.

"Come along," Delahunt said briskly. He herded Mason toward the vault. Mason pushed through a gate in a low railing separating the officers' desks from the lobby and faced the vault. He swallowed hard. Fortifications back in San Francisco at Fort Point weren't this stout, and that Civil War fort commanded the span across the wide Golden Gate. He stepped forward and ran his hand over the thick concrete walls, as if testing them for give. Giving up trying to budge the walls, he shifted his attention to the steel portal. The heavy vault door with a complicated mechanism was beyond his ability to understand. Sliding bolts operated by the combination lock on front fastened securely in the concrete walls.

"There's a special time device to be certain the door only opens during banking hours," Bronfeld said proudly. "Even knowing the combination will not allow anyone to enter until the timer allows it."

"Even you?" Mason was impressed.

"Even me, sir."

Mason and Delahunt examined the walls around the vault. It shared no external wall. The four walls were as secure as anything Mason had ever seen. He let Delahunt boost him up to examine the top of the vault. He had thought the bank building's roof was secure. The vault was even more secure. If the building collapsed, it would hardly scratch the vault itself.

"Do you see any fire hazards?" Delahunt poked around the desks and shuffled papers into stacks, but otherwise did nothing significant.

"I might be able to blow open the vault with enough explosives, but there's no threat of fire I can see." Mason rubbed his hands against his pants legs and took a final look at the sturdy vault.

"You know of such things? Dynamite?"

"I'm a chemist," Mason said. "I also work as a geologist, so I know a little about it, but I've left such things to mining engineers."

"You give the bank a good grade, then?"

Mason looked at Delahunt, wondering why the fireman wanted to hear his report. If he was a fire marshal, he had more expertise, but Mason had seen no hint of a way to breach the vault. Fires could be set inside the bank and the stolid construction insured the contents were safe.

"I do," he said.

"That's a relief, gentlemen," Bronfeld said. "The mines will start storing their shipments here in a few days."

"Is the vault large enough to hold a ton of silver?" Mason tried to estimate the size required for such a vast weight. Without seeing the vault interior he was at a loss.

"Easily that," Bronfeld said. "And that's not an accurate weight."

Mason smiled. "Less?"

His eyes widened when Bronfeld replied, "More. Much more." He handed Mason back his six-shooter.

The Comstock Lode was bursting at the seams with silver destined for San Francisco and banks beyond.

"That's fifty dollars, sir," Delahunt said. Mason watched the banker count out two twenty-dollar gold pieces and ten cartwheels. The fireman stuffed the money into his vest pocket and, as before, herded Mason ahead of him.

They stepped out into the cool evening. Even the trace of smoke that had lingered from the afternoon fire was gone.

"I appreciate your help. Without you, I couldn't have gotten half that from him. Saying you know about explosives and soothing his feathers over anyone blowing open the vault doubled my fee."

"Glad to be of help." Mason untied his horse's reins, but had no chance to mount. The fire brigade captain pressed close.

"Let me buy you dinner. There's something more I'd like to discuss with you."

"What's that, Captain?" Mason wondered if he might

work as an assistant fire marshal. Seeing how much Delahunt had received for a cursory examination of the bank might have him rolling in the clover if he could share in that wealth. What Delahunt said surprised him even more.

"I'd like to recruit you as a volunteer fireman. Fire Brigade No. 1 can use men of your expertise and honesty."

Mason struggled to answer. He saw how the firemen were held in high esteem in Virginia City. They were at the top of the social ladder. Putting out fires was dangerous work, and the adulation was deserved, but everyone had told him this was an honor above all others in the town.

"If you buy me dinner, you're likely thinking that I'll say yes," he said.

Delahunt was agreeable, and Morgan Mason thought not only of food in his stomach but increased social standing to impress Emma Longview.

CHAPTER FIFTEEN

A HEAVY BOOT POKING insistently against his ribs
woke him. Morgan Mason rubbed sleep from his
eyes and sat up, slumped forward. For a moment he
didn't remember where he was. Then everything tumbled back. He jerked upright, then got to his feet to
face Captain Delahunt.

"Good morning, sir. Thanks for letting me sleep in
the fire station last night."

"Find yourself a permanent spot to sleep from now
on. Don't make it too far away, since all of No. 1's volun-
teers have to be ready to man the pumps and get to a fire
in less than ten minutes. That's how we beat the other
companies and save Virginia City every last time!"

Mason looked around. He hadn't been the only one
sleeping in the main room of the firehouse. This was
where the social had been held. Now pumpers and
other pieces of equipment he didn't quite recognize

were parked here. In a stable connected to the fire station, a half-dozen horses, including his Victoria, kicked and cried for food.

"I need to tend my horse," he said.

"That you do. See to all the others, while you're at it. Feed, water, curry. When you're done, come back in and one of the members will begin your training. You need to know how to use the pump and the hook and ladder and wrestle the hose about. It gives quite a kick when the water begins to spew."

"I've got a job at the telegraph office. I'll lose it if I'm not there in two hours."

"Better hurry and get started. There aren't any slackers in Fire Brigade No. 1!" Delahunt made the rounds, rousting the others. Some he talked to for a minute, others he hardly disturbed.

"Why's he play favorites?" Mason asked a smallish man who struggled to get into his pants. Somehow he had put them on backward. Mason wasn't sure if he ought to point this out or let the man discover it for himself the first time he had to unbutton the fly.

"Not favorites. Some of the men were up all night watching for fires. The captain's lettin' them sleep a bit longer."

"You look like you had a hard night. Were you on watch, too?" Mason finished buttoning his shoes and got to his feet. The last muzziness of his deep sleep had passed.

"Out carousin'. Let me give you a hand with the horses. If you got a job, maybe you can put in a good word with your boss. Since we're both firemen and all."

"I'll see what Mr. Ammer has to say." Mason doubted the telegrapher would consider the man if he drank like a fish and ended up still half-soused in the morning. "Were you celebrating anything special?"

"Every night you don't get burned up is special," the man said.

They took care of the horses, Mason watching what the other man did since he'd never owned a horse before. Other than the boy at the livery stable, he hadn't even seen how horses were groomed. Living in a city like San Francisco had advantages. He hadn't needed a horse to take the trolley across town. A few times he had hired a hansom cab. Getting a gentle mare like Victoria allowed him to climb up and ride without fear of being thrown off, though he was unsure about riding at a gallop. That appeared more difficult than simply keeping his seat as the horse walked along or even cantered.

"I wish I had time to go to the doctor's office. A friend of mine's in a bad way after a mine collapse."

"Happens all the time. Did he get out in one piece? If he did, that's unusual. Mostly, if the cave-in's bad enough, they seal the shaft and drill a new one." The man finished grooming the last of the team that pulled the pumper wagon. He stepped back and nodded in approval at the sheen he had brought to the horse's flanks. "Not a bad way to go, if you ask me. Who wants to be buried down in the cemetery under a tiny marker, if you get that much, when you can have an entire mountain as a monument?"

"Doesn't the brigade provide a decent burial?"

"Not really. Too many of us get burned up. Who wants to bother with burying a cinder? I've got to go." He paused at the mouth of the stall. "Don't forget to ask if there's a job for me. One fireman to another."

"Wait!" Mason tried to stop him. If the man wanted a job, he could apply in person. But he had vanished as if made from smoke. Mason made sure Victoria got an apple from a crate of the treats, then indulged himself. The horse appreciated the bitter apple more than her owner, but it was going to be the only breakfast he could expect. He tucked another apple into his pocket before returning to the firehouse for his first lesson in firefighting.

It turned out to be an hour of polishing brass and cleaning the fire hose with no real instruction in putting out fires. He resigned himself to doing the tedious work passed off to him by others. There had to be an apprenticeship before acceptance as a full-fledged member of this Virginia City elite society.

"Be back by sundown," Delahunt called after him as he rode away. He waved, then fished out the apple he had taken from the bin. A single bite convinced him to give it to his horse. Victoria was far more appreciative of this treat.

The door of the telegraph office stood ajar when he rode up. At first he worried that something was wrong since the Wells Fargo office and the bank were still closed. Then he heard the click-click of the telegraph key inside. When he stopped just outside, the heavy sulfuric acid odor made him giddy. Ammer kept the door open for ventilation. Mason stepped in and saw the telegrapher working furiously on the key.

"Lot of traffic today. There's a stack of 'grams. Deliver them, then get out on the south wire again. I'm getting static with traffic from that direction. Did you repair that line properly yesterday? Never mind. Go, go."

Mason got. He snatched up the stack of yellow envelopes stuffed with telegrams. A quick riffle through them showed deliveries had to be made all over town. That suited him fine. A few minutes rearranging the envelopes gave him the chance to make a wide circuit through town without having to backtrack. Down one street, drop a level and back along it, then zigzag once more on still lower levels.

Three hours of riding later brought him to Dr. Sinclair's office. He had intended to see how Duggan fared before this, but too much had happened. Telling Duggan all his news puffed him up to the bursting point. He needed someone to share all the events of the past couple days.

He poked his head in and looked around.

"Doctor? Dr. Sinclair?"

"He ain't here. Miz Gomez is having a baby. She'd call the midwife, but that's her. I mean, she's the midwife and doesn't have anyone to help her bring yet another squalling brat into this miserable world."

Mason pushed through the curtains. Duggan still sprawled on the bed, his head heavily bandaged.

"You sound like you're back to your normal cantankerous self. Why's the doc letting you lay about back here when you should be working?" Mason pulled up a chair and sank into it. He gingerly found a more comfortable position. Riding, even an easygoing horse like Victoria, took getting used to. But he was getting the hang of it and was nowhere near as sore as he had been the night before.

"I'm raring to go, but that quack says my head needs to heal. I busted my skull, and he wants to be sure my brains don't come pourin' out one ear."

"Too late for that," Mason joshed. He launched into all he'd done and why he was able to come visit in the middle of the day. When he got to the part about meeting Emma Longview and how they had gotten along so well, he hesitated. Some things were too personal to share, even with someone like Duggan whom he considered his friend.

The old miner was quick to pick up on something missing.

"What's her name? Working for Ammer and being an apprentice fireman's all well and good, but neither of them things causes a man to grin like a damned fool."

"She just got into town from . . ." His voice trailed off. He didn't know where Emma hailed from. The truth was what he knew of her he had guessed. Her firm muscles, callused hands, the way she walked and looked and . . .

"No need to go into details now. Just invite me to the wedding. Miz Gomez is the best midwife in the Comstock. Keep that in mind."

"You're jumping the gun. I just met her."

"Women in this part of the country are rarer 'n hen's teeth. Don't let her slip through your fingers, boy."

"That whack you took to the head's worse than I thought. Advice like that isn't what I'd expect from a bachelor miner."

"You're a citified cuss. Not like me at all. You're content to work for Ammer and be a volunteer fireman. They'll pin medals on your chest when you find who's settin' those fires you go on about, too. Mark my words." Duggan slumped back and kept talking, but his words faded away. He had worn him out. When the miner started snoring loudly, Mason pushed the chair back and left.

It had been good talking to Blue Dirt Duggan again and seeing that his condition was greatly improved. Not many men endured having a leg cut off and their head bashed in. Duggan was tough enough to take it all and still demand to be set free so he could rip more silver from his mine.

Mason finished delivering telegrams, the last of which went to the Fire Drake Brigade station. He was pleased to see Jasper Jessup working there, patching a hose. Jessup looked up and waved him over.

"What brings you back here?" Jessup made a point of shoving out his belly to show his brass buckle with the numeral 2 on it.

"I came to see if Captain Finley had come to his senses and kicked out a slacker named Jasper Jessup," Mason said. "It looks as if he passed you over again for getting the axe."

"You're a clever one, Mason. Real clever. You know I got my own axe." Jessup hooked his thumbs under the suspenders adorned with yellow stripes. "I'm in line to get another stripe, making me a senior fireman."

"We're rivals now. I'm apprenticed at No. 1."

"Do tell? You'll get a lot more learnin' if you stand around and watch how *we* put out fires. We got the fastest horses and hardest-pumping pumps in the whole Comstock Lode. That's why we always get the fire out first and have our pick of the purtiest girls in town."

Mason started to brag on how he and Emma Longview had hit it off, but he held back. There wasn't time to get into a tall-tale-swapping contest with Jessup. Besides, when he found out on his own, it'd be all the sweeter.

"Got to get out on the telegraph lines and do some repair work. You can get back to patching No. 2's decrepit hose. Be sure to use a big patch. That's a monster-sized hole you're working on."

"Get out of here before I test the hose on you!"

"Deliver the 'gram for me, will you? It's for Captain Finley." Mason passed over the telegram, shook hands and mounted.

As he rode away, he heard Jessup call out to the fire captain, "Here's news about our new axes. When will we get 'em?"

He felt good seeing the people he counted as friends in Virginia City, even when two hours later he found an entire pole broken off south of town and lying on the ground. The wires had remained attached. It took him the better part of the afternoon to dig a new hole and wrestle the downed pole into it. The wires strained when he finished because the lower two feet had rotted off the pole, but they were hot to the touch, showing electricity still coursed through, carrying the dots and dashes of news and information from all over the country.

As the sun sank low over the Sierras, he rode back to the telegraph office. Ammer appeared not to have moved all day long. He still worked the key. A new pile of envelopes gave Mason pause. Captain Delahunt had told him to report for duty at sundown. If those had to be delivered, he'd be on horseback until midnight. Just as he decided not to disturb Ammer, the telegrapher looked up.

"That man you sent around for a job? I fired him. Just because he's a fireman doesn't mean he wants to put in a day's work. I caught him sleeping and not delivering." Ammer nodded in the direction of the telegrams.

Mason wondered if this was the fireman from the morning. He didn't even know the man's name, but denying he knew him was futile.

"Sorry, sir. I . . . I'm supposed to report to the firehouse now." He looked significantly at the undelivered telegrams.

"Go on. Be back here tomorrow. You repaired the southern line. Best signal on it I've had in a month of Sundays. Head west tomorrow, up and over Gold Hill. That's the San Francisco connection, and I don't want it down when . . . when . . ." He turned from Mason and scribbled quickly as a new telegram message clicked into the office.

"When the silver shipment is sent," Mason finished. Ammer nodded brusquely. "What about these telegrams?"

"I'll deliver them."

The way Ammer spoke made Mason glance at the top telegram. He grinned. If the gossip he'd heard was right, the top telegram went to the madam of the biggest cathouse in town.

"Yes, sir. Have a good night." Mason kept from laughing out loud when the telegrapher mumbled under his breath and shooed him away.

The ride to the station house ended far too soon. After a day in the saddle Mason ached all over. He had hoped for a few hours to rest, but the fire captain had other plans.

"You're on first watch tonight," Delahunt said. "You walk along C Street, drop down and do D Street. When you've gone from one side of town to the other, work your way back. It takes about four hours. Someone will relieve you."

"And in the morning I get to tend the horses?"

"And," added Delahunt with a hint of cruel glee, "you learn how to roll and unlimber the fire hose. It weighs close to a hundred pounds, and every one of us has to be able to handle it alone."

Mason started to lead Victoria to the stables. Watch required being on foot to poke about in alleys and other tight spots for any sign of an ember or untended fire. Delahunt stopped him.

"Here. As fire watcher, you need to show some authority." The fire captain held out a belt with a brass buckle, suspenders and a red shirt. "Go on, try them on."

Mason surprised himself with the excitement he felt putting on the uniform. He held out his arms and looked. Then he buttoned the collar.

"It fits perfectly," he said in amazement.

"We get our uniforms from Miz Logan. She said she already had your measurements. How's that?" Delahunt looked skeptical.

"She's got a good eye, maybe," he replied. He had not realized she'd taken his measurements—or why she had bothered—when she'd given him his work clothes after he'd rescued her children.

"She's the best tailor in town. That's why No. 1 uses her services. Now get out there and do us proud on fire watch." Delahunt handed him a whistle. "Give that three sharp toots to call out the company if the need arises."

He slid his thumbs under the snowy white suspenders and let them snap back. Unlike Jasper Jessup's with yellow stripes, these lacked any ornamentation. Others in the station house had brass buttons fastened onto their suspenders. He couldn't get a close look but thought they were awards of some kind. After enough procrastinating, he did a long, slow stretch that pulled tired muscles back into place. He was in as good a shape as he'd be that night.

Mason set out on his circuit. He trooped along, went down Union to C Street and began his lookout. As he walked, he fingered the whistle, wondering if he would have to use it. A heavy pall hung over the area he patrolled. It was as if the smoke from the last fire clung to walls and waited for a new fire to add to the odor. Fifteen minutes of prowling about convinced him the captain had been right. Riding would have been easier, but working his way through the tight spaces between shops, poking through piles of trash and then returning to the main street would have been impossible. He'd either have to mount, ride to the next alley, dismount and go through his routine, or simply leave his mare tethered while he walked.

An hour into the watch, he dropped down to D Street. The evidence of even more fire damage tore at him. This part of town was sadly in need of renovation—of complete rebuilding in places. He started to walk past a gunsmithy when he saw furtive movement in the deep shadows. Rather than going immediately to investigate, he broke stride, stumbled and went on to the next alleyway. He darted down to the space behind the shops and turned back. Mason reached for his six-gun, but he had left it in his saddlebag after work riding the lines. The silver whistle went to his lips, but he hesitated to blow it. This was the alarm for a fire.

He pressed against a wall and edged along. Whoever prowled about behind the gunsmith's ship might have a legitimate reason for being here. The thought kept haunting him that there were jars of gun oil inside. And gunpowder. The gunsmith loaded cartridges and did a brisk business. If the powder went up in a fire, the explosion could send sparks all over town.

Mason moved closer. He caught his breath when a lucifer flared. The whistle pressed cold and ready against his lips, but the match snuffed out. A low curse, hardly more than a whisper, followed. Then the man took off running.

He had been seen! This was the firebug, and somehow he had scared him off before learning his identity. Mason swung around and began pursuit, falling over the debris. He hit so hard it knocked the wind from his lungs. Pain racked his chest as he took in air again, but he got to his hands and knees, panting.

"There he goes. Get the varmint!" Two men burst into the alley. For an instant Mason thought they meant him, but they lit out after the firebug.

"I'll string him up when I catch him," growled the second man.

Mason tried to point, to offer help. By the time he was gasping in fresh air, they had disappeared in the same direction as the firebug. He got his feet under him and ran after them. At the side of the gunsmith's store, he cut back to D Street.

He caught a snippet of one calling to the other.

". . . same one that tried to set the bank on fire."

Mason looked around, trying to spot the two men. They had to be deputies out on patrol, too. Finally, the marshal had proof that Mason's accusations weren't hot air. Two of his own officers had stopped the arsonist from sending the gunsmithy up in flames.

He hurried along, hunting for the two deputies to help them out. Three of them stood a better chance of finding the firebug. After a full minute of running, he slowed and finally stopped, out of breath. He bent forward, hands on his knees to recover. Mason came upright with a start when a hand pressed into his back.

"Are you . . . ?" He stared, not at deputies or even a firebug, but at Emma Longview. "What are you doing here?"

"That's no way to greet me," the brunette said. She was dressed in a dark riding outfit, with a split skirt and bolero jacket that caused her to fade into the night. Even at arm's length she was difficult to see.

"Miss Longview, I thought you were a deputy chasing a man who tried to start a fire. Back there." Mason gestured back down the street.

"There're lawmen out tonight? Here?" She sounded a little surprised. Or was it fright in her voice?

"I spotted a man trying to set a fire"—he held up his whistle, showing his interest was official—"and they scared him off before I could. They saved the town from a nasty fire."

"That's . . . nice," she said uncertainly. "I see by your outfit that you are now a member of Fire Brigade No. 1. Congratulations, Morgan. It's a great honor."

"And responsibility. I need to find those men. They chased the firebug, but unless they caught him, there's still some danger."

"I should go back uphill, then. To avoid the danger." She pressed her palm against his chest to hold him at bay when he tried to step toward her. "Find me later. I want to hear all about your heroism." Before he answered, she pushed away, turned and hurried off. Her dark clothing caused her to vanish in the night within a dozen yards.

Confused at all that had happened, he turned in a full circle, then threw up his hands in frustration. He had lost the trail of both deputies and the arsonist, and why had Miss Longview been walking in a part of town shuttered and dark for the night? He rubbed his chest and worked out the lingering pain, then continued his fire watch. The final hour went by uneventfully. Mason returned to the fire station to pass over his whistle.

At loose ends when the other fireman left, he decided to see if Marshal Benteen's men had run the firebug to ground. The jailhouse door stood open for ventilation. The marshal and two deputies sat at the large desk playing cards. Benteen looked up when Mason entered.

"What do you want?" The marshal's tone warned Mason to make his query quick.

"Your men? Did they run down the arsonist? I wanted to see what kind of man sets fires that endanger lives and the entire town."

"What are you talking about?"

"Your deputies, these two?" Mason pointed to the men clutching cards close to their vests. A pile of nickels and dimes on the desk showed the pot was better than two dollars. "Were they the ones who chased the firebug down on D Street an hour ago?"

"There's no call for them to chase anybody, much less this mythical firebug of yours. They've been here all night. It's been quiet. Not even a fight in any of the saloons. I'm going to mark it on my calendar, just like I will to celebrate me winning with this." Benteen glanced at his hand. "They've been cleaning me out until now. I finally got 'em dead to rights. Call me or fold," the marshal said to his deputies. One folded, but the other pursed his lips and ran his fingers around the edges of his cards, thinking on the play.

"Then there are other deputies on patrol?" Mason was puzzled.

"We're it tonight." To his men, he said, "What'll it be? Am I getting back my stake?"

"You're bluffing, Marshal. I feel it in my gut," said the deputy across from the marshal. "I call." He laid down a full house.

Marshal Benteen made a strangling sound.

"Beats my ace high flush. My best hand tonight and you jinxed it by flyin' in here. Clear out. Now!" He glared at Mason and pointed at the door.

Mason tried to find the right question to ask, but the lawman wasn't in any mood to answer. He stepped into the night, wondering what was going on. The elusive firebug, those two unknown men chasing him, Emma Longview acting quite strange, and the marshal laying down another losing hand.

He had no idea what to make of it.

He set off uphill, going to the Crazy Eights hoping to find Miss Longview, but wherever she went after their encounter, it wasn't here.

CHAPTER SIXTEEN

T HE BULLET DANCED off the rock to Morgan Mason's right. He threw up his arm to keep flying granite chips out of his eyes as he ducked. New lead whined through the air above him. Then came the roar of a shotgun. The impact against the rock shielding him was great but, with his back pressed against it, the vibration turned into an earthquake.

"Stop shooting, you old fool!" He poked his hat up over the top of the rock. A more accurately aimed round sent the bowler flying. He stared at the hat lying in the dust a few feet away. "That was a new hat. Almost. I bought it before I left San Francisco."

"San Francisco? Who's out there?"

"It's me, Duggan. It's Mason. The idiot who saved your life twice. Why are you shooting at me?"

"Morgan Mason?"

"Yes!"

A long pause weighed heavily, as if the world had gone mute. Then Mason heard scraping sounds. He chanced a quick peek over the rock. Blue Dirt Duggan hobbled from the mouth of the mine, leaning heavily on a crutch. He was festooned with six-shooters and had two rifles slung over his back. Bandoliers crisscrossed his chest and he held a long-barreled shotgun better suited to goose hunting alongside the crutch as he came forward.

"Why didn't you say so?"

Still wary, Mason rose and thrust his hands high in the air. If the crazy old miner was going to kill him, it'd have to be in cold blood. He wasn't making any move that could be misinterpreted as hostile.

"I did. You opened fire. It gets mighty tiresome the way you shoot at me." Mason circled the rock, keeping his hands held high.

"Put your fool hands down, boy. You look like a complete horse's behind walking around like that."

"What's got you all het up? Did the claim jumpers come back? Robbers?"

"You snuck up on me. Took me by surprise. A man in my condition's got to be careful." Duggan hobbled to a rock and sank onto it. He balanced the goose gun at his side and took a few seconds rearranging the arsenal dangling from shoulders and hips.

"Getting around wouldn't be such a chore if you left half that iron back in your cabin."

"I'm working the Mira Nell just fine with it at hand. They'll come for me, mark my words."

Mason found himself a spot to sit. He had left his six-gun in his saddlebag and Victoria comfortably stabled in the shed behind Duggan's cabin. Facing so much firepower, he felt downright naked.

"You owe me a new hat, at least."

"You just want an excuse to see that purty Miz Logan, don't you? She's not running a haberdashery shop. Just tailoring, but for you I bet she'd be more 'n happy to pick something out real special."

"I know that," Mason said, irritated at how Duggan shifted from murderous old fool to meddling old fool. "She did a right fine job on my fireman's shirt. Captain Delahunt gets all the brigade's uniforms done there."

"Smart man, Delahunt. I'd think he was sweet on her, too, but him and her husband—her dead former husband—didn't see eye to eye on much of anything."

"What happened between them?" Mason had no call listening to gossip, but he was curious in spite of his better instincts.

"Delahunt wanted him to join the brigade and got turned down. There was personal pizzen between them, maybe over Miz Logan, but I don't think that was it. Might be Delahunt feels a tad guilty over Mr. Logan's death and that's why he pays the widow woman to do No. 1's uniforms. Can't say, though."

Duggan unlimbered both rifles and lined them up next to the shotgun. Mason considered how much this looked like an arsenal more fitting for a lawman's office. The four six-shooters still stuffed into holsters both at the miner's hips and under his armpits only added to the feel of a war about to commence.

"You're trying to work the mine?" Mason stared at the guns. Trying to claw out silver chloride at the best of times was a grueling job. Doing it weighed down

with so much iron showed determination beyond anything reasonable. For a one-legged man to do it meant
the head injury was worse than even Dr. Sinclair thought.
Duggan had gone around the bend and had found
plumb loco there.

"Doing, not trying. Since I got back a couple days
ago, I carted out close to two tons of ore. That pocket
you found is so rich, the silver 'bout falls out of the
rock onto the ground for me to scoop up."

"It's as rich as anything I've ever seen. Or heard of,
for all that. You need to hire someone to help out.
You're rich, Duggan. Set back, drink a beer and watch
others do the work for you."

"That's too much like them starched collars back
where you come from. They don't work, they let their
money buy other folks' work."

"When you've got enough, that's the way you make
even more," Mason said.

"You do it. I trust you. You come out here to dig for
me. I'll pay you good wages."

Mason hesitated. When Wilson had turned down
his application to work in the assay office, he would
have jumped at this chance. But now? He pressed his
hands into his belly. In hardly more than a week it had
shrunk to a decent size, and what was there turned to
muscle. Riding all day, working on the telegraph wires,
then lugging heavy fire hose and working the pump on
the pumper truck and all the other chores required to
be a volunteer fireman had trimmed off the fat and
given him some bulk. Muscular bulk. Working in the
mine would keep him fit, but it was underground and
solitary.

He had come to like the outdoors. But trading being

in Emma Longview's company for the Mira Nell wasn't something to fill him with happiness. He hardly saw Miss Longview but when he did, it gave him something to think about all night long and the entire next day riding the telegraph lines. A prison of rock, even rock laden with untold wealth in silver, wasn't a fit way to live.

He wasn't Blue Dirt Duggan. He wasn't a miner or a geologist content with poking around in caves.

"I'll be glad to help out how I can, but not scratching out ore to send to the smelter."

"I never took you for a lazy lout," Duggan said. "But you can still be a help." He looked around and rested his hands on two pistol butts. In a lowered voice he said, "I hid all the silver from the mine around here. It'll be a week 'fore the big shipment. You can guard it whilst on its way into Virginia City."

"I'm not much of a gunman," Mason said. "I can ask the bank president to loan you a few men from the army he's recruited to guard the main shipment."

"Bronfeld's a crook. He forecloses on mortgages and puts women and children out in the cold, he does. I wouldn't trust anybody he'd send."

"You're trusting him to oversee the entire shipment to San Francisco."

"I'd ride along, if I could. But I can't."

Mason looked at the pinned, empty pant leg, but that wasn't what Duggan meant.

"I don't dare leave the Mira Nell for a second or varmints would move in. Claim jumpers. You tangled with a pack of them. You know." Duggan half drew his pistols, putting Mason on edge. If the miner got carried away in his worry over being robbed, he might throw down and start firing again. This time Mason didn't have a big rock between him and the guns' muzzles.

"How long will it take you to round up all the silver you've squirreled away? I can see that it gets to the bank vault. From there, you'll have to believe Mr. Bronfeld and that company of guards he's hired will be able to escort it safely."

"Two days," Duggan said. "I'll stack it yonder, behind the cabin so nobody can see it. You get yourself a big wagon, at least two mules. Oxen would be better for pullin' up these hills. You come back in two days. I trust you, Mason. You've saved my life twice."

"Make that three times. You reminded me how I pulled your fat out of the fire when the robbers tried to hijack your mine."

"You saved me back there? That's rich! It was the other way around. You fired that gun of yours—the one you took off the dead owlhoot—like you'd never seen one in your life. You cringed as you fired it."

"Did not," Mason said, though every word the old miner uttered was true. He wanted to engage Duggan and keep him from using all his rifles and shotguns and pistols anymore.

They made their way to the cabin and shared a couple shots of whiskey from a bottle that Mason had brought from town. Dr. Sinclair had allowed as to how this would be medicine for Duggan. As the potent alcohol burned down into Mason's belly, he knew it was equally as good medicine for what ailed him.

An hour later, he left agreeing to return in two days to cart the silver into town and the safety of the Wells Fargo bank vault. How he'd work that into his crowded schedule was something of a poser. Mr. Ammer wasn't the sort to let an employee take a day or two off when lines needed fixing and telegrams delivering. Not being available in the case the brigade was called out was less of a problem. Most of the firemen worked in the mines. He counted at least a dozen Ophir Mine employees, though they were closer to Virginia City than others. Calabasas Creek was way out of town. Riding hard it'd take him a couple hours to answer the clarion call. Mason was particularly intent on being able to help at his first fire since apprentices required several call-outs before they could be given full membership.

He touched the brass belt buckle and traced over the relief figures. He wanted the full uniform, and that included a helmet with his own special number on it. That was as functional as it was special. If a fireman got trapped or burned beyond recognition, that helmet might be all that identified his body. A shiver passed up his spine. Why he had wanted to volunteer for such a dangerous hobby was beyond him.

And a hobby it was. He got no pay, other than a drink or two after a fire was successfully put out. The way Texas Jack treated him at the brigade's favorite watering hole made that less an attraction, but if Emma Longview showed up, that made it worthwhile. He had a job and he had prestige most in town lacked. A few extra minutes with the lovely woman and conversation beyond geology would surely reveal his sterling character to her.

He reached the firehouse and dismounted, tended Victoria and put a nosebag on her. The grain was scant, but he found enough oats to make it seem a treat for his mare.

"Get a move on, Mason!" Delahunt's strident voice

lit a fire under him. Mason rushed into the main room. Four others worked on the steam-powered pump, cursing and blaming one another for its repeated failure to produce a powerful stream of water. It had broken down more than a few times as they practiced with it.

"Will they repair it anytime soon?" Mason tried to figure out what the men did to the equipment but couldn't.

"It doesn't look like it. Any fire tonight will be fought by bucket brigade and the hand-pump truck," Delahunt said. "You know how to fix a steam engine?"

Mason shook his head. He wasn't mechanically inclined.

"Too bad. We need an engineer." Delahunt fished around in his pocket and drew out a silver tube on a short chain. "Here's your whistle. Get out there and do No. 1 proud!"

"I will, sir." Mason took another couple minutes to settle into his bright red shirt and white suspenders. These as much as his buckle marked him as someone in authority. He placed the string with the whistle around his neck and hurried out onto his watch.

Less than halfway down C Street, he spied the telltale flickering that caused a knot to form in his stomach. He rounded a darkened building and found a waist-high fire already chewing away at the store wall. Mason ran to the pile of fiery debris and tried to kick it apart and rob the fire of its fuel. Too late. The hungry flames already ate through the wall and hopped into the store. Paper and furnishings inside exploded in a wave of heat that forced him back. Cut off from C Street, he ran down the alley behind the buildings.

He fumbled out his whistle and put it to his lips,

then stopped. Behind another store fifty feet away he saw the telltale flare of a lucifer. It blazed brightly, momentarily casting shadows of the man holding it.

"Stop. Don't!" Mason reached for his waistband, but as before he had left his six-gun in his saddlebag. The man dropped the match, igniting another fire. Then he ran pell-mell away from Mason.

Caught between chasing down the firebug and sounding the alarm, Mason knew his duty. He filled his lungs with air and blew on the whistle as long and hard as he could. His ears rang from the shrill notes, but he continued blowing on the whistle as he returned to the larger street.

His eyes widened when he saw a fire wagon clattering toward him. Captain Delahunt had responded in amazing time, bringing not only a pump but the hook and ladder as well. Firemen clung to the handholds as the wagons careened around and bore down on him.

"Here! The fire's here. And another, smaller one down the street!" Mason blew his whistle until he gasped for breath to make certain he'd be heard over the clanging bell mounted on the pumper wagon.

The fire trucks skidded to a halt and the firemen jumped to work. Mason's eyes went wide when he saw the men working diligently to pour water into their steam pump and rush to use axes to break their way into the burning store.

"Jessup," he said in amazement. "What are you doing here?"

"The Fire Drake Brigade's the best. You just leave it to us. Tell your buddies at No. 1 they got here too late to be the heroes. Don't take it too hard." Jasper Jessup slapped Mason on the shoulder, then cringed when

Captain Finley shouted at him to get to putting out the fire.

By the time Delahunt and the hand-pump truck arrived, No. 2 had the fire contained and were rolling up their hose to return to their firehouse.

Delahunt and Finley argued for a few minutes before Mason's captain spun around and stalked off, ordering his men back to the station.

Mason watched them retreat, then waited until Finley's men drove away, laughing in triumph, ready to accept free drinks and accolades from the grateful citizens of Virginia City.

CHAPTER SEVENTEEN

I'M ACTING AS Mr. Duggan's agent," Morgan Mason said, "and will bring in the silver he wants shipped."

The bank teller looked up and shook his head.

"He has to sign off on the forms in my presence. I'm a notary and all the papers require his signature."

"What if I get a power of attorney?" Mason saw this didn't budge the man. "Let me talk to Mr. Bronfeld. I've worked for him on security matters. He knows me."

"You?" The teller looked Mason over. "Well, you're a fireman. That counts for something, I reckon. Go on inside, but if you're lying about working for him, I'll have you clapped into jail for impersonating somebody important so fast your head will spin." The teller motioned Mason away to deal with the next mine owner in line.

Mason went to the bank's double doors, where he was stopped by a deputy.

"I know you," the deputy said. "You spent some time in a cell."

"It was a mistake. Jasper Jessup and I were released when we got it squared away. Both of us are firemen," he added, almost as an afterthought. That had worked with the teller. He hadn't expected it to work with the deputy, but it did. He tucked his thumbs under the white suspenders and thrust out his now-diminished belly to display the brass belt buckle. All that acted like he had given the secret password to get inside. The deputy stood back.

Mason found himself in a crowded lobby. Everyone around him wore six-guns at their hips as well as carrying a rifle or shotgun. Blue Dirt Duggan would be right at home here, up to the instant he started slinging lead. Then all hell would break loose. From snippets of conversation he overheard, these were part of the army of guards hired to protect the shipment. There wasn't a one of these rough-looking desperadoes that Mason would ever want to tangle with.

Memory of what the saloon patron had opined about outlaws hiring on and then stealing a single wagon while letting the rest roll on came back to him. If Duggan's silver trove was in the wagon stolen, then what would the bank do about it? Mason thought he knew.

"Have you come to check out our security, sir?"

Mason shook himself out of his worries and faced the bank president. Pleading Duggan's case faded and was replaced by the notion of being sure the shipment was secure. If necessary, bringing the miner to the bank with his silver was preferable to losing the hard-won treasure.

"I hadn't examined the inside of the vault. Let me

take a quick look before it starts filling up." He gestured at the guards milling about. "Just be sure none of them light up a smoke while they're inside."

"I hadn't thought about that. Uh, any suggestions on that, sir?" Bronfeld eyed the red shirt and buckle and somehow relinquished his authority to the fireman.

"Get more cuspidors. They can spit rather than smoke."

"Oh, yes, of course. A good idea. But then, of course it is. This way." The bank president led the way to the freestanding vault.

Mason eyed the exterior critically. Nothing had changed from his and Delahunt's earlier inspection. Now the vault door with its complicated locking mechanism stood open. He caught his breath at the sight of so much silver already stacked in anticipation of transport.

"That's quite a sight," he said, eyeing the silver bars.

"We're contracting to ship more than we expected." Bronfeld lowered his voice and said, "In confidence, if I can trust you. We are adding two more freighters to the wagon train."

"With more guards?" Mason saw how uncomfortable this made Bronfeld and guessed the answer. Wells Fargo intended to hire the original number, possibly keeping the added heavily laden wagons a secret. It hardly mattered. If a hundred armed men weren't enough to guard the original train, additional wagons were in no more danger. Would two hundred armed guards do any better protecting the shipment?

"We've sent a request to the cavalry. I'm sure they will respond favorably since several Wells Fargo officers in San Francisco are adding their voices to the request."

"That's sure to work," Mason said, not bothering to hold down the sarcasm. He entered the vault and, for a moment, felt overwhelmed by being surrounded by the waist-high walls of pure silver. It took all his willpower not to reach out and touch the bars. Instead, he actually examined the walls for any weakness, any spot where a fire might burn through. The concrete structure was secure all around.

Overhead, he saw how steel bars had been worked through the concrete to give further strength. Cutting through the walls or ceiling would take days, possibly a week. Any explosive made short work of even those stout walls, but with the horde of guards prowling about as the silver came in, stealing anything silver-bar heavy was almost impossible.

"You've done well, sir," Mason said. "There's no way any fire—or explosive—can endanger the contents."

"Will an additional further fee be required?" Bronfeld's tone dictated his response.

"Not at all, Mr. Bronfeld. Your payment to Captain Delahunt covers my work." He hesitated, then plunged ahead, "I am overseeing shipment of some miners' silver. Will my signature be adequate for you to accept the bars?"

"An assemblage of independent miners? Well, it will speed up our acceptance if a single signatory is responsible rather than a dozen or two," the president said dubiously.

Mason knew how to seal the deal.

"Having so many of those, well, shall we say uncouth, gentlemen crowding in with the representatives of the largest mines is certainly troublesome. I can remove that problem." He ran fingers over his white suspenders. Doing this filled him with confidence that communicated to Bronfeld. Who was a savior of Virginia City and who was merely a banker?

"I'll let the tellers know, Mr. Mason. Yes, a fine idea. I'm glad you volunteered." Bronfeld smiled wanly. "That's kudos for your work with the fire brigade, too, of course."

"Of course. Thank you." Mason made a point of vigorously shaking the president's hand in full view of the tellers. He had sealed his presence in such a way that delivering Duggan's hoard wouldn't be a problem. The old miner could remain at his mine, guns cocked, waiting for the invasion of thieves he vowed were after him and his silver. Considering that claim jumpers already stalked Duggan, such an armed presence might not be out of the question.

He left the bank and found himself caught in a turbulent swirl of men on horses, others on foot waving six-shooters around and a general roar that deafened him. Mason wished he had his own six-gun, though another pistol added to the crowd might be just the push needed to tip everyone into violence.

"What's going on?" Mason shouted the question to a man waving a rifle in the air but who looked less het up than others.

"They stopped hiring."

It took Mason a few seconds to understand. The offer to pay a hundred dollars for a month's time guarding the silver shipment had drawn a steady stream of men. Being this close to the actual shipment had produced a flood of latecomers. From the sound of their chants, they demanded to be hired.

Mason edged away and circled the knot of men.

Marshal Benteen and two deputies did their best to disperse the crowd. The lawman finally shinnied up a lamppost and signaled his deputies to fire in the air. Both men came close to emptying their guns before the crowd settled down to listen.

"I got news for you all," Benteen shouted. He clung to the post with both hands, and his boots scrabbled for traction. He was a funny-looking figure, but he faced down a dangerous crowd. Still, Mason found himself thinking the marshal was in a position to take away his job of climbing telegraph poles with the skill he showed clinging to the lamp. "The jobs are all gone. Wells Fargo has hired all the guards they need. Now get on out there, have a drink, find other jobs. There's plenty of mines looking for miners."

The crowd turned ugly. This wasn't what they wanted to hear. A hundred dollars riding all day in the saddle for a month was better than filling their lungs with rock dust for thirty dollars earned monthly from fourteen-hour days, six days a week underground.

"Don't make me start throwing you in jail. What's that get you?"

"You're in cahoots with them thieves, Marshal," someone shouted. "They're the crooks. Aren't they?"

The man rousing the crowd's ire got no farther. A deputy slugged the man with a drawn six-shooter. The agitator dropped to his knees. Before he uttered another word, the deputy slugged him even harder. This laid him out on the ground. The deputy stepped over the fallen dissenter, straddling him and pointing his six-gun at the man.

"Don't you go making this uglier than it already is," the marshal shouted. "Disperse. Get out of here. I don't want to see any of you buried in the potter's field downhill from here."

The deputies worked to shove any would-be ring-leader away. Mason was more interested in a half-dozen men at the edge of the crowd. All of them carried long guns or sawed-off shotguns. From the way their eyes danced around, they'd come into any fray on the side of the law. But they didn't have badges. Mason wondered if Wells Fargo had authorized use of the men already hired to shepherd the silver to protect the bank before the shipment.

Mason perked up when Emma Longview made her way through the crowd to its far side to face a tall, thin man with a hatchet face, scraggy beard, and eyes and nose like an eagle. His clothing carried more dust than could be expected from someone on the trail for a week. Mason tried to see him as a miner but "gun-man" kept popping up as more likely from the way he stood, held his gun, missed nothing around him.

Emma Longview moved close to him and spoke rapidly. The man shook his head, causing Emma to react sharply. She drove her index finger into his chest and pressed him against the bank wall. Mason tried to hear what she said, but the sounds of the protesting crowd breaking up muffled her words. He bounced from one man to another to go to Emma, but by the time he got there, she was gone and the hawklike man was rounding up a half-dozen henchmen to leave.

Mason watched them march off. His curiosity burned like a fire. What was Emma Longview's con-nection to these men? She wasn't in the least cowed by them. In fact, she seemed to order them around. But those orders escaped Mason. If anything, they had been ready to come to Marshal Benteen's aid if the crowd had gotten out of control. From their clothing and dusty condition, they were miners and not interested in signing on as guards.

But they carried their weapons like they knew how to use them.

Mason wasn't able to piece any of it together. The only way to settle it was to find Emma Longview and ask. A smile came to his lips. Finding Miss Longview was worth the effort, no matter what.

"Marshal! Can I have a word with you?" Mason ran to catch up with the lawman. Benteen's two deputies had roughed up the man in the crowd, dunked him in a water trough and then sent him stumbling on his way. When Mason called to the marshal, the deputies rested their hands on the butts of their shooting irons.

"What do you want, Mason?" The marshal took him in with a quick glance. Mason thought a hint of admiration went with the appraisal. He made sure his belt buckle was seen by all three lawmen.

"You did a good job back there calming down the crowd."

"Tell the mayor. Maybe he'll pony up last week's pay. He's late with it." Benteen started away again. Mason matched the lawman's long stride. At least he had been at this altitude and was fit enough now not to gasp as he exerted himself.

"The men lined up against the bank wall. Who were they? They were ready to come to help you out, if you'd needed them."

Benteen looked at Mason and sneered.

"That more of your fairy tales? There's nobody else in this town who'll come to my aid. In fact, I lost another deputy only this morning. He was about the final one hired onto the posse guarding the silver shipment."

"I was thinking they might be Pinkertons hired by Wells Fargo. Or part of the guards from the shipment."

"I don't know anything about that." Benteen walked a few more steps, then said, "I'm usually the last to know, but if they were Pinks, your boss Ammer would have twigged to it from 'grams and told me. Don't you go spreading that around or I'll see he fires you so fast your head'll spin."

Mason had wondered how secure any telegram coming into Virginia City was. His boss at least kept the news held close to his chest unless the marshal needed to know. That made Mason feel a tad better. But nothing sent along the wires was secure because a man had to send it and another had to decipher the code and see that the written 'gram was delivered.

"Have you spotted anybody trying to set a new fire?"

Benteen stopped dead in his tracks and spun on Mason. He grabbed a double handful of Mason's coat and lifted the shorter man onto his toes.

"I warned you about saying things like that. You go around scaring people and they start shooting first and thinking about it later. Texas Jack warned me you had this bee in your bonnet. I don't care if you are a fireman—you go spreading rumors like that and cause panic and I'll tar and feather you."

"I think I saw the firebug when he was setting fires earlier. And there's something I can't explain."

Benteen dropped him down and thrust his face within inches. Mason wanted to tell him his razor was nicked and left tiny cuts and patches of beard, but he didn't. He realized everything snapped into focus for him because he was afraid not only of the lawman but the accusation he had to make.

"The other night. That fire. I was on fire watch and blew my whistle, but Fire Brigade No. 2 got there while I was still giving the alarm. There wasn't any way they could have reached the fire that fast, not coming uphill with a pumper wagon."

"You've got something else to say?"

"Marshal, I saw a fireman setting fires. I think it's someone in No. 2 trying to burn Virginia City to the ground."

"Who was it?"

"I only saw his belt buckle. It . . . it was a fireman's brass. I didn't see his face, but he was setting the fires."

"So we've got a firebug fireman, eh? How do I know it's not you? You came to town and got accepted mighty fast. Most gents take a year to even get noticed. The lure of men you don't know buying you drinks and women you get to know better all nuzzling up against your flank. That's more than most men could resist. All you have to do is drop a lucifer and whoosh!" The marshal clapped his hands together and lifted his hands like rising smoke.

"There's no reason for me to tell you if I was the one. Besides, the fires started before I got here."

"Get lost, Mason. Don't stir up any more trouble, and keep out of my sight. I don't give two hoots and a holler if you're a fireman or the owner of the Ophir Mine! You're wasting my time." Marshal Benteen shoved Mason back and stormed off. His deputies trailed away after him. One looked back at Mason, said something to his partner that made them both snicker, then they rushed to catch up with the marshal.

Mason felt the currents flowing all around him in Virginia City, and he had no idea what any of it meant. If he didn't figure it out by himself, no one else would.

It was time for his fire watch, and for the next two hours he stewed over all he had seen. None of it made a whit of sense. None of it.

CHAPTER EIGHTEEN

J UST GO ON and shoot me. Put me out of my misery, you old galoot." Morgan Mason rose from behind the bullet-nicked boulder and lifted his hands. If Blue Dirt Duggan noticed the six-shooter strapped to his waist in a brand-spanking-new holster, it might be over for him. He stepped away and worked his way up the rocky slope toward the mouth of the Mira Nell Mine.

"That you, Mason?"

"You know it is. Put the rifle down. Put away all your guns or I'll turn around and go back to town."

"You can't do that!" Duggan hobbled from the mine, using the rifle as a crutch. Mason worried that enough dirt clogged the barrel that it would blow up on Duggan's face if he tried firing without first cleaning the rifle. "You promised!"

"And you promised you wouldn't take potshots at me when I came with the wagon. There. See it? Down by your cabin? I even rented two mules like you asked, though I cannot see why. You don't have enough silver for me to take to the bank."

"Are them real sturdy mules? Able to pull a quarter ton or better?"

Mason lowered his hands and stared at the miner. The blow to the head had left him a mite loco. Considering how he had been before getting his skull bashed in, he hadn't changed all that much. But the ring of real concern in the old miner's voice made Mason question his own sanity.

"You've got more than a quarter ton of silver to transport? That's nigh on five hundred pounds."

"Well, good for you, boy. You weren't asleep in the third grade after all."

Mason finished the hike to the mouth of the mine. He sank to a rock and studied Duggan. The old miner looked about the same as he had a couple days ago when Mason had visited him and agreed to transport what silver had been mined here.

"Most of the mines are signing over a hundred pounds or less—lots less. The two at the Lost Cause said they had close to ten pounds, and that sounded like a fortune to me."

"It would. You think small, boy." Duggan used the rifle as a support to sink to the edge of a turned-over, corroded ore cart. From the rust stains on the seat of his trousers, he sat here often. "Why didn't you believe me that the good ole Mira Nell was the richest mine along Calabasas Creek? The Ophir and some of them company mines claw out more than I do, but I don't have a dozen floors and a winch-powered elevator for all my miners, either."

"They've opened up close to twenty levels at the Ophir, or so they tell me."

"They, they, they. Go on and say it outright. You mean Delahunt." Duggan spat at a lizard and missed. The lizard scurried away to find a better rock for sunning.

"We have to be ready if there's a fire in the mine. Those are hard to fight, or so they tell me." Mason bit his lip to quiet himself.

"If there's a fire down there, more 'n miners will die. Anybody damn fool stupid enough to go down to put out the fire will die. Did Captain Delahunt tell you that?"

"The Yellow Boy fire," Mason said, recollecting all the captain had said. "That was a bad one."

"They're all bad ones. The miners slosh around in knee-deep hot water, then hit a gas pocket. The damp fills the mine, chokes the men, then explodes. I don't have that trouble since I don't have to dig that deep."

"You just have the roof caving in on your head," Mason said. "I don't have much time off. I promised Mr. Ammer to deliver a passel of telegrams later on. Being only four days from the wagon train shipment leaving, there's a lot of telegraphic traffic between here and the San Francisco bankers."

"Listen to you, spouting all that lingo. 'Telegraphic traffic.' What else can you try to dazzle me with?"

Mason heaved to his feet and said, "Your silver for the shipment. Now. I'm heading back right away, whether it's loaded or not. And you're going to pay me for renting that wagon and those mules, two of them balky, cantankerous mules!"

Duggan clutched his rifle to his chest and looked

around as if a million robbers were thundering down on him.

"You hear that?" He cocked his head to one side.

Mason's hand went to the six-shooter in its holster, but he didn't draw. Instead, he pressed his hand down hard against the rock where he sat.

"Earthquake?"

"Blasting. Somebody's doing some powerful blasting." Duggan looked back toward town and used his rifle to point. "There. Behind Gold Hill."

"There's no reason for anyone to be blasting now. Everyone's anxious to get their silver to the bank," Mason said.

"Just because we're sending off our silver doesn't mean anybody's giving up on finding more and digging it from the ground."

"For the next shipment," Mason mused. "That makes sense," he agreed. "Ship the silver and smelt more. Only the smallest mines have reason to shutter now."

"The ones what with a single miner working the claim," Duggan said. "At the Mira Nell, that's me. And you're the one carting my precious metal into town. Are you sure it'll be safe?"

Mason hesitated. Freighting the silver into Virginia City was the riskiest part of the trip to San Francisco. If a half-dozen road agents jumped him, he'd have a fight on his hands he wasn't likely to survive. Once in Bronfeld's vault and then onto wagons bound for San Francisco, there was an army of men ready, willing and able to defend it to the death. The largest outlaw gang Mason had ever heard of hardly numbered twenty. That was a five-to-one superiority for the guards. And after the ruckus in town, Wells Fargo might have hired a few more of the crowd to help protect the shipment.

More than a hundred men could hold off any attack possible. There weren't enough Paiutes in the territory, and why would they bother attacking? Silver meant little to them, but to road agents? This was where a full couple companies of gunmen mattered most. Even with Gatling guns and military determination, the fight would be too costly to contemplate.

But between Duggan's mine and town? Mason fingered his six-shooter. He had been practicing and was good enough to hit what he aimed at now. Usually. In an all-out gun battle, though, he'd be overwhelmed.

He considered asking Duggan to ride back with him. The miner sported enough armaments for a squad of men. Then he discarded the idea. Duggan was as likely to shoot him as he was an outlaw. Better to load the silver and get it back to town as fast as possible. The less time he spent on the road, the less chance an outlaw gang had of robbing him.

"Do you have the silver ready to load?" Mason wasn't looking forward to the work required, even for stowing a few pounds.

"Got it stashed all around. Some's under the floor of my cabin. Got another bag hid out in the shed. Then—"

"Let's start with those," Mason said, resigning himself to a long afternoon of treasure hunting. "I'll dig up the cabin floor. You can root around in the shed." He suspected Duggan had hidden it where the horse dung accumulated the fastest.

"Do you think it'll be all right for me to leave the mine unguarded? I don't want them varmints sneaking in and stealing anything from me." Duggan's guns clanked as he swayed on his one good leg.

"We'll check every now and then. Come on. Let me help you down off the hill." Mason let Duggan lean heavily on him all the way to the cabin, where he made the miner show him the spot where the silver was buried.

"I'll get on over to the shed. There's a hoe leaning in the corner you can use to dig up my silver." Duggan reluctantly made his way to the shed, glancing back over his shoulder several times to make sure Mason wasn't hightailing it.

With a sigh, Mason set to work scraping away the cabin's dirt floor. He'd gone down a foot and started wondering if Duggan had forgotten where he had buried the trove. Then he hit a piece of wood. Digging away the lid surprised him. This was a goodly sized crate. When he pried off the top, his eyes went wide.

He started to say something, but words failed him at the sight of so much wealth. He began lifting bars from the cache. Twenty heavy bars piled up on the floor. He tried to judge their weights and decided one hundred ounces per bar was about right.

"Two thousand dollars," he whispered in awe. "Duggan has been one lucky miner. And he's about to be a rich one."

He began moving the bars to the back of the wagon. The mules brayed, realizing they'd soon be pulling the wagon back to town and resenting the effort ahead.

"I got the next one yanked out of where I hid it." Duggan pointed to another stack of bars. Mason was speechless. The miner had at least as much as was already loaded. By the time Mason had settled it into the wagon bed, Duggan motioned to him from up on the hill, about halfway to the mine and off the trail.

"What is it, old-timer? I want to get this to the bank."

"You can't give up, not when most of the silver's left to be loaded. Come on up here and get it."

"Most?" Mason wanted to scoff, but something told him Duggan wasn't pulling his leg.

By the time he had loaded all the silver into the wagon, he was as jumpy as a long-tailed cat beside a rocking chair. One hundred bars caused the axle to creak and protest. Close to a quarter ton of silver was his to deliver. Ten thousand dollars was more than he would earn in a lifetime or at least a couple decades of diligent work. Larcenous thoughts flashed across his mind and disappeared as quickly as mist in the bright morning sunlight. Duggan had risked his life for this. He had lost a leg and part of his skull bone and was about half-crazy. He deserved the wealth.

But for the first time Mason understood the lure of being a road agent. To become this rich with one daring robbery!

"You really should ride shotgun with me," Mason said. "This much silver is a powerful temptation."

"To you?" Duggan cocked his head to one side and squinted, peering at Mason. "You're thinking about it. I can tell. I can also tell you'll do the honest thing."

"I'm a Virginia City volunteer fireman," Mason said as a joke. He discovered there was less of a joke there than there was truth. He had an oath to uphold about defending the city and its people against fire. Somehow, that included being honest in the face of great temptation. It buoyed him and his determination to do right.

"Then get on back to town and deliver my silver. Be sure to get an accurate receipt. Them bankers are all crooks and will try to rook you out of a penny. Given temptation like you got in this wagon, they'll do anything to steal me blind." Duggan backed off, muttering curses on the head of the bank president and every teller. Mason noticed that Duggan knew them all by name, so he wasn't merely firing blindly at the banking class.

It took a little coaxing, but the mules began to pull the heavy wagon. Mason drove at the excruciatingly slow pace dictated by the mules. He wanted them to gallop wildly and knew that wasn't possible. As he drove, he looked around constantly. If he had thought, he'd have asked Duggan for the shotgun or one of the rifles he toted. Arguing with himself what he would do if road agents held him up passed the time.

Before he knew it, the wagon strained to go up Union Street toward the Wells Fargo office and the bank alongside. Mason worried less now about being held up and more about the wagon breaking down. If any of the passersby had a chance to grab a silver bar, they'd take it. He had been in town long enough to know that temptation drove most of them. Otherwise, they wouldn't have come to the Comstock Lode to make their fortune. Prospectors and miners lived by their wits. Grabbing a hundred-ounce silver bar and running away with it because the driver got careless or had bad luck and broke down was to be expected.

Again, all his worry got him to the bank. A dozen armed men milled about as the bank president and two tellers tallied the contents of a wagon ahead of him. Not being able to move should anything happen made Mason even more anxious. He almost collapsed when Bronfeld and his two employees came over.

"Filling the vault, are you? I've got more for you."

"Blue Dirt Duggan?" Bronfeld almost spat the name. "He always manages to confound me with his bull-headed ways. I'd loan him money, if he actually needed it, but I won't give it to him interest-free." The bank president looked up sharply at Mason. "The last time he wanted a million dollars! Or he said he did. He only came to bedevil me. That's how he entertains himself."

Mason noticed how Bronfeld and Duggan were similar in their regard for each other. That told him they enjoyed needling each other, asking the impossible and then detailing why it wasn't going to happen. He watched the tellers carefully weigh each bar and enter the amount in a ledger. When they finished the tally and Bronfeld signed it, one gave Mason a copy.

"Your receipt, since you are acting as Duggan's attorney. That's right, isn't it?"

"This is credited to his account," Mason said, looking over the document. "That's the way it should be. Thank you."

"Roll along, sir. There's another wagon coming in. This one has *real* silver in it."

A heavily loaded wagon from the Ophir came to a halt. While this likely had a great deal more silver for the wagon train, Duggan's bars were hardly to be sniffed at. Mason maneuvered the mules around and started down the street to return them to the wagoner who had rented him the team.

He pulled back hard on the reins and secured them on the brake handle when he passed by the assay office. Forgetting the samples he had brought in from both the Mira Nell and the Lost Cause Mines almost two weeks earlier had been easy because of so much happening. He ran his fingers over his white suspenders. That was just part of it. The silver being shipped, the fires and trying to track down an arsonist all had filled his time. Fire watch six nights a week also left him short of time to do such things. Not for the first time he wished he had kept some of his chemicals to do the analysis himself. Stringing telegraph wire was a decent job but not one he intended doing the rest of his life. He had trained as a chemist and geologist and intended to pursue those fields.

"Good afternoon, Mr. Wilson." The clerk sat behind his desk reading a newspaper. He looked up and pushed his eyeglasses back along his nose.

Mason saw several boxes of rocks on the counter, ready to be picked up. Sheets showing the analysis were tucked under the rocks. A quick look made him shake his head in wonder. The nearest box was filled with worthless stones. Granite. Not a trace of quartz or even pyrite. He stood on tiptoe to sneak a peek at the other two boxes. They, too, were nothing but paltry rock. From the look of it, someone had expended too much effort digging it from the side of a mountain. Even a greenhorn prospector ought to know rock like this wasn't worth digging out, much less bringing in for assay.

"Not ready."

Mason turned his attention back to the bespectacled clerk.

"But it's been ten days. Why aren't they ready?"

"There's a rush on other assays. The Ophir opened a new level. Those rocks get done first since they're my biggest customer."

Mason's anger flared. He pointed at the boxes of rock on the counter.

"But it's almost two weeks! You're wasting time with dross. Worse, if those are from the biggest mine in Nevada. There's no way those rocks will ever show even a hint of silver chloride or—"

"And it might be another two weeks for your assay, if you don't let me get back to work." Wilson folded the paper and stuffed it into the center desk drawer. "Now get out. I don't need you taking up valuable space in my office."

Mason almost asked if being a fireman got him any special favors. The way Wilson glared at him gave the answer.

"I'll check back in a few days."

Wilson made some comment, probably obscene, under his breath. Mason almost asked for the samples to be returned. He had some money now from working and could get a few more dollars from Duggan. Chemicals sent from San Francisco might take a few weeks to arrive, but from the way Wilson worked, it might be quicker to see the assay that way.

He walked to the wagon, his muscles stiffening both from riding on the hard bench seat and from loading the silver. Working hard lifting and carrying had given him a considerable amount more strength than when he'd arrived in Virginia City, but it took more than a single day's freighting to get him into whipcord-strong condition.

He started to climb into the driver's box when he saw the hawk-nosed man who had captured Emma Longview's attention at the almost riot. Mason dropped back and watched the man go into the assay office. He wasn't carrying any samples when he went in but juggled the three boxes that had been on the counter when he came out.

Mason frowned. The gaunt man took a rock out and tried to scratch it with his thumbnail. He held it up and examined it, then read the report with it. Most amazing to Mason, the man wasn't disappointed at the lack of pay dirt. If anything, he was happy at what he read in the report.

Worthless rock. The man must be more gunman than miner, Mason decided, to be pleased with the report. Or had he wanted to get back an assay of only granite?

That made no sense. Unless he was salting a mine with the intent to sell it to some unsuspecting investor. Why sell a mine that had real potential if he dug a shallow hole and salted it to some greedy speculator? This was the Comstock Lode, and all manner of swindles were rife.

Mason wondered if he ought to report his suspicions to the marshal, then decided against it. Anyone willing to fork over a huge amount of greenbacks for an unproven hole in the ground should be smart enough to get mining experts to verify the claim. Still, letting the man bilk an unsuspecting man out of his money rankled.

And what business did Emma Longview have with him? A shiver passed up his spine thinking she might be the one being cheated. Then the shiver went down as he wondered if she wasn't the one doing the cheating.

CHAPTER NINETEEN

Mason drove at breakneck speed, the empty wagon swaying as he swerved from side to side going down the steep hill without applying the brakes. The mules realized they'd be run over if they didn't gallop at full speed. Even then the pressure of their harnesses against their rumps prompted great braying. They weren't keeping up with the wildly careening wagon. When they reached the bottom of the slope, Mason drew back on the reins to slow the all-out rush.

When the mules saw their stable, the speed picked up again. They were happy to be rid of their crazy driver. Mason jumped down, lashed the reins around the brake and waved to the wagoner.

"Thanks. I'll be back to settle up later."

"You gotta pay now!" The man hitched up his drawers and came after Mason.

"You can find me at Fire Brigade No. 1 anytime. Or ask at the telegraph office. I'll pay, I promise, but I've got a job right now that needs me."

"Fire? You telling me there's a fire?" The wagoner looked around in panic. Mason tried to calm the man's fears. He saw how the man thought that a fireman in a hurry meant "in a hurry to put out a fire." But there wasn't enough time.

Mason was gasping and out of breath when he got to the firehouse. He was required to sign in so the officer of the day knew how many firemen were available and where to reach them. Mason waved as he went to the stable, saddled Victoria and tore out at a full gallop. Pedestrians scattered as he cut through town and struggled back uphill to the assay office.

He had taken so long he worried he had lost the hawk-nosed man. He hit the ground running and stuck his head into the assay office. Wilson looked up, startled.

"Where'd he go? The man who picked up those rocks?" He pointed to the empty counter. Only a little dust remained to show what he meant, but Wilson's mouth opened and closed.

Before he realized he even spoke, he pointed and said, "Over the hill."

"The other side of Gold Hill?"

Wilson nodded. He was gone before the assayer got back his usual peevish attitude. Outside, he vaulted into the saddle and wheeled his mare around.

There was only one road leading up Gold Hill and over to the other side. Victoria strained to reach the top, which gave a view of miles along the road away from town. As he caught his breath and let Victoria rest, he scouted the winding road down the far hill-side.

This wasn't the route the silver caravan would take. The road was too steep. When they left the bank, axles creaking under the precious load, they would wind around and take close to a day to reach the spot on the main road far below him.

"There!" Mason stood in the stirrups and involuntarily pointed when he saw a dust cloud miles away. He settled down and wished he had field glasses to be sure he had found the hawk-nosed man and his bundle of worthless rocks. But he felt it in his gut that this was the man Emma Longview had badgered and who had picked up the rocks from the assay office. If Wilson had blurted out the truth, the man had come over Gold Hill.

Mason hunted but found no one else on this side of the hill. Judging distances and the time it had taken him to hand over the borrowed wagon, saddle up and ride to the ridge, he felt confident he was on the right trail.

Only he had no idea where that trail might lead. He had to admit he would never have taken notice of the dust-covered man if he hadn't seen Emma Longview talking with him. Too many unanswered questions caused him to start down the road. Victoria almost balked, but he let the mare pick her own way on the steep slope.

Turning the trail over to his horse, he stood in the stirrups to keep the rider below him in sight. As the road made a quick switchback, he lost sight. When he rode back, the man had disappeared. Mason started to berate himself for losing his quarry, then thought it through. He knew how far down the mountain the man had eluded him. There wasn't that much foliage and only small outthrusts of rock.

"More than enough to hide a rider," he said, "but why would he try to hide? He had no idea I was trailing him."

Even if the rider spotted him, he'd have no reason to believe Mason was after him. As he continued down the winding road, he thought up a dozen excuses if the man stopped and braced him. Mason tried to keep himself from worrying, but he touched the butt of his six-gun more often than he liked. Anyone watching him would see how nervous he was.

He took another cut back, but Victoria reared. Once he controlled the horse, he hunted for what had spooked the mare. A rattler in the road would have caused the reaction, but he saw nothing. There wasn't even a rabbit or larger animal in sight. He looked over his shoulder and saw that Victoria had paid more attention to his quest than he had. Branching away from the larger road, a trail more like an animal run cut off in the opposite direction.

A closer examination showed freshly broken branches on low brush, what had to be a hoofprint in the dry dust and a large pile of horse flop drawing flies.

"Apples," Mason promised his horse. "Not those bitter crab apples, either. Something I'd like, too."

He tugged at the reins and set Victoria on the trail. By now the sun was sinking into the Sierras to his left. A chilly wind picked up, and twilight made picking his way along the rocky trail more difficult.

Mason considered returning to Virginia City. He had fire watch tonight. Delahunt would have a conniption fit if he missed it, but Mason had to decide what was more important. The questions posed by a man looking cheerful over a box of unprofitable rocks only multiplied when he wondered how Emma Longview was in cahoots—and they might, for some reason, be mixed up in the arson around town. He had seen the woman and a couple men after the firebug had tried to start a new blaze.

Figuring out who was setting fires and turning him over to the marshal would placate Captain Delahunt. Missing one fire watch to eliminate dozens of future, deadly fires was a decent trade.

Victoria stopped so suddenly Mason almost somersaulted over the horse's head. He caught himself in time and rocked back, hanging on to the saddle horn. Before chiding the horse, he caught snippets of men talking caught on the evening breeze. Go back to town?

No! He was getting closer to answers. The hawknosed man had met up with others out in the middle of a barren hillside. There wasn't any reason for such a get-together, no honest one when they could pull up chairs around a table in some Virginia City saloon, have a drink and chew the fat.

Dropping to the ground, he secured Victoria's reins around a low, sturdy bush and continued down the trail on foot. Each step was placed carefully. To turn his ankle or kick a stone and reveal himself was most likely a death sentence. He had no proof for that, but this was another gut feeling.

". . . shows we done right setting the charges."

"Cover your ears," came a deeper, gravelly voice.

Mason tried to see who spoke when a deep shudder ran beneath his feet. He stumbled and fell. He winced as skin tore off his knees. He felt blood oozing from the cuts and sticking his pants legs to his body.

"When'll we be able to see how it went?"

"The dust will settle in ten, fifteen minutes. We might set a new charge right away. We're falling behind."

"She was right in how to set the last charge," said a third man. "We blasted through more 'n ten feet by putting the bore holes in at an angle, sending the shock wave against a single point."

Mason's entire body tensed. He had told Emma how to more effectively blast in a mine like that. The "she" these men were talking about had to be her, and she must have passed along his expertise to these men after cleverly wheedling the information out of him.

"The rock breaks like she said it would, too." This had to be the hawk-nosed man speaking. Mason recognized his voice from the assay office.

Creeping forward, he found a spot to flop belly down and peer farther down the trail. Dust settled, but what he saw appearing startled him. A well-traveled road cut downhill toward the main road around the mountain. Three wagons were parked to one side. A dozen horses penned in a crude corral pawed the ground and tried to run because of the explosion that shook the ground so violently.

Mason looked past the three men huddled together against the cascading dust uphill to the mouth of a mine. Dust still rolled out from the explosion deeper in the mountain.

"We'll make it just fine," the hawk-nosed man assured his partners. "The assay showed less granite and softer rock."

Mason wanted to shout that neither the granite nor "softer rock" held one speck of silver or gold. He jumped when a half-dozen men came from inside the mine. They waved to the trio in the road.

"Let's see if we really are on schedule," the gravel-voiced man said. He hiked uphill, hawk-nose and the other man following. They discussed something that Mason caught only a word here and there about how many horses each team should use.

They meant the wagons parked behind them, and the horses were sturdy enough to pull a fully laden wagon.

He wiped dust off his face. The men had the look of road agents to him. They weren't miners. But how were they intending to hijack the silver shipment due next week? Mason considered every speculation he had heard or thought. If only a single wagon was cut out of the silver caravan, a lot of men would be very, very rich. But stealing a half ton or more of silver and running away with it wasn't possible, not with a hundred armed guards ready to give chase. If the wagon was brought up here and somehow hidden away in the mine they blasted, then the mouth closed, they'd have all the time in the world to split up and scatter to the four winds. In a week or month or even a year, they returned and dug out their precious metal.

Stealing the silver wasn't a problem if they had a big enough gang and enough guards helped out. Getting away with it was the problem. This scheme made sense to Mason. He worried that Emma Longview was the mastermind. He was quite taken with her, and she had shown interest in him, too.

But was it only to pump him for blasting techniques? She had perked up when he'd told her he was a geologist. Meeting her was something of a blur of conflicting sensations, but he was sure she had said she was a geologist, too. His experience had been in surveying and assaying mines across the Bay. There were many other things a geologist studied. Emma's expertise might not be in mining or assay, but that didn't mean she wasn't knowledgeable about the strength of various rocks, how they laid down in strata and even the crystals formed in the rocks themselves.

Mason brushed himself off and cautiously went up the trail to the open mine. The road that had been cut this far was cleared for a full-sized wagon. They intended to load the rock in and cart it off. He reached the mine and pressed flat against the mountainside, listening hard. Voices echoed along the mine shaft, amplified so he made out what they said as clearly as if they stood in front of him.

"We need to sweep aside the loose rock and extend the tracks."

"What we need is another crew," complained another.

"Your share has already been reduced twice doing that," snapped the hawk-nosed man. "What we take out of here won't be worth spit if we hire more miners."

"That's not a problem," the gravelly voice man declared. He laughed harshly. "We got to worry now about too many of the crew getting drunk and bragging about how rich they'll be."

"We don't want anyone cutting in on our silver," hawk-nose said.

"You're right, but if you want to clean off the floor and get tracks down for carts, get them back from town. They're not doing anything but what you worry about most, getting drunk and running off at the mouth."

"We need them guarding the bank," hawk-nose insisted. "If they catch that firebug, we can get them all back here. We don't dare take a chance of a fire getting out of control and burning down the bank."

Mason frowned. He tried to make sense of what he overheard. Miners supposed to be working in this mine patrolled Virginia City doing *his* job as fire watch? Chancing being seen, he entered the mine and fell to his knees. He winced. The bloody knees almost caused him to betray himself by calling out in pain. Mason dropped to hands and knees and wiped away the fresh layer of dust blown from the depths of the mine.

Iron rails vanished into the dark distance. They intended to run ore carts. To get rid of the dross? The assay denied the existence of silver or any ore with silver-bearing deposits. They ran a full-scale mining operation to mine . . . granite? That didn't make any more sense than sending a flock of miners into town to stop the firebug.

At least someone else believed such an arsonist existed. That relieved Mason a little. He stood and braced himself against the wall. A cascade of rock and debris created a small hill on his boots. In panic, he looked at the roof. They had blasted the mine shaft but had done nothing to brace the walls or overhead. Continued use of explosives would cause the entire mine to collapse on their heads because they had failed to do the simplest shoring.

The voices from deeper in the mine grew louder. Mason kicked away the rocks and dust and beat a retreat. He popped from the stuffy mine out into the fresh night air. A quick look around showed a place to hide. He dived into a narrow gully and lay still, fingers crossed that the exiting men overlooked him.

They argued over details that made no sense to him as they made their way downhill to the wagons. Mason propped himself up on his elbows, then sat up when he saw a banked campfire. They shielded the fire from the main road but left the side toward the mine open.

"They don't want anyone traveling to Virginia City to see them," he mused. This was yet another fact piled onto a heap that made no sense—or very little. When the aroma of brewing coffee drifted up to him, he knew they were settling in for the night. Coffee, a meal, bedding down.

He stood and slowly moved to the mine shaft. With a quick spin he entered the mine and faced the darkness. Mason slid one foot ahead and followed it with the other until he found the shelf with miner's candles and a few lucifers in a metal tin. He stuffed several half-used candles in his pocket and lit the only new one. Yellow light flared and momentarily dazzled him. When his eyes adjusted, he followed the tracks deeper into the mine.

Walking slowly and steadily, he studied the walls and the rock strata. For the first fifty feet or so, the rock was soft and easily dug away. Then the formation turned harder. A hundred feet deeper he reached the solid granite that had been such a concern to the men clawing their way into the hillside. He walked faster, hunting for any hint of blue dirt.

"Nothing," he said softly, shaking his head. "Why so much effort to drill the tunnel?"

After the candle began burning down and spilling hot wax over his fingers, he switched to a half-used stub. As it flared, his eyes went wide. The tunnel entered a broad fault. No digging or blasting was necessary here. Miners had widened the crack. The ore cart rails still stretched ahead.

Mason almost ran getting through this section. The crevice narrowed, and a granite plug showed where the most recent blasting had occurred. He slowed and saw the boundary between the granite and softer rock.

And nowhere along the shaft had he seen a speck of silver. There hadn't even been quartz that might yield silver or gold.

Mason scooped up bits of rock and put them in his pockets. The miner's candle gave enough light to see but hardly enough to closely examine the rock. He must have missed something important for them to put in so much work. Why dig all the way through the mountain just to hide a silver wagon cut out from the rest of the train? A few yards into the mountainside would have been enough to bury their ill-gotten gains.

Returning as fast as he could without falling down, Mason picked up chips of stone until his pockets bulged. He wasn't sure he'd find anything at all. For all his nasty demeanor, Wilson at the assay office seemed to be competent enough. If his analysis showed common rock, then that's what all this was.

Mason snuffed the candle and dropped it onto the shelf near the mine opening, then froze.

Voices. Coming back uphill from the camp toward the mine.

He touched his six-gun, but shooting his way out was a sorry tactic. He was in the mine. A million ideas jumbled in his head as hawk-nose and a voice he remembered all too well neared. Frozen in place, he awaited to be discovered.

CHAPTER TWENTY

H<small>E COULD RUN</small> fast and try to leave the mine before they spotted him. But they were too close now. He had hesitated too long. Or gun them down when they silhouetted themselves against the mouth of the mine. Mason's hand trembled as he touched his six-shooter. He might be able to cut down the hawk-nosed man, but not his companion.

Mason recognized the other voice.

He wasn't able to shoot Emma Longview in cold blood.

A full frontal charge was out of the question. Fighting wasn't in the cards. He'd be the one ventilated by every round in the gunman's six-shooter if he stood his ground. There was only one thing to do. He turned and ran back into the mine. As he passed the ledge with the candles and matches, he scooped up more of each. Fumbling as he ran, he finally lit one candle. Its wan, flickering light was hidden by his body, but if he didn't stay far enough ahead of those behind him, they'd see even a faint candle burning in the Stygian darkness.

Mason had studied the walls both entering and almost leaving. There wasn't much in the way of a crevice to hide in. Not successfully. Most mines followed ore veins and wandered away from the straight central shaft. This one had drilled and blasted straight as an arrow into the mountain.

As much as the pair behind him seeing his candle, he worried he made too much noise as he ran. Everything, anything, could betray him. They unwittingly had him trapped. If he warned them of his presence, they wouldn't even need to finish him off themselves. There were others in the camp to provide the firepower.

Mason plunged on. More than once, the candle almost blew out. Since he had one stub only a quarter as long as a new one, he had to replenish and use other candles.

He slowed once, trying not to gasp too loud. Blood pounded in his ears, but as his heart settled down, he heard Emma Longview and her henchman far behind him. Their words were indistinct as they whispered rather than spoke, but he knew the woman's voice. And by now he recognized the hawk-nosed man's as well. The only consolation he took was that they hadn't brought others along with them. Clanking, rumbling noises smothered them entirely. He tried to figure what that sound was. Whatever it was, it was metallic and drowned out the two approaching.

Wild ideas of gunning down Emma's companion and forcing her at gunpoint to leave with him filled his imagination. Once he got her back to Virginia City, he could sort out this mess and find what her role was. Somehow, he doubted her explanation would satisfy him. As much as the idea horrified him, he had to let Marshal Benteen figure it all out.

Only . . . only . . .

If he shot down the man with Emma and took her back to town, he'd be guilty of murder and kidnapping. And what crime did he accuse her of committing? There wasn't anything she had done that would convince Benteen, nothing they could properly see, anyway.

Morgan Mason would be the criminal, not Emma or her companion.

This made him break stride and almost fall. He caught himself and scraped more skin, this time off his left palm. More cautiously he continued deeper into the mine, through the crevice and to the other side, where the granite plug had been blasted to gravel. He reached the end of the mine shaft and hunted for a hiding place. There wasn't one, even with rubble from the blast piled against the end of the tunnel. Mason scrambled to the top, thinking he might burrow through to an open space beyond.

Solid rock.

He slid back down and sat, sweat beading his forehead. A rattling sounded that brought him to his feet. Holding the candle up high, he looked back along the tunnel in the direction of the approaching man and woman. An ore cart swayed along the tracks and came to a halt a few yards from him.

Mason pressed the candle against his chest, snuffing

it out. Remembering where the cart stopped, he took three quick steps, banged into it and fell forward. He landed on his side inside the cart. Twisting about, he fought to get his six-gun from its holster, but he had landed so his entire body weight pinned his right arm down against the cart's rusty metal bottom. He stopped struggling when Emma and the man neared.

"It worked just like you said," hawk-nose said. "Should we repeat it?"

"This is closer to schist. It's not as hard as granite."

Mason held his breath. Over the edge of the cart appeared long, slender fingers. Emma's. They slipped along the rusted edge as the woman went closer to the tunnel end.

The cart rocked as the man pressed between the cart and wall on the other side. Mason winced as a drop of hot wax spattered into his cheek. He bit his lip to keep from crying out. The man sidled past but didn't look down.

"Look here, Slick," Emma called. "This is what you need to do. I'll mark the spots to drill."

Mason almost cried in relief. The man pressed on and joined Emma. Slick?

"Do you think we'll make it?"

"We have to," she said. "I'll get the survey equipment in here tomorrow and see."

"You're quite a peach, you know that?" Slick's voice became husky. "That's why I love you."

"You're just saying that." Emma spoke with a hint of amusement.

"Who else could lay out a scheme like this, find men to do it?"

"Do you mean who else could find a man like you to help me with such an audacious scheme? I suppose that makes me special, doesn't it, Slick?"

Mason swallowed hard when he heard them kissing. Moving painfully, a fraction of an inch with every jerk to reposition himself, he ended up on his back. His legs were doubled under him. No amount of effort brought him to a kneeling position. Aware that he might be seen, he reached up and caught the edges of the cart. He pulled hard and raised his head enough to look over the end of the cart toward the rock plug.

He blushed at what he saw as flickering candles cast shadows dancing in unison. He sank down and wondered what to do next. His six-gun was handy now, but what did he do after he got the drop on them?

He heard the rustle of Emma's dress and the thud as Slick dropped his gun belt. The chance of the gunman drawing went away now. Mason held the upper hand, if he wanted. The question remained. What would happen after he leveled his six-gun at the pair?

Their sounds became more passionate. Mason rose once more and peered over the edge of the rusty ore cart. There was almost no chance they would hear him, even if he made some noise. It was now or never. He turned and flopped over the far end of the ore cart. Slithering like a snake, he dropped to the mine floor, got his feet under him and began creeping away like a spider. Only when he was in complete darkness did he slow and hunt for the candles and matches in his pocket.

Lighting the candle wasn't much of a risk now. The ore cart hid him from the pair, if they'd notice anything at all going on around them. He turned his face away from the bright candle flame until his eyes adjusted to it. Then he started walking quickly, holding the candle close and at waist level to hide as much of the light as possible. After ten minutes of hiking, he breathed easier.

Wind slipping into the mine from outside caused his candle to sputter and dance about. He cupped his left hand and protected the flame. But Mason concentrated too much on the candle not being extinguished and not enough on watching where he went.

He almost collided with one of Slick's partners.

"Watch where you're going, will you?" The man shoved Mason back a step.

"Sorry," he said. He blew out the candle to keep from revealing his identity.

"Wait." A strong hand clamped down on his shoulder. "Who're you?"

"I was with Slick and"—Mason struggled to name the woman properly—"Miss Longview."

"Who?"

"Slick and Emma," he corrected, hoping this played a trump card in a deadly game.

"Oh, sure. Why'd you call her Longview?"

"That's what she's calling herself in town. I want to keep comfortable with it."

"Yeah, that makes sense. I didn't know that was what she called herself this time."

Mason started past the man blocking the mine mouth and was again stopped.

"You didn't answer who you are. I've never seen you around before. Are you one of the men they recruited in town yesterday?" The man rested his hand on his gun, ready to throw down and shoot.

"Dynamite," Mason muttered. "I'm supposed to get into town and bring back more dynamite."

"More? We got enough stashed to turn the whole mountain into pebbles."

"The final blast, Emma said. She knows about these things. She told me what to fetch, and was specific about it."

"She does know what she's doing," the man admitted, nodding in admiration. He relaxed and slid his hand away from his gun. Mason considered going for his own. The crazy notion vanished for the same reason he hadn't held Emma and Slick at gunpoint. What was he supposed to do after they surrendered? Shoot them in cold blood? Taking prisoners was useful only if he had somewhere to lock them up right away.

"I'm riding to town right away, so I can be back before sunup."

"Time's running out for us, that's for certain sure," the man agreed. He paused and said again, "Do I know you? You look familiar."

"Emma said not to stand around lollygagging. You want to come into town and give me a hand? There's going to be a ton of supplies to load."

"A ton? Oh, you're joshing me. There's no way a ton of dynamite'll be needed for the last blast or two." The man pushed past Mason and pointed downhill. "There's Henry and a couple others. If you want help, ask him."

"Thanks," Mason said, stepping around and starting downhill. He felt the man's eyes on him, but when he looked back, the man had gone into the mine. If he found Emma Longview and Slick and mentioned someone sent for more explosive, the game would be over. Mason had to hope that Slick was taking his time. That'd hold questions at bay.

Halfway to the camp, Mason stepped away from the road and cut across the barren mountainside. He tried to figure out where he was by finding stars, but a thick layer of clouds had moved in, obscuring the Big Dipper and Pole star. He walked until his knees turned wobbly, then he made a right and slipped and slid downhill to the trail. He wasn't sure where he had left Victoria. Finding the mare took another ten minutes. Every passing second made him more nervous.

Slick or Emma or something he had said or done would betray him if he lingered too long. Whatever they were up to wasn't legal. The sooner he hightailed it, the more likely he was to see the warm sun of a new day.

Victoria's whinny led him to his horse. He patted the mare's neck, then mounted quickly and turned away from the mine, backtracking to a place where the winding road over the hill guided him to Virginia City.

He turned over everything he had seen and heard at the mine, but the memory of Emma and her beau kept intruding. No matter how he tried to concentrate on what the gang accomplished digging such a shaft into the hill, the two lovers' more titillating goings-on derailed his thoughts. What bothered him most was how he had fallen for the lovely brunette. He had thought she was interested in him. She had even approached him before he became a fireman.

"Using me, that's all. She wanted to know how to best blow the granite reef."

He looked up suddenly and went cold all over.

Four riders blocked the path.

"What's this about blowing something up?" The question cut through the cold, still night and straight into Mason's heart. He had run into more of Emma's gang.

CHAPTER TWENTY-ONE

Run. Fight. Morgan Mason had been faced with the same decision repeatedly. He went with what had worked for him before. Rather than slapping leather or running, he walked his horse forward and touched the brim of his bowler.

"Evening, gents. Or should I say good morning?" He guided Victoria off the trail for the men to pass. They didn't budge.

"What're you doing out here?"

"I'm heading into town," he said slowly. It took all his courage to keep the quaver from his words. His mouth felt like the inside of a bale of cotton, and if he hadn't gripped the saddle horn so tightly, his hand would have shook like he had the palsy.

"Who are you?" demanded another of the riders.

"I was just delivering a report."

"Who'd you give it to?" Two of the men reached for

their sidearms. The other two sat ramrod straight. The one doing all the speaking sounded like their boss.

"You're mighty curious. I don't know any of you. Does Slick know you?" Dropping the hawk-nosed man's name caused them to exchange looks.

"You take this supposed report to him? To Slick?"

"Of course not. Emma wanted it. Work in the mine was at a standstill until she saw it." Mason waited. The men were wavering now. He put as much exasperation in his voice as he could muster. "They hit a granite reef with high tensile strength. The assay report gave the mechanical strength she needed to know how best to blast through it."

"If you gave her the report, why are you heading into town?"

Mason reached for his pocket. Three of the men whipped out their smoke wagons, ready to shoot. The leader held up his hand to keep them from filling Mason full of lead.

"Here," Mason said, holding up a handful of rocky debris he had taken from the mine. "This'll be the last time Emma needs a report. The last time until . . ." He let his words trail off, hoping the leader finished the sentence for him.

His luck was running high, but not that high.

"Be sure to get back real quick. We'll need every hand we can drum up."

Mason grunted, not trusting himself to make a coherent reply. He tapped Victoria's flanks and rode past the riders. He imagined eyes boring into him, but when the trail took a small dogleg, he glanced back in their direction. They had ridden on to the mine. Mason let out a breath and enjoyed the feel of fresh air gusting back when he sucked in a deep breath. His luck was still good. Only he began to think of it as something else. He had bluffed his way past the gunmen who'd kill him if they thought for an instant he wasn't one of them. Only Emma recruiting so many men who didn't know one another had saved him.

He urged Victoria to greater speed, though it was dangerous in the dark. Putting as much distance as possible between him and the mine mattered now if the men compared encounters and someone asked who he was. If they described him, would Emma recognize him and send Slick back to Virginia City to kill him?

Mason looked down and realized he wore the suspenders and Fire Brigade No. 1 brass buckle. None of the men at the mine had noticed. Or if they had, they hadn't commented. It went a ways toward identifying him. There weren't that many firemen in town. All they needed to do was loiter around the fire stations until he was identified.

He laughed aloud. They wouldn't do that, and it had nothing to do with luck. Whatever their scheme, it was coming to a climax. That meant it had something to do with the silver shipment. This was Thursday, and the wagon train was leaving as soon on Monday as the bars from the bank vault could be loaded. He didn't know when the time lock opened, but it was probably not more than a half hour before the usual bank hours.

Victoria found the road leading over the hill back to Virginia City before he spotted it. Mason rubbed his eyes. He was half-asleep now. He gave the mare her head and tried not to fall out of the saddle as he dozed. When they reached the ridge overlooking Virginia City, he snapped awake.

He rubbed his eyes some more. The blur faded. He fixed on a small fire burning at the base of the town. He thought he heard faint fire bells ringing out their alarm, but the distance was too great to be sure. As he worked his way down the road, the fire disappeared. The Fire Drake Brigade had responded; it was close to their station. He sent good wishes outward that Jasper Jessup wasn't injured. Even the smallest of fires was dangerous—deadly.

Mason rode to the marshal's office. The door stood ajar, letting him peek inside. Marshal Benteen slept at his desk, head on crossed arms. A deputy Mason didn't recognize cleaned his six-shooter. He considered waking the lawman since the deputy wasn't inclined to listen to his tall tale, then he rode on.

What was there to tell the marshal? Some miners had eaten loco weed and worked to drive a shaft into a mountain without a hint of silver? That they were a gang of road agents fixing to hijack one of the silver wagons? Or maybe there was a bigger ambition. The shaft was long enough to hide all the wagons. If the gang ambushed the guards, and some of the guards were in cahoots, all the wagons could be driven into the mine.

Mason frowned as his tired brain worked on that. Something was wrong with the idea. Then he remembered the size of the mine wasn't enough to drive wagons in. He wasn't the tallest man in the world, and the ceiling had brushed the top of his hat in places. Even lifting the wagon bed from the wheels, there wasn't clearance enough to hide stolen wains.

He needed sleep, but the sun was poking up in the distance. Letting Captain Delahunt chew him out for missing his fire watch seemed less attractive than telling Blue Dirt Duggan that the silver had been turned over to Mr. Bronfeld and giving the miner the receipt.

Mason's hand flew to the pocket. Again he had been luckier than he deserved. If the bogus miners had caught him, they'd have found the receipt. With it they might have been able to withdraw Duggan's silver from the vault. The miner would have been robbed, and it would have been Mason's fault.

He rode faster. Even if Delahunt was mad at him for shirking his volunteer duty, there was no reason to add the telegrapher to that list. He wanted to keep that job, even if repairing wires wasn't something he looked forward to doing when winter came whistling down from the higher slopes. Freezing to death on a telegraph pole wasn't too appealing.

Victoria kept a steady pace all the way out into Calabasas Creek and to the Mira Nell Mine. He hoped Duggan wasn't inclined to take a potshot at him. The way he felt, he might return fire.

"Duggan!" He dismounted, secured his horse and started the climb to the cabin. "I've got your receipt. You in there?" Mason rattled the rickety door. When he heard nothing but rats scurrying around, he shoved the door open just enough to peek in. Then he put his shoulder to the balky door and almost tumbled to the ground when it gave way unexpectedly. "Where have you got off to?"

Duggan wasn't the greatest housekeeper, but his bed hadn't been slept in. The blanket was smoothed out as good as possible. There wasn't a fire laid in the stove. From the amount of ashes, Duggan hadn't had a fire overnight.

A quick look around convinced him the miner was decked out with all his guns. Mason stepped outside, shielded his eyes against the rising sun and hunted for movement near the mine. He called a couple more times. The only response came from the horses in the shed. Duggan had to be upslope since he hadn't ridden away.

Since the horses were in their stall and the cabin was more or less neat, it hadn't been searched and Duggan wasn't victim of robbers again.

Mason trudged up the hill and slowed when he came to the mine entrance. A single scuffed boot poked out from deeper in the mine.

"Duggan!" He ran to kneel beside the prostrate miner. "What happened?" He rolled him over. With a trembling hand, he pressed his palm into the man's forehead. "You're burning up with fever. What's happened?"

Duggan's eyelids fluttered, and he peered up. His cracked lips moved. Mason bent lower to hear.

"Too hot. Can't see good. Eyes ain't workin' right. I tried to go to work. Fell."

Duggan shivered uncontrollably.

"Were you up here all night?" Mason got his arm around razor-thin shoulders and sat Duggan up.

"You deliver my silver? Is it on its way to San Fran?"

"I've got the receipt in my pocket. Come on, can you stand?" Mason quickly found out the answer. Duggan tried and collapsed. Wrestling the miner down the hill turned out to be easier than he thought. The once-huge Duggan was so skinny if he turned sideways he'd disappear.

When Mason dropped Duggan onto his bed, the old man heaved a deep shuddery sigh and lay deathly still.

Frightened that Duggan had died on him, Mason put his finger under the bulbous nose. A ragged, hot gust came out often enough to let him sit beside the bed and feel some assurance he was still alive. He put his hand on the wrinkled forehead. If anything, Duggan felt hotter than up in the mine.

Mason began taking off the gun belts and bandoliers and laid them aside before covering the frail man with a blanket. He applied a cold compress to his forehead and tried to remember all the things he had heard about reducing fever. If it raged too long, it was like a fire set in a building. The fire went out when the fuel was all burned up. Duggan would die when his body exhausted the last of his reserves.

As Duggan slept, Mason well nigh passed out from all his own exertion. He came awake hours later in the middle of a nightmare. Trapped in a collapsing mine shaft, unseen outlaws shooting at him—and Emma Longview laughing. Her mocking laughter was worse than the threats from cave-ins and bullets. He shook himself awake, reapplied the compress and tucked the blanket around Duggan to keep even the slightest chilling breeze from reaching his body. As he finished patting down the blanket, he stared at the empty spot where the man's leg had been. The amputation might be the cause of the fever, but he suspected it had more to do with getting his head bashed in. That wound was half-healed, but Mason imagined he saw infection rotting away the forming scar tissue. The only way to be sure was for Dr. Sinclair to examine him.

"Don't let 'em take the Mira Nell. Don't. It's all I got." Duggan thrashed about weakly. Mason held him down.

"Got the receipt for all your silver. And I'll keep the claim jumpers away. I promise. Just you rest."

Duggan's eyes popped open and fixed on him with a sharpness that belied his condition.

"I'll make you a partner. That way, if I die, it'll all be yours."

"But the Mira Nell is one of the richest mines in the Comstock!" Mason protested. He knew how it'd look if Duggan signed over part interest and then died. Benteen and most everyone else in Virginia City would think he had killed the old man. "Besides, I have a job. Mr. Ammer will be wondering what's become of me."

Duggan muttered something about the telegrapher, then louder, "Work the mine and take the silver. As payment for tending me until I'm not feelin' so puny."

Mason nodded. That made some sense. Getting Duggan into town wasn't possible until he was stronger. Leaving him was out of the question, and he needed to make some money to keep alive. Virginia City prices were exorbitant, and he thought Ammer would hire someone else this very day when his lone lineman failed to show up for work.

"I can do that. This is a rich mine."

He did what he could for Duggan, made sure he sipped some water and then slipped out. Duggan snored loudly. Mason took that as a good sign. At least his lungs were strong enough to make the sawmill noise.

His legs threatened to give out by the time he climbed up the steep slope to the mine. How Duggan managed to get to work from his cabin on one leg was a testament to the old man's staying power.

"When you're determined enough, anything's possible," he told himself. He looked out from the mine down Calabasas Creek toward Virginia City. Tendrils of smoke rose, but that was normal. The smelter, the forge, hundreds of cooking fires, but no huge cloud warning of a new town-devouring fire.

Mason hefted a pickaxe and started into the mine. For a moment, he thought he'd caught the fever. His knees wobbled. He braced himself by pressing his hand into the wall.

The powerful tremor died down quickly. He knew it wasn't an earthquake now. Emma Longview and her crew had detonated another explosion, and this one was the strongest yet.

Whatever she was up to continued, so he had plenty of time to poke around further to find what she was up to. Later. Later, after Duggan was all healed up. He lit a candle and made his way into the bowels of the Mira Nell Mine to dig out enough silver to pay for looking after Blue Dirt Duggan.

CHAPTER TWENTY-TWO

MASON WAITED TWO days for Duggan's fever to break. The old-timer lay limp as a rag and breathing raggedly, but he was still breathing—and alive. Mason was amazed at the miner's stamina. How Duggan clung to life and then actually grew stronger was nothing less than a miracle.

The times he left Duggan, he went up to the mine and worked the richest pockets of silver chloride. The silver was almost in nuggets, the ore was so productive. A single ore cart showed enough silver to more than pay him for the time and effort spent tending Duggan. It still rankled that he hadn't been able to get word to Mr. Ammer that he was taking care of a sick friend or to Captain Delahunt what was going on.

Most of all, letting Marshal Benteen hear what he had found on the far side of Gold Hill seemed most important of all. Telegraph wires could be restrung by anyone, and enough men in Fire Brigade No. 1 walked the fire watch that there was scant chance of a fire getting away from them.

On that point, Mason considered telling the marshal yet again his suspicions about the firebug, but convincing the lawman a gang boring a hole into the side of a worthless hill posed a threat to the silver shipment was as unlikely.

Mason loaded the silver ore into gunnysacks and dragged them down to the cabin. To his surprise, Duggan was sitting up and taking a drink of water from a glass Mason had put on the table. The miner used both hands and looked frail, but his eyes were bright and sharp. He fixed them on Mason.

"You scrabble enough ore from my mine to make it worth your while?"

"There might be as much as twenty ounces in the ore. It's rich, the richest I ever did see."

"You fixing on riding into town?" Duggan swung his feet over the edge of the bed and tried to stand. He didn't make it, even using the table for support. He settled back to the bed.

"As soon as you're better."

"Ain't going to be anytime soon. I hate to say it, but Doc Sinclair's the one what can do me the most good. I can ride, a little. You see me into town, then you can go about your business. I can see it's been eating you alive, worrying over something. Is it that girl?"

Mason started to answer, then only nodded numbly. Emma Longview was constantly in his thoughts, but not the way Duggan meant.

"You want to get into town to see the silver wagon train leave," Mason accused. "You don't trust me that I turned it over to Wells Fargo for transport."

Duggan held up the receipt. With it were a few other pages, scorched from a fire.

"Those the sheets that cost you your leg?" Mason started to pluck them from Duggan's grip, but the man was too quick for him. He twisted and held the papers away from Mason's grasping fingers.

"They are. I'd have traded both legs to retrieve these."

Mason tried to read through the pages, but there wasn't enough light behind Duggan, and the scorched paper made the sheets even more opaque.

"I can't imagine what a mule-headed man like you'd risk his life for."

"And I can't imagine why a fraidy-cat like you would risk life and limb to pull me out. You go saddle up my horse. I want to get to town."

"For church services? We'd probably miss them since it'd be early afternoon when we got in."

Duggan made a few disparaging remarks and tried to stand again.

"I need the doc. It pains me to say it, but I need that sawbones something fierce."

Mason helped Duggan from the cabin to a stump outside where he could sit until his horse could be saddled and brought by.

"It looks like everything pains you," Mason said. "Set a spell. I'll be back before you know it."

He prepared Duggan's horse and cut a few lengths of rope in case he had to tie the old man into the saddle. That would be humiliating but not as bad as slinging him belly down over the saddle and taking him into

Virginia City that way. From all the man's previous ranting about doctors in general and Sinclair in particular, Duggan had to be in serious pain to relent. But as Mason helped him up into the saddle, he didn't seem too uncomfortable.

They rode into town at a steady clip. Duggan kept up his side of sporadic conversation, but Mason saw the ride was draining the energy like water out of a leaky rain barrel. Nothing much showed at any instant, but mile after mile Duggan became less sharp and clung to the saddle horn with both hands. Just as Mason considered tying him down, they arrived at Dr. Sinclair's office.

To his relief, Mason saw the door was open for ventilation.

"We're here. It's a good thing you left your arsenal back at the cabin. Otherwise, you'd be too heavy for me to help you down without dropping you." Mason caught Duggan around the waist and lifted. The miner was as light as a feather.

"Didn't expect to see either of you again," the doctor said from the doorway. He leaned against the doorjamb, smoking a cigarillo. He studied Duggan as Mason helped him over. "What can I do for you?"

"I'm just looking for a cheap place to sleep tonight." Duggan tried to spit, but his mouth was too dry.

"You still owe me from your last visit, but there's something to what you say about getting a bed. The town's overflowing with miners come to wave goodbye to their silver tomorrow morning bright and early. There's not a hotel room left in Virginia City. There might not even be any beds in the cribs, since I've heard some folks are shacking up with the soiled doves overnight because of the hotels being so crowded." Sinclair stubbed out his smoke. "That'll be more business for me in a week or two, maybe next month."

Mason looked at him and raised an eyebrow. Sinclair grinned crookedly and helped with Duggan as he said, "The new cases of the clap and the drip and the French disease will be impressive in size. I've put in an order from San Francisco for mercury skin inunction and as much astragalus as I can find. No pharmacist has any cypridol, so—"

"What can you do for him, Doctor?" Mason had no desire to hear all the cures the doctor considered.

Sinclair's face lost all emotion. He steered a quiet Duggan to the back room. When he returned, he looked grim.

"I've seen men look this way before. There's nothing I can do for him, I'm afraid."

"But he got over a fever. And came back strong after losing his leg and getting his fool head bashed in!"

"That," the doctor said, "is the problem. Each sapped his strength just a little. Rattling along one after the other like cars on a freight train, well, he wasn't able to recuperate. Did you see his eyes?"

"They looked yellow."

"Jaundice," Sinclair said. "I have some liver remedy that might let him rest easier. It's got enough cocaine in it to calm a bucking bronc. Otherwise, there's not much to do but to let him rest." Sinclair brightened a little. "He might snap back. He's a determined cuss."

"On the ride in, he kept saying he wanted to die with his boots off. He thought that was the mark of a rich man." Mason saw that Duggan was convincing himself to die, and no one could blame him after all he had been through.

Sinclair said nothing, but the glum expression told of hearing such things from other patients. Mason guessed what the outcomes were in those cases. Sometimes a man knew when his time was up.

But his wasn't.

He bade Duggan goodbye, though the man was drifting off to sleep. He dropped a sack of silver ore on the doctor's desk and said, "That covers his bill."

Sinclair peered into one and said, "You dig it out yourself? I noticed the broken nails and dirt worked into your palms."

"It's his ore. It came from the Mira Nell." With that, Mason left. It was twilight, and Ammer was either closed for the day or fixing to close. He needed his job back, but after even a few days where he failed to show up for work, the telegrapher had replaced him. With any luck, he wasn't entirely cast adrift again.

He presented himself at the fire station, where Delahunt shouted and carried on as he sent the fire watchers out on their nightly vigils. Mason wondered if the captain would ask for his belt buckle or suspenders first. The shirt would come off his back later.

"You!" Delahunt pointed. "You get on up to A Street. There and Howard. Look sharp. There's a passel of men waving their six-shooters around."

"The silver caravan leaves in the morning," Mason said.

"Get going. I've got to be sure the pumper is working. The seals are leaking."

Mason stared in wonder. Luck? Or had Delahunt

simply not noticed he'd missed so many nights on fire
watch? Whatever the reason, he threw the fire captain
a quick salute and headed uphill. When he started his
fire watch, this would have been considered a promo-
tion. These streets were lined with saloons and busi-
nesses that ran around the clock. Only at the extreme
ends of the streets were the buildings closed and dark
and less likely to have anyone see a fire and give alarm.
He touched the whistle as he walked away from the
Wells Fargo office and bank, into more deserted territory. He patrolled an area where he wasn't likely to
need to blow an alarm.

Two hours into his watch, Mason hiked along Howard Street and considered passing along the duty to
another volunteer. The loud music and boisterous
laughter from saloons at the other end of the street
drew him, but something caused him to feel uneasy
enough to make one last check on a particular building. Mason saw a shadow moving about inside. It might
be the shop's proprietor, but if so, the man moved fur-
tively, hiding the candlelight and turning away from
windows if there was a chance he might be seen.

Mason realized he might imagine all this since he
was certain a firebug was running rampant in Virginia
City. He was the only one who did. Edging closer to a
window, he chanced a quick peek inside. He caught his
breath.

The shadowy figure worked to pile paper and other
debris in the middle of the room. The candle guttered
on a nearby table. With this much fuel, the smallest
spark would ignite the shop and take the buildings
next to it in a flash.

Not thinking of personal danger, he turned sideways and flung himself through the window. With a loud crash and a groan he hit the floor. Mason got his feet under him and yelled, "Stop! Stop or I'll shoot!"

He went for the six-gun at his hip. His fingers brushed his leather holster, but he couldn't drag out his iron. The firebug crashed into him and knocked him backward. They landed in a heap. Powerful fists pummeled his head and shoulders as he writhed about. Somehow he drew and jerked back on the trigger. The loud report deafened him and startled his attacker. The brief cessation of punches gave Mason the opening he needed. He arched his back and heaved hard. The man rolled away.

"Stop. Give up or I'll shoot." Mason lay on his side, but his gun hand was free now, and he pointed his pistol at the arsonist.

"You don't have it in you, you yellow belly!" The man reared up like a bear on its hind legs.

A thousand images flashed through Mason's mind. Fists hammering at him. A boot sliding forward in an off-balance kick. Dark clothing. And a bright brass buckle. A fireman's buckle.

He fired point-blank into the man's belly. Mason was shocked when the round didn't stop his attacker. A brilliant streak of white lightning exploded off the man's body instead.

"My buckle!" The fireman attacking him reached to the spot where Mason's slug had ripped away part of the buckle, saving him from injury.

Mason shook off his shock and fired again. This time his attacker grunted in pain, but his meaty fist was already on the way. Bone connected with the side of Mason's head, knocking him flat. A boot followed.

Then a rain of blows fell on him like retribution from heaven above. He got off another shot, but it went into the floor. Then came a punch that drove him around the bend into blindness.

He shook his head to clear it, but the muzziness remained. In the dark it was hard to tell, but he thought his eyes refused to focus. Everything looked doubled. He moaned and tried to sit up, only to find his arms and legs refused to move.

With a convulsive jerk, he flopped around like a fish out of water. His wrists and feet were securely tied. Straining with all his strength to break the ropes did nothing but cut his wrists and cause blood to sluggishly flow. Mason kicked and got himself upright to lean back against the table.

He coughed and as he blinked his eyes in an attempt to clear them, smoke burned until tears ran down his cheeks.

"Fire!" He shouted at the top of his lungs, but who was there to hear him? Wrenching about, he tried to get the fire whistle between his lips. It flopped about on its string around his neck. As he twisted, he fell onto his side.

The smoldering pile of paper and debris lit up as sparks turned to flames. He was trapped and unable to escape or even warn anyone.

CHAPTER TWENTY-THREE

MORGAN MASON WIGGLED like a worm toward the fire. The heat first warmed his face, then raised blisters as sparks landed on his cheeks. He ignored it as he half lifted himself from the floor and then landed smack in the middle of the fire. For an instant, he thought he had scattered the fuel. Then the flames leaped up all around him, burning his clothing and tearing at his exposed flesh.

If he had flailed about before, now he fought like a trout being reeled in. To no avail. He felt his strength fading as pain grew all over. In a strangely detached fashion, he wondered why his red shirt wasn't even smoldering. Then he remembered hearing someone— Jasper Jessup?—make the outrageous claim that the shirts were woven with asbestos to protect firemen.

"Chrysotile," he gasped out. The geologist in him died hard. But it would die. *He* would die.

He cried out as he flew through the air and landed hard, stunning him. He barely saw through his smoke-teared eyes, but someone moved above him. Past him. To the fire.

"There," came a familiar voice.

"All of it?" Another familiar voice but he wasn't able to remember where he had heard it before. His brain was too jumbled.

"Of course, all of it. This is no time for half measures."

Water cascaded over him and onto the fire like a tidal wave. He sputtered and shook off the droplets like a wet dog. His eyes were free of the burning smoke for the first time. The pile of rubble sent up white curls of mist. The fire had been put out by being deluged with the contents of a rain barrel.

"Come along now. You need some fresh air." Strong hands slipped under his armpits and dragged him out into the street. He gasped and took in several deep breaths of revitalizing air. In the distance came the clang of an approaching fire engine. He heard the horse pulling the truck, the loud shouts of firemen hanging from leather straps on the sides, the creak and groan of wood as the pumper came closer.

"All taken care of," he said. "But I didn't blow the whistle. I . . . I shot him. The firebug who set this fire. He left me to die."

"Here's your pistol." As if by magic, his holster filled with three pounds of six-gun. "It won't do to have them find you all trussed up." A knife snick severed the ropes on his feet. The strong hands that had lifted him inside the shop again pulled him upright.

He staggered along into an alley across the street,

but a dainty foot thrust out and tripped him. Mason rolled onto his back. In the light from along Howard Street, Emma Longview stared down at him.

"You saved me."

She cracked her knuckles, stepped closer to avoid being seen by the firemen and towered over him. She rested her fists on flaring hips and shook her head slowly, disapprovingly.

"Whatever shall I do with you?"

He almost blurted out he had seen her and Slick in the mine, then realized he might have his six-shooter back but his hands were still secured behind his back. Mason said nothing.

Emma looked down the street and said, "There wasn't much of a fire for them to put out." She stamped her foot, then motioned. "Get in here. Don't let anyone see you."

"They're off to get soused," Slick said. "You're such a brave man, putting out a fire this one started." The gunman came into the alleyway and shoved his captive hard. He sent Captain Finley to his knees.

"You're the one," Mason said. There wasn't much light, but he saw where his bullet had ricocheted off the fire captain's belt buckle. "You set the fires and tried to kill me."

"You shouldn't have meddled."

Mason started to demand an answer to why the fireman set the fires, but he knew.

"You wanted the glory. You wanted *all* the glory and couldn't stand that Captain Delahunt was a better fireman."

"He's a Johnny-come-lately. What's he know? This was my town until he started his rival company."

"But his is number one," Mason said, then realized this was part of the battle between them. "He was voted in the top spot, and you weren't."

"Our good captain here found a way to be first at the fires. He started them himself. His men were told to go out at a certain time." Emma fished around in the captain's pocket and pulled out a large watch. She held it up so it turned slowly in the dim light. "This is a very precise watch, I suspect. Whoever your partner is had a duplicate and was told to get the company rolling at a precise time to a location you both agreed would be torched." Emma seemed mesmerized by the spinning gold watch.

"You don't have anything on me. His word? Pah! Who'd believe an apprentice against a fire captain?"

"I don't understand why you stopped him," Mason said. "All you needed to do was let the marshal know. He'd believe you."

"Yeah, sure, tell the marshal," scoffed Slick. "Come on, Emma. We've got to get back to . . ."

Mason almost blurted out, *The mine!* He had learned to hold his tongue.

Emma pressed her finger against her lover's lips to silence him.

"I know, I know."

"We should take care of him." Slick drew his six-shooter in a move so fast Mason saw only a blur. The pistol was cocked and pointed directly at Finley.

"Go on. I'll handle this," she said. She shooed him off. She balanced the watch in her left hand. "You don't need to know anything, Morgan."

He swelled a bit. She remembered his name.

"Why did you save me?"

"I had to put the fire out. This fool kept setting fires closer to the bank. Burning it down was never in the cards."

"You're a Pinkerton agent. You and Slick and the rest?" It didn't make sense, and yet it did.

"You know his name. Oh, my. Perhaps I should have let you burn, Morgan. But no. You don't deserve that."

"Your hired gun's gone off. How are you going to stop me?" Finley stood, a hulking man made stronger by his work as a fireman. He reached for Emma Longview.

She laughed lightly and stood her ground.

"Men like you never learn, do you?" She mocked him.

Mason jumped when a gunshot rang out. Finley took another step. A second shot brought him down. Emma held a .45 derringer in her right hand. She tucked it back into the folds of her skirt and looked at him.

"Here's a souvenir, Morgan." She tossed Finley's watch into his lap and blew him a kiss. With a swirl of skirts, she spun and disappeared, leaving Mason with the dead fire captain.

He heaved himself up to his knees, then used a wall to stand. He propped his shoulder against the building until he was steadier. Twisting and turning failed to loosen his bonds. Mason looked with distaste at the dead fire captain. A knife in a sheath at the man's belt gave the only way to get free, but he had to drop back and wiggle over the corpse to get the knife.

Mason kept telling himself he had done braver things. Rescuing Duggan from the burning building, fighting the claim jumpers back at the Mira Nell Mine, all his daring exploration on the far side of the mountain.

"Emma," he whispered. "What are you up to?" His fingers closed on the hilt. It took forever to slip the

blade from its sheath and even longer to brace the
knife against the dead body so he could cut the ropes.

Mason gasped in relief when the last strand parted
and circulation rushed back into his numbed fingers. He
rubbed his hands and then shot to his feet to get away
from Finley's body. Emma had shot the fire captain
twice, the bullet holes only an inch apart. She was a true
marksman and had not panicked when attacked. Mason
remembered how he had felt when he had been in the
gun fight. *Panic* hardly described it. And afterward—
still—he felt remorse at taking a life.

Emma Longview hadn't batted an eye when she
shot Finley. If the death was anything to her, it was a
mere inconvenience, nothing too important.

Mason picked up the watch and held it as she had,
wondering if the spinning gold timepiece somehow
hypnotized and allowed such easy killing. The movement did nothing to fill him with courage. He tucked it
into his pocket and backed out of the alley, as if Finley
might come to life and accuse him of murder. The fireman never stirred. He was dead, very dead.

Without a good idea what to do, Mason headed for
the other end of the street. Not turning Emma Longview
in for murdering Finley seemed like a dereliction of
duty as a fireman or even as a citizen. But Marshal Benteen might think he was responsible and throw him into
a cell. Emma was a bright, sociable creature adored by
everyone. Accusing her of the murder wasn't likely to be
believed by anyone. If she even came to trial, batting her
long lashes and shedding a tear or two would be all it
took for her to get off on all charges.

Mason was more likely to be strung up, just because
he was convenient.

He acknowledged another fireman from No. 1 coming to take over the fire watch. The man said something, but Mason hardly heard. He passed over his alert whistle and continued toward the bank. His successor called out something, but Mason ignored it. Something was happening, and he had no idea what it might be.

At least the firebug was no longer a threat. Captain Finley had set fires when his brigade was already on the way to minimize damage and make his own heroism soar. Resentment of Captain Delahunt was one thing, but risking major conflagrations in a firetrap like Virginia City was completely outrageous.

Emma and Slick had opposed Finley's firebug ways. They did the right thing, but Mason wondered why, when they were clearly taking part in their own suspicious activity digging out ore they knew to be worthless.

He stopped fifty feet from the Wells Fargo office. The guards on the silver caravan camped out all around. A few campfires provided warmth against the cool night, but men sat by those fires and passed bottles around. They might get drunk, but they were vigilant about not letting their fires get out of control. There wasn't any call for him to make mention of them.

"You come to check on the fire situation?"

Mason turned to face the bank president. Bronfeld had a self-satisfied grin that showed teeth gleaming in the firelight.

"Something like that," Mason said, fingering Finley's watch weighing down his coat pocket. "There been any trouble?"

"Captain Delahunt made another check earlier. He only charged half what he did before." Bronfeld winked broadly. "I think he appreciates being part of this marvelous endeavor. There's never been a bigger silver shipment in the history of the West. Not even by train."

"Is the marshal checking the security, too?"

"He has two deputies on patrol all night long, but there's no reason for them to be here. The entire company of guards is already on duty. I started paying them to watch over the silver this morning." Bronfeld snorted. "Some few of them objected because they didn't like missing Sunday service, but I hinted that replacements were easily had. Missing one Sunday is not going to send their eternal souls to purgatory, not at all. If anything, they are doing the Lord's work holding road agents at bay."

"Did the captain check the fancy lock on the vault?" Mason tried to ask enough questions to satisfy his worry. Something felt wrong, and he couldn't put his finger on it.

"The time lock is functioning perfectly. Friday afternoon the locking bolts slid into place and the timer began. It is set to draw back those bolts at exactly six a.m. With all these men lending a hand, we will have seven wagons loaded and on the way in an hour."

"That quick?" Mason was impressed.

"I have offered a bonus of ten dollars if they arrive ahead of schedule. There's not a solitary man who didn't applaud my generosity."

"Or that of Wells Fargo," Mason said.

"Yes, well, there is that. Now, sir, I must go home and get what sleep I can so I will be here bright and early to open the vault. The timer only releases the bolts. I must personally dial in the combination to

open the steel door." Bronfeld strode off, whistling a
jaunty tune that Mason almost recognized.

That bothered him as much as everything else. He
felt answers were within his grasp—almost.

He walked the perimeter of the impromptu en-
campment, idly counting heads. He didn't tally one
hundred, but some of the men had bivouacked away
from the Wells Fargo office and the bank next to it.
Their horses were stabled in a makeshift corral down
the street, with seven empty wagons waiting for their
silver and a chuck wagon already filled with trail supplies for the drivers and guards. Once they started rolling, there wouldn't be any reason to slow down.

Rather than return to the fire station and sleep
there, he settled in a chair set out in front of an apoth-
ecary. Rocking back and bracing himself, he tipped his
hat down over his eyes and slept, dreaming of silver
bars and gunshots and confusion all around.

CHAPTER TWENTY-FOUR

MORGAN MASON JERKED awake and almost fell from the chair. He pushed his hat back up on his head and righted the chair. He came to his feet and looked around in panic.

"Seven? Eight? Bronfeld said there were only supposed to be seven wagons." A quick survey of the men camped around the bank showed a few were stirring. One had put a pot of coffee onto a fire to boil. None of them was the man he wanted.

"Where's the marshal?" he bellowed again and got the attention of a deputy. The man wore a badge, but Mason had never seen him before. He had to be another recently hired lawman, possibly one of the rejects from the army of a hundred guards.

"Don't go yellin' like that, Mister." The deputy came over. He carried a rifle resting in the crook of his left arm and a six-shooter swinging at his right hip. Mason took it all in with a single glance. The man wasn't a gunfighter, not without using a rawhide strip to tie down his holster. There was a softness to him, also, that Mason recognized because he had looked the same way a couple weeks earlier. The deputy was citified, and not the rawboned frontier type filling Virginia City to overflowing.

"I need to talk to Marshal Benteen. There's going to be an attempt to steal the silver."

The deputy raised his left arm high and waved it in a circle. Mason stepped to one side and saw the marshal hurrying toward them. Mason's mouth went cottony. The marshal cowed him, but he had to stand up to him right now.

"What do you want, Mason?"

"You know him, Marshal?" The deputy repositioned his rifle in his arm.

"Get on back to patrol, Guthrie. Yeah, I know him. He's the one with the wild-eyed ideas about there being a firebug flittering around town."

"Eight, Marshal, there are eight wagons. Mr. Bronfeld said there were only seven signed on for the wagon train. Six and a chuckwagon."

"What? So?" The lawman brushed it off with a wave of his hand.

"What if outlaws drove a wagon up to the bank with the legitimate wagons, filled it and went off? Who'd know?"

"The bank president would. The Wells Fargo station agent would. The guards would, that's who."

"You mean they're gonna sneak in ahead of the last

wagon, get the silver and off they go? Then pretend to break down or have some other mishap along the road and take the silver?" Deputy Guthrie scratched his chin and nodded. "That's real clever, Marshal. In all the excitement and with a hunnerd newly hired men, there might not be anyone keepin' track."

"They'd never load the wagon."

"Ain't nobody over there knows anybody else. You think that there bank president knows every one of them hunnerd guards? He prob'ly don't even know the drivers."

"Or the chuckwagon cook," added Mason.

"What chuckwagon are you going on about?" Marshal Benteen looked perplexed. "You telling me there's a chuckwagon going along?" He shot a hard look at his deputy, who only shrugged. There wasn't a great deal of communication between the lawmen.

"If you don't know, then none of the Wells Fargo officials do, either. This wagon train's too big with too many new faces for them to know."

"Show me, Mason. And if this is another of your harebrained ideas, I swear you'll spend the next month in the lockup." Benteen jerked his head in the direction of the corral where the horses waited to be hitched to the wagons. Deputy Guthrie trailed his boss and Mason like a puppy dog.

"I think I know one of the men who's responsible, Marshal. His name's Slick." Mason held back on naming Emma. One detail at a time. If he flooded the marshal with too much, the lawman wasn't likely to believe any of it.

"Slick? Don't know anybody with that moniker," Benteen said.

"What about Slick Sid Underwood, Marshal?" The deputy caught up so he walked on Mason's right side and his boss was on the left. They had him bookended.

"I don't recollect anybody with that name," Benteen said. "How'd you come by him?"

"I read through all the WANTED posters," Guthrie said.

"There must be a hundred of them. You remember one out of them all?" Benteen sounded skeptical.

"I remember him 'cuz he's from Boise, just like me. I never heard of him robbin' or stealin' back home, but then I wasn't nuthin' but a law clerk." Guthrie looked sheepish. "Havin' a good memory's important for a clerk. I can recite all the US laws dealin' with open range and—"

"So you're sure Mason here hasn't been eating loco weed?"

"See, Marshal. Seven wagons. And over there's the chuckwagon." Mason pointed. He hunted for any sign of Slick. Slick Sid Underwood, the deputy had called him.

"Hold on there!" Guthrie brought his rifle to his shoulder. Two men in the driver's box of the third wagon started to run. A single shot in the air stopped both men in their tracks.

Before the marshal and deputy got to them, they were babbling and blaming each other.

"You confess that you meant to rob the bank of the silver shipment?" Benteen had his six-shooter out and trained on the men. They raised their hands a mite higher. They looked in pain at how stretched out they were. Mason almost drew his own six-gun to see if they'd go up on tiptoe.

"Let's get these owlhoots to the jail, Deputy. I want to hear everything about their fool plan." Benteen looked at Mason and shook his head. "You're proof that a stopped clock is right twice a day. You saved Wells Fargo a powerful big loss, though how these two figured on making off with their treasure is beyond me." Benteen hitched up his drawers. "But I'll find out." He rushed after his deputy, leaving Mason behind.

Drivers for the other wagons began arriving. Mason watched for Slick Sid or Emma, but neither showed their face.

"Hey, Mister, get that wagon out of line. You're holding up the entire train." The driver in the fourth wagon held his reins expertly. Tiny ripples up and down the leather straps told the horses to prepare for some real work.

"I'll do what I can," Mason said. "I've never driven a wagon before. Well, I have, but it—"

"Move it!" This time both drivers behind in line yelled. Mason had no call telling them of his inexperience and how the only real time he had driven a wagon was to bring Duggan's silver in to the bank.

He hopped into the box and took the reins. Sawing a bit, he got the horses pulling off to the right to let the other wagon roll past. When he had gone far enough, he looped the reins around the brake. A quick wave to the other drivers brought him curses and obscene hand gestures. Mason sighed. They had a job to do, and as far as they were concerned he was preventing them from the adventure of a lifetime.

He turned to jump down when he saw the tarp in the back had come loose. A corner lifted in the fitful morning breeze, and Mason went cold inside. Scrambling into the wagon bed, he pulled away the tarpaulin and gasped. Six cases of dynamite and a box of detonators had already been loaded. The two outlaws hadn't intended to steal the silver by stealth. That was too clever. For whatever reason, it looked as if they had intended on blowing up the vault. How they'd make their getaway was beyond Mason.

It might have been something the two hadn't planned.

He secured the tarp and jumped to the ground. This was one more detail to pass on to the marshal. Mason hadn't reached the now-empty corral when a shriek of pure anguish went up from the direction of the bank. He whipped out his six-shooter and ran to see what caused the commotion.

The bank president stood in the doorway making sounds a trapped, dying animal would make. He finally choked out, "The silver's been stolen!"

The crowd murmur died to complete silence. Only sounds from other parts of Virginia City intruded. Then a tumultuous cry of disbelief and anger went up. Through it all, Mason pushed his way forward. By the time the guards were firing their guns in the air and stamping their feet, he reached a spot directly in front of the bank president.

"Mr. Bronfeld, let me in to check the vault."

The bank president sputtered, but shock held him stationary. Mason took the opportunity to push past. Behind him stood four tellers, all staring past the open steel door into the vault.

"How much has already been loaded on wagons?" Mason shook the nearest teller. The man broke down crying.

"None," the teller said, bending over at the waist

and holding his face in his hands. "We're ruined. They'll hang us all!"

The other tellers shared his opinion. Mason grabbed the teller standing closest to the vault and demanded, "Tell me everything that happened. Everything. Now!"

Responding to someone who seemed in charge, the teller said in a choked voice, "The time lock clocked off. Mr. Bronfeld dialed in the combination, and I swung the door open. To . . . to . . . that!"

"No one moved the silver Friday before the time lock was set?"

"No one could," the teller said. "Mr. Bronfeld, me, the marshal and a couple deputies, we all saw the door locked. The silver was there at five o'clock on Friday afternoon."

"No one tampered with the lock?"

"Not a scratch," the teller said.

Mason checked for himself. If any tools had been applied to the steel, bright, shiny scratches would have jumped out. He ran his hand over the cold, slick metal to be sure such scratches hadn't been filled in or painted over. The original steel-strong door slid past his fingers.

A loud shout outside quieted the crowd. Marshal Benteen had returned from taking the two would-be robbers to the jailhouse. The thought raced through Mason's head that, if those two had been successful opening the vault, they would have been thwarted by an empty box. Knowing he had little time, he stepped into the vault and examined the walls and ceiling.

Mason's time for studying the vault ended when Benteen and his deputies crowded in.

"What're you doing in here?" The marshal started to have Mason taken away when a deputy pointed to the ceiling.

"Marshal, is this how they got in?"

Benteen and the other deputy stared at a crack in the ceiling. The marshal took out a thick-bladed knife and shoved it into the cranny. Mason had already seen and dismissed the blemish as a possible entry point. Instead, he looked at the floor. Stacks of silver had been dragged over the floor, leaving metallic streaks. His quick eyes went to the far back corner. Part of the floor curled up. Mason stepped down on that section of the floor and heard a hollow echo.

Everything fell into place for him. Emma, Slick and their gang must have tunneled through the mountain to a spot under the bank. Digging up into the vault allowed them to take the entire weekend to empty it of silver. They had replaced the floor to give themselves a few minutes more to load the silver into that rusty ore cart and push it repeatedly through the mountain and out to where they had wagons waiting to haul off their plunder.

They didn't even have to haul away all the silver to strike it rich.

Mason saw the lawmen arguing over the crack in the ceiling. Benteen had pried loose a section of the board to reveal the solid steel that made up the ceiling and walls. Mason wanted to see if the floor also had a steel plate to protect the contents, but he suspected it didn't. The vault designer had never considered it possible for someone to attack the contents from below, only from the sides and above.

He overheard one deputy mention him and saw how that discussion went. Benteen would think he and the two already locked up were in cahoots to divert attention from the real theft. Even if the marshal came to his senses and realized Mason had nothing to do with the theft, he was likely to be ignored.

Or taken out and hanged if he pointed out the tunnel under the bank. That would seal his fate with the crowd outside. They wanted someone to blame, and that sentiment would only grow worse when the mine owners' voices joined those of the guards. Not only would he have pointed out the tunnel, he had inspected the vault earlier and declared it secure.

"They need to discuss everything in private," Mason told Bronfeld. The bank president looked less flustered now and more frightened. He realized his neck was going to be stretched, too, if the crowd took it into their collective mind to deliver some rough-and-ready justice.

He slid through the partially closed doors. Two men pinned him against the wall and demanded to know what was going on. Mason blurted the first thing that came to mind: "Get Captain Delahunt. His help's needed inside."

Murmurs of fire spread and helped disperse the crowd enough for him to bull his way to the back. There, he broke out in a run. He had a desperate idea that no one would ever go along with. The wagon loaded with the dynamite was still hitched up.

A quick jump landed him in the driver's box. He took the reins and snapped them to get the sturdy horses pulling. Rather than drive past the still sizable crowd around the bank, he cut away and headed for

the steep road going up and over Gold Hill. Unloaded—
or only carrying a few cases of dynamite—he thought
the horses could get him up and over to the far side.

The side where Emma and her gang must already
be escaping with the stolen silver.

CHAPTER TWENTY-FIVE

M ASON HAD NO idea what he was doing. Driving a wagon required skill and experience he did not have. He balanced at the top of the steep downhill slope. The horses nervously pawed the ground. A quick look back down the deserted road leading to Virginia City showed he had time. The marshal wasn't after him. Yet. Mason felt in his gut the lawman would get around to forming a posse. By the time that happened, Mason had to stop Emma and Slick Sid and the rest of their gang.

Another look back, this time at the dynamite in the wagon bed, gave him a thrill of impending death. The only thing he could do with so much dynamite was to blow it up. Where?

"Giddy-up." He snapped the reins and started downward, faster and faster. The wagon inched closer to the galloping horses. He reared back, braced himself and shoved his boot against the brake to slow the wagon. For a few seconds, he thought he was winning. Then he realized the horses were pulling, too, adding to the downward speed.

He stood on the brake with both feet now while he gave the horses free rein. If he didn't, the wagon would run over them. The smell of burning wood rose, along with an ominous white curl of smoke from where the brake pressed into the front wheel. A new threat rose. The brake worked all too well and caused the wagon to skew to one side.

A quick release let him right the wagon, then he applied the brake again. His back ached, and his legs threatened to pop. Then he flopped backward, resistance gone. The brake handle broke off. He scrambled about, reins still in hand. The only thing he could think was to slow the runaway horses. He pulled back on the reins as hard as he had applied the brake.

The wagon began to slow. The harness creaked with the strain of pressing into the horses' rumps. The breakneck descent became more manageable, and finally he brought the wagon to a dead stop.

Mason flopped forward over the driver's seat, gasping for breath. His arms and shoulders burned with the fury of a thousand wildfires, and his legs turned to water under him. Mindful of how he moved with the reins still in hand, he climbed from the wagon bed back into the driver's box. Simply sitting a few seconds calmed him enough to hunt for the trail around the mountain to the mine shaft disgorging a thousand pounds of silver stolen from the Wells Fargo vault.

Much of the landscape was still cloaked in night. It'd be another half hour or more before the sun crested the mountain and warmed the western slopes. Mason hoped this twilight hid his approach to the mine. Hearing the horses complain of the mistreatment he gave them, the rattle of chains and the creak of wheels, he gave up on the idea of sneaking up on the robbers. The other course of action was plain.

The trail was narrow and rocky, but he brought the horses to a quick step, bounding around and to hell with the dynamite in the rear of the wagon. Speed mattered. He either got to the road leading up to the mine and made a stand, or he didn't.

By the time the sun peeked over the mountaintop, he pulled the wagon around to block the road. This was the best he could do, and it was futile. All the outlaws had to do was drive across the desert around him. The road was hardly more than a scraped-off patch of desert, and telling the difference in places wasn't possible.

He considered all the things he could do and none of them looked promising. Driving the wagon into the mouth of the mine and setting off the dynamite was his best chance, but did he want to bury Sid Underwood and the others in the mine? And Emma Longview? Did he have it in him to bury her alive? He'd heard stories of miners trapped underground. The few who escaped were never the same. The ones who didn't quit mining turned wild as the wind. They had cheated death and hunted for new ways to laugh at the Grim Reaper. Whether they thought they were invincible or simply sought to kill themselves wasn't anything Mason had considered too closely.

The horses balked when he tried to get them up the steep slope to the mine opening. He saw deep ruts in the ground where at least two wagons had already rolled down, straining under the silver piled into them. Was it worth killing the gang if they'd made off with most of the silver?

"Trap them. I've got a gun." He touched the six-shooter at his hip. Penning them up inside and waiting for the law to arrive was something that didn't involve crushing them under tons of rock. "Let them stand trial. And tell what happened to the silver already moved out."

Somehow the plan made sense until gunfire from the mine caused the horses to rear. The wagon rolled back down the hill. Without a brake, he had no way to slow it. The weight of the wagon pulled the horses backward until they fell. Then they were dragged, amid kicking hooves and wild cries of pain.

The wagon fetched up against a tree and saved the animals from further torture. They climbed to their feet and strained against their harnesses. Mason fastened the reins around a front wheel, hitched up his britches and started the climb alone. He reached the level area at the mine's mouth and cautiously peered into the depths.

He flinched when a foot-long tongue of flame disturbed the darkness. Loud cries followed. Then Emma and Slick Sid backed from the mine.

"Got it?" The gunman emptied his pistol into the mine, did a border shift and drew a second six-gun from his belt. He began firing methodically, one round every five seconds. A cry of pain from the mine warned of his deadly accuracy.

"Right here," Emma answered. She held up a single stick of dynamite.

"Hurry up. I need to reload." Slick Sid jerked to the side as return fire came from in the mine.

Emma Longview drew out a match, struck it on a rock and lit the fuse. The black miner's fuse sputtered and then flared. She tossed it into the mine.

"How long before it blows?" Slick Sid tossed an empty six-shooter to her and began reloading his second pistol.

"They're rushing us!" she cried out. Her derringer appeared in her hand and sent two .45 slugs into the mine. "The fuse burns at a foot a minute. That was about a foot long, so—"

The explosion knocked Mason to the ground. It was far more powerful than any single stick of explosive ever invented. Emma had cached more dynamite just inside the mine and used her single stick to detonate whole crates.

Dust and debris gushed forth as if the earth exhaled mightily. Mason shook himself and sent new clouds of dust flying. He got to his feet and advanced, six-gun drawn. The explosion had sealed the mine permanently. Digging it out would require as much work as had originally cut the tunnel.

"You buried your own men," Mason called. "Get your hands up. I've got the drop on you!"

Emma and Slick Sid turned, she slowly and Underwood with a practiced spin that took him into a gunfighter's crouch.

"Why, I do declare, look at who's joined us, Slick. It's Mr. Mason. Did I make a mistake saving you from that arsonist?" Emma's cool, collected manner did more to unnerve Mason than the gunman training his pistol on him.

"Reach," Mason said. "I've got the drop on you. Both your six-shooters and that derringer are empty. You killed your own men." That kept coming back to shock him. He had planned on doing that very thing, but they weren't his partners. Even then he hadn't come to a solid decision about what to do.

These two had solved one problem for him. All he had to do now was bring in the pair of them.

"You are correct, Mr. Mason. My two-shot is empty. And so is this six-gun." Emma held it up high.

Mason made the mistake of following her movement and took his eyes off Slick Sid.

"Mine's got bullets in it. I reloaded." The gunman fired twice.

Mason winced as a fiery streak crossed his side, going between his chest and inner arm. The second round went wide because Mason doubled over in pain. As if from another country, another world, he heard Slick Sid's hammer fall on a spent round. The outlaw had only reloaded two chambers. Mason forced himself to stand, aim and fire.

Slick Sid dived for cover while Emma remained standing, as if she didn't have a care in the world. She carefully reloaded her derringer, then reached down and took cartridges from a box on the ground and began reloading the six-shooter.

"Drop the gun," Mason commanded. She looked up and smiled. That expression burned itself into his brain. She was amused. She came close to laughing out loud. And then she closed the gate on the six-gun, cocked and fired it at him.

Mason reacted instinctively—or his legs simply gave way. He sank to the ground so all her slugs tore through thin air.

"Oh, Slick, this is becoming tiresome. Take care of him, will you?"

"We've got to get the wagon on the road fast," he said. "If he found us, the law's not far behind."

"Don't be so pessimistic. Mr. Mason is quite a clever man. Aren't you, Morgan? He figured this out all by himself and never shared it with the marshal. After all, he and Benteen did not get along too well. Am I right, Morgan?"

Mason slid a few feet downhill, hunting in vain for a target. Emma stood exposed, reloading her six-gun. Her partner was out of sight. Mason trained his gun on her but couldn't pull the trigger. She was going to kill him if he didn't shoot her first, but he couldn't bring himself to gun her down.

A new curtain of lead flew down toward him. Almost in relief, Mason turned back to see Slick Sid standing beside a pile of bushes some distance from the mine. A few shots forced Slick to back off. When he did, the brush pulled away from a wagon. The team was facing the mountainside, and all Mason saw was the lowered gate in the back.

The bright flash of silver—bars and bars of silver—dazzled him. Other wagons had removed early loads from the vault. This had to be the final treasure.

Bullets dug tiny craters all around him. Emma walked forward, taking care to aim every time. Mason rolled left and right, then tumbled down the hill. This did nothing to stop the robbers but saved him. He rolled out of range.

"Get in, Emma. There's no need to kill him." Slick Sid settled in the driver's box and wheeled the wagon about.

"I suppose you're right, Slick. You usually are about such things. Still, he's such an easy target."

"Get *in*." Slick Sid snapped the reins and got the team pulling, slowly at first, then with greater speed as he turned downslope. Emma gauged her distance, took a running step and vaulted up to sit beside him. She rested her six-gun in her lap, ready to take another shot at Mason if the opportunity presented itself.

Mason's brain worked at top speed. He couldn't outgun them. They were escaping with the last of the silver. From the ponderous sway, hundreds of the stolen bars might be in this wagon. He scooped up the reins on his own team and launched himself upward, landing with teeth-jarring impact on the hard bench seat. Mason got the team racing along the trail ahead of Emma and Slick.

With a lighter load, he outdistanced them and reached the main road, the one where the silver caravan was supposed to have traveled by now. The wagons driven by others in the gang must have rattled this way already. Mason wasn't able to do anything about that, but he could stop the last load from being driven away.

He could stopper them.

The wagon began to fall apart from how he drove along the main road. He took two switchbacks and came to the narrowing in the road he had seen days earlier. The builders had blasted into solid rock here for a road with a sheer drop-off of a hundred feet on one side and the solid rock of the mountain on the other, barely a wagon wide. He reined back the horses and let the wagon slew about onto the constriction in the road.

Working forward, he unhitched the linchpin, setting the horses free. They stood for a moment, then realized galloping away was in their best interest. Mason climbed back into the driver's box and drew his six-shooter.

He looked back. Emma and Slick had reached the main road and whipped their team to cross this neck in the rocky road. The expression on her face was one of pure fury. The gunman hunched over, intent on controlling his team.

Mason cocked his six-gun, aimed and fired. The explosion lifted him up into the air even as it blew away the road, leaving only a gap and a hundred-foot drop.

CHAPTER TWENTY-SIX

A GENTLE FRAGRANCE, A soft breeze blowing across his face. A distant, nagging sensation of pain every time he took a shallow breath. Morgan Mason forced his eyes open. It took a few seconds to focus, then he smiled.

"I've died and am seeing an angel." His voice was low and ragged but audible.

"You're so sweet." Mrs. Logan bent over and lightly kissed his cheek. The touch burned like fire and brought him fully awake. "Oh, I'm sorry. Your face lost some skin in the explosion, and you broke three ribs." She brushed over his cheek with her feathery touch. This was better. "And your arm's broken."

"Otherwise, I'm all right," he said. He tried to laugh, but it hurt too much.

"Oh, yes, you're all right," she said. Her radiant smile made him try to reach out to her. He failed.

"I see he's finally decided to join us." Dr. Sinclair came into Mason's field of vision and pressed a finger into his left wrist to take his pulse. "Strong. You'll live."

"He's so thin," Mrs. Logan said. "He needs food. I can get some chicken soup I whipped up for the children."

"Tommy and Iris," Mason said. "Did Captain Delahunt let Tommy play with Smudge?"

"You remembered their names," she said. "How clever of you."

"Not hard to do," Mason got out.

"Let me fetch that soup. I'll get some for you, too, Doctor."

"Finally. Someone thinks about the man tending everyone else."

"Oh, Doctor, you know everyone thinks well of you. I do because of how you've treated Mr. Mason." She turned and blew Mason a kiss and blushed. "I'll be back in two shakes of a lamb's tail."

Sinclair left with her, giving Mason a moment to sink back in the bed. Even this small interaction wore him out. Mason's eyes began to lower when a shuffling sound brought him back fully awake. He turned slightly and saw Jasper Jessup in the doorway, shifting nervously from foot to foot and holding a fire helmet in both hands. He looked like a schoolboy caught throwing spitballs.

"You're back among the living. That's good, Mason, that's real good. I worried 'bout you."

Mason looked Jasper Jessup over. He wore a full volunteer fireman's outfit, with brass belt buckle and red shirt and helmet with a number on it. His suspenders carried the three yellow stripes of a senior fireman, and now there was an added brass button awarded for some heroic deed.

"What time is it?" Mason watched Jessup fumble in a pocket, open the case of a large gold watch and peer at the hands.

"Purty near two in the afternoon. Why do you care? You're not going anywhere for two weeks or so. Least-ways, that's what the sawbones said."

"My watch. In my coat pocket. I want to be sure it's keeping good time. Get it, will you?"

Jasper Jessup rounded the bed and searched through Mason's coat until he found the watch. Mason saw him stiffen when he drew out the watch.

"I got it, Mason. It needs winding. You've been here two days and nobody wound it."

Jessup came back to the bed and laid the watch on Mason's chest.

"Why, Jasper? Why'd you do it? You and Finley could have burned down the whole town."

"No, no, Mason, you got it all wrong. Captain Finley had it all figgered out. You know we had our watches all lined up. We'd agree when I'd call out the brigade and where to go. The fire'd be just startin'. Nothing big, but enough for folks to appreciate us. Finley was sick of Delahunt bein' number one, always gettin' to the fire first and puttin' it out, no matter how fierce. The Yellow Boy Mine fire was put out by Delahunt's crew. That made him a hero."

"You did it just to cadge a free drink and have women think you were brave?"

"Even knowing what we faced, puttin' out fires is dangerous. You know that." Jasper Jessup swallowed a lot more now and shifted from foot to foot, considering the best time to turn and run away.

"One fire getting out of control could burn down Virginia City. You risked that. For what, Jasper?"

"For this, Mason. For this!" He held the helmet high. "Finley made me his second in command. This is the first time in my life anybody thought so highly of me. I command respect!"

"We were friends, Jasper. I respected you." Mason closed his eyes and summoned strength. "If you're right, the doc said I'll be up and about in a couple weeks. The first thing I'm going to do is tell Marshal Benteen what you and Finley did. Your captain's dead. You've got at least a week's head start before you'll end up the same way. If the citizens don't string you up, your fellow firemen will for betraying their trust."

"You're askin' me to give up bein' a fireman!"

"One week, Jasper. That's only because you were the solitary soul to show me kindness when I came to Virginia City."

Jasper Jessup stood straighter and left without another word. Mason closed his eyes. Turning in one of his few friends in Virginia City would be hard, but he'd do it. Too many people had lost property and lives had been put at risk. He tried to remember Tommy and Iris Logan huddled under the table, fire all around them. The frightened looks on their faces were etched in his mind. Whoever caused such fear had to be brought to justice.

His eyes opened as he felt the gold watch on his chest slip to one side. He thought his breathing had caused it, then he realized there was a different cause.

"Hello, Mr. Mason," Emma Longview said. She

held up the gold watch and examined it. "This is an expensive watch. Somehow, you don't seem the type to really use it. It's not like it's an heirloom."

"Why aren't you in jail?"

"How rude, Mr. Mason, how very rude of you. Slick is locked up, but I found a way to live up to his name. I proved slicker and got away from the marshal. He's a very determined man, much like you. But he's not very bright." Emma walked around the bed, forcing Mason to shift about to watch her. "He's not at all bright—unlike you." She drew her derringer and pointed it at him. "You cost me three wagons loaded with silver. Whatever should I do to punish you for that?"

She cocked the derringer.

"Three? That means you still have one?"

"Ah, I was right. You are smart. Yes, I have one that drove off late Friday night and was many miles down the road by the time you chose to butt in." She aimed the derringer directly at him. The .45-caliber barrels looked like dual fire hoses pointed at him. Her finger tightened on the trigger.

Then she lowered the hammer and tucked the pistol away in her flowing skirts.

"You were a worthy opponent, even if you cost me a great deal of money."

"An entire wagon filled with silver's not a bad day's work," he said. "If you aren't caught."

"Several months of effort went into the tunneling, but splitting the silver four ways is still good."

"If your partners haven't double-crossed you."

"That, Mr. Mason, is always a risk in my profession." She held up the watch, then added it to the pocket where her pistol resided. "I'll keep this as a reminder."

"I'll have Marshal Benteen after you before you can get out of town!"

"Oh, Morgan, you may be smart, but you are so naive." She blew him a kiss and left.

She pushed past Dr. Sinclair, who turned to eye her as she exited. He shook his head and came to sit on the bed at Mason's feet.

"You don't have to be a fireman to draw the ladies to you like flies to—"

"Doctor, please. I'm very tired."

"One more thing, Mason, and I'll let you rest. This one isn't as pleasant as a sweet young thing hanging on your every word."

"She—never mind." Mason had no reason to explain Emma Longview to the doctor. He hated to admit it, but he was still just a little sweet on her. More than this, Sinclair looked as if he was in no mood to hear anything at all.

"You haven't had a chance to ask the obvious question." Sinclair ran his hand through his thinning hair and summoned up courage to press on. "That's Duggan's bed you're in. He didn't make it. I did everything I could, but he was too weak."

"But he survived having a leg cut off and his skull bashed in!"

"All took their toll on his strength. The fever was more than he could tolerate. I warned you before that I thought he wanted to come here to die. It's hard to believe such a thing, especially when talking about a strong-willed man like Duggan." Sinclair drew out a sheaf of papers from his coat pocket. Mason recognized the scorched sheets as the ones Duggan had saved from the fire where he had lost his leg. "You saved his life two times, maybe three. Maybe four, if you count the attack on the Mira Nell by the claim jumpers."

"He told you about that?" Mason was surprised. Duggan had acted as if this was what Mason should have done, nothing unusual, nothing out of the ordinary. Mason realized he might make more of it since he had never shot anyone before that day.

"He spent most of his time talking about you, Mason. This," Sinclair said, holding up the papers, "is the registered deed to the Mira Nell. When he knew he wasn't going to make it, he signed it over to you. It's witnessed and notarized. You're rich, Mason, maybe the richest single mine owner along Calabasas Creek."

"But he must have family."

"Not that anyone ever heard. You're as close to someone he trusted. Thinking on it," Sinclair said, looking away into the distance, "you might be the richest man in Virginia City, since the Ophir and other mines are owned by big companies."

"But I don't want to be a miner!"

"Be a telegraph wire stringer, then. Or a full-time fireman. Captain Delahunt is bragging all over town how you're one of his brigade. If you object to filling your lungs with dust and never seeing the sunlight, why not hire those two ne'er-do-wells from the Lost Cause?"

"They seemed like honest men," Mason said. He had never finished the assay on their ore, but from what he'd seen of their mine, they were digging into a worthless hole. Paying them a decent wage to work the Mira Nell was possible.

"Your life's changing, sir. It is. You've gone from not having a bed to sleep in, to . . . having your choice. Choose well." Sinclair rose and said in a louder voice,

"Come on in, Miz Logan. He's been complaining something fierce about being lonely. And hungry."

"I can help out with both, Doctor."

"I'm sure you can." Sinclair winked at Mason and went to the door. "Good, you brought me some of that fine soup. You're a peach, Miz Logan."

She came to Mason's bedside and placed a pot of her soup on a low table.

"Let me spoon it in, Mr. Mason," she said, lifting a tablespoon dripping with soup to his lips.

"Thanks," he said. "And please call me Morgan."

Ready to find
your next great read?

Let us help.

Visit prh.com/nextread